PAST
CONTINUOUS

ALSO BY K. RYER BREESE

Future Imperfect

PAST
CONTINUOUS

K. RYER BREESE

Thomas Dunne Books
St. Martin's Griffin
New York

This is a work of fiction. All of the characters, organizations, and events portrayed in this novel are either products of the author's imagination or are used fictitiously.

THOMAS DUNNE BOOKS.
An imprint of St. Martin's Press.

PAST CONTINUOUS. Copyright © 2011 by K. Ryer Breese. All rights reserved. Printed in the United States of America. For information, address St. Martin's Press, 175 Fifth Avenue, New York, N.Y. 10010.

www.thomasdunnebooks.com
www.stmartins.com

ISBN 978-0-312-54772-1

First Edition: November 2011

10 9 8 7 6 5 4 3 2 1

PAST

CONTINUOUS

PROLOGUE

In the dream it's summer.

Days away.

I'm at the beach again. Cherry Creek reservoir.

What do you call déjà vu of your déjà vu?

And there's a guy whispering in a cell phone at my ear.

He says, "Destroy everything. Leave nothing behind . . ."

The chemical smell is strong. Reeks, really.

It's the rubber of the tennis courts. And I home in on it like the million moths that crash through the night to the phosphorus light of the court. Light as bright as the moon.

What's funny is I haven't smelled that rubber smell in years.

I haven't picked up a racket since sixth grade.

But in the dream it's stronger than ever. The tennis courts must have been repaved. I follow the rise and fall of the water. The dunes. The collapse of the reservoir. The wind in the reeds. The buzz of insects.

I know this place like the back of my hand but haven't been here since the whole Jimi thing. After changing the future, there really wasn't a point.

It's like being back at a battlefield.

And the cell phone glued to my ear hums endlessly with variations on a theme. It's a mantra. It's a totem. The guy is chanting, "Destroy everything. Leave nothing."

He says, "Destroy everything you encounter. Leave no witnesses."

He says, "Destroy everything. Nothing shall remain . . ."

I get the point. But I instinctively know that if I hang up, he'll just call again. I also know that it's his cell. It's his minutes he's wasting.

"Leave nothing behind . . ."

I get to the court and notice her immediately.

Vauxhall. Beautiful dressed down. Jeans and a black sweater. Her hair up.

She's not playing tennis but standing in a halo of light and she's with an older guy. Hair slicked back. Looks like old money. Wears a cardigan.

"Destroy it all . . ."

I walk onto the court.

Vauxhall turns and looks at me and smiles. But cardigan says, "I don't think so."

The cell phone is talking in my pocket.

The voice says, "Nothing left . . ."

And the cardigan guy steps up to me and raises his hand but doesn't touch me. He doesn't need to 'cause I go flying back onto the court as though he punched me.

He smiles. Super proud.

Vauxhall looks down at me sadly.

"Destroy it all . . ." the guy on the cell says.

I pull myself back up and step closer to Vauxhall. She shakes her head. And then she raises her hands to the sky, to the moon. A shadow falls over the court, something massive moving over us. I don't bother looking up.

I can hear Vauxhall's breathing. I want to kiss her but I can't get close.

Focused in on the love of my life, I say, "You can't do this."

"She can and will," the woman standing near her says. This woman is wearing sunglasses and a hat. It's hard to tell how old she is but she's so pale.

The man on the phone says, ". . . everything. Destroy it all . . ."

Again the cardigan guy steps over to me and sends me sprawling across the court without even touching me. This time I have trouble breathing but I pull myself up.

Whatever is floating in the sky above us, it makes a humming noise.

The cell phone in my hand buzzes with a saintly voice.

Like a divine cricket kicking out the heavy word of God.

I tell the person on the other end of the line to wait a minute and shove the cell into a pocket. On the phone: "Everything will be destroyed. But before then—"

I walk back onto the court and stand in front of Vauxhall and say, "I love you and I won't let you do this. No matter what happens next, I'll get you back again. Even if it takes a thousand years."

And that's when I pull a gun from my pocket.

Vauxhall says, "Don't."

I pull back the hammer.

The cardigan guy raises his hands and Vauxhall's face falls, her lips tremble.

I close my eyes and that's when I wake up shivering. I feel terrible about the dream and decide to erase it from my mind as soon as possible. Screw whatever psychology went into creating it. Forget whatever anxieties led to it.

By mid-afternoon the dream is gone.

I don't remember any of it.

Wait, what dream?

CHAPTER ONE

ONE

Hey, Heinz—

Awesome seeing you at the swim meet this past weekend. Can't believe I almost came in third. No doubt that was due to some of the astral plane stuff you've been doing. Keep it up, brother! At this rate, what with all the lesser demon saliva and minor devil bones, I'll make the city B finals this spring.

Anyways, I'm writing to get your advice. I'm in a major bind here.

Let me try and explain it up front, just give you the background, before I get to the actual problem. I'm hoping you'll be sympathetic. Can't imagine that most folks who become Satanists didn't mess around with other forms of antisocial behavior as kids.

There's this crew. They call themselves the Pandora Crew and really it's just two dudes. Both of them are total morons. Both of them are like me, gifted, and yet neither of them does anything more than "foment revolution." That's their deal: chaos for the sake of chaos. Anyhow, I somehow wound up in Gordon's and Jeremiah's orbits. Actually, that's not true. It wasn't somehow. These guys used to hang with the LoDo Diviners. They were part of the scene like two years ago. Clean-cut and productive, though I still don't know what abilities they actually have. Both were kicked out by Gilberto and that's when I met them at a show at the Blue Bird. We got to talking. One thing led to another. Now I'm a part of the crew. Now I'm doing the most unbelievable stuff and it's only getting worse. It has only slightly been illegal so far. No one's gotten hurt, I mean.

But soon it's going to cross a line. That line.

I can just tell.

Here's the thing: The stuff we're doing, it makes no sense. It's just destructive and wild and fearless and, honestly, I'm loving every minute of it. It's liberating and I don't know why. This isn't me, Heinz. I'm not this guy. Sure, when I was knocking myself out every other day, crashing cars and diving off roofs, that wasn't the sanest business either. But I don't do that anymore. I'm not that person. I'm stable. I'm sophisticated. And when I did that concussion stuff it was for a reason. It was for the future. This? This is just nihilism.

And I kind of like it. My abilities, now they're boring in a way. Just touch someone and see their future, it sounds totally exciting. It sounds incredible. But it isn't. Think about the people you know. The guy who checks your bags at the grocery store or the chick who drives your bus. The mall security guard. The ticket guy at the movie theater. None of these people have surprising futures. Bumping into them, the future you see is like spending a weekend watching the Home Shopping Network. Predictable. Dull. I'm longing, *really, for a concussion. To see myself back in action and not every-one else.*

Thing is: I've promised myself I wouldn't. I promised Vauxhall.

The Buzz is gone so what's the point, right?

That's why there's something about being out with the Pandora Crew that kick-starts my demon. A new Buzz. Something I'm calling the Delirium 'cause that's honestly the way it feels. You know me; I'm not religious. But the feeling I'm getting when I do something so out of control that it hurts to even think about it is like nothing I've felt before.

I think I'm possessed, Heinz.

Seriously.

I need you to help me exorcize myself.

Your pal,

Ade

TWO

I'm having a great evening.

And by great, I mean I'm with Vauxhall.

We have dinner at a steak place downtown.

Nice place. Nicer than kids our age, kids like us, should be allowed in.

That's because it's the first of the month.

Date Night.

Tonight, the steak house dinner scene, is Foolish Romance.

We're both dressed up. Over-dressed up.

Vaux's wearing this prom gown that she found at a yard sale. Orange and frilled and gaudy and all bejeweled. The story we made up is that this monstrosity was from the late '70s and was worn by a faded starlet. Maybe her name was Marjorie. Or Babette. To fit the dress, Vaux has her hair curled. She's also got makeup caked on.

Me, I'm wearing a sky-blue suit. Have my hair all slicked back. Also alligator-skin boots just to knock the look out of the ballpark.

Last Date Night we went to the art museum on a moped. Raced through traffic, screaming and hollering. We decided this particular Date Night should be called Head Over High Heels.

Me in a tux and her in a slinky red dress.

At the museum, on the third floor, we sipped from a flask I snuck in and sat and talked in front of a sculpture of an enormous duck that had a swastika on its side. Modern art, right? More people took cell pictures of the two of us than of the duck.

Month before it was the race to the airport.

We called it Heart of the Party.

Vaux was at the airport, sunglasses on and suitcases packed, and she was in line, ready to buy a ticket, when I came barreling down the concourse in one of those golf carts. I acted all panicked and the guy who was driving it, the employee, he jumped right out and just let me drive. He shouted after me, "Go get her!" And I did.

I drove that cart right up to the line she was standing in and jumped off it and ran over to her and we hugged and kissed like we thought we might both die and everyone around us just burst out into applause.

We ran off hand in hand, all the travelers hooting and hollering.

You see, this summer Vauxhall and I have decided that we're going to live Hollywood. We're going to live in a Romantic Comedy World.

She came up with the idea.

She said, "In all those terrible romantic comedies, there's always this one scene, usually right before the big fight that happens at the eighty-minute mark, where the couple has some amazing, jet-setting date. Like they fly to Paris and sip wine beneath the Eiffel Tower or they go to San Francisco and hang glide to a picnic on a hill in the Mission district. They always look amazing, so happy and in love. That's the Hollywood moment and you never, ever see it. Right? I mean, you're never downtown and see one of those couples race past you, all decked out, on a Harley or in a biplane? Well, we're going to be that couple this summer."

So far, so good.

You should see the way people look at us on Date Night. It's like we've flown in from another dimension. Like we've stepped off of the stage for a life among the audience. Demigods among the mortals. We are the story that people go home and tell. The story they try and finish.

For one night, we are the stars. We are the people no one really knows.

The people who, for the most part, don't even exist.

Even better, we are the story they'll tell tomorrow over breakfast.

The one they'll post online.

The one they'll sigh about when they're lonely.

Tonight, Date Night number four, Foolish Romance, is going

just swimmingly. Despite the getup, we've decided to keep the drama on the low end. Just us being dressed up and being out. Just us happy being in love. And eating.

We finish our crab wonton appetizers when Vauxhall leans forward and puts her hands on mine, smiles, and says, "You weren't at Jimi's birthday party this morning. I didn't say anything to you but did you forget?"

"Shit!" I smack my forehead. Fake. Totally exaggerated but I do feel bad.

"Yeah, he was bummed." Vauxhall pulls her hands back from mine.

"I forget a lot of things, Vaux. It's kind of like my thing. You can't just expect—"

"He's your brother."

"Yeah, exactly. My half-brother. The same half-brother who I didn't know existed until four months ago. Same exact half-brother who not only stole my childhood but tried to make me kill him so I wouldn't exist anymore."

Vauxhall says nothing. She's so disappointed.

"Look . . . I'll give him a call later, okay? I'm sure he's not sobbing over it or anything, right?"

Vauxhall shrugs. That means that I don't get it.

I try to change the subject, move us on. "Have you seen Paige this week?"

Vaux nods. "Yeah, of course."

"Well I haven't. I don't know what it is but ever since she started dating, like really dating, it's like she doesn't have time for me anymore. Remember how we used to watch our shows and just—"

"No. I wasn't there, Ade. Remember?"

"Right. Okay."

Then she gets this serious look. Like a cloud passing over the sun.

"What's going on?"

"What do you mean?"

"You know. You, you're different. Ever since you started hanging out with Gordon and Jeremiah. What's funny is that I'm used to you being forgetful, but this is different. This isn't you forgetting things, it's you purposely not remembering."

"How can you purposely not remember something?"

"Ask yourself."

I groan. "Why isn't it okay for me to hang out with other people? I mean—"

"Don't even. Don't even start that. I'm not keeping you in a cage, Ade."

And like that Date Night turns into Fight Night.

This had been happening lately. Neither of us wants to admit it, recognize it, but we're starting to get all crabby. Me, mostly. It's like we're becoming an old married couple. Only in high school. Only when we're not even eighteen yet.

"I know that, Vaux. It's not like I really believe that."

"Then why say it?"

"Ugh. Seriously? Listen, I'm sorry and I won't ever open my mouth again. Can we just get back to having fun here? Whatever happened to having fun? It's just—"

My foot-in-my-mouth, making-it-worse non-apology is interrupted by a goofy fool banging on the window at the front of the restaurant. This guy has a weird beard but he's young. Googly-eyed and probably wasted.

Half the restaurant starts freaking out over the madman.

They drop their forks, make all sorts of kitchen clatter, and whisper and point at the mugging idiot at the window. This isn't supposed to be happening at a fancy steak place like this one. Dudes like the fool at the window aren't supposed to be here.

The riffraff is never invited.

Vauxhall, she just looks at me and shakes her head. "I thought this was Date Night."

I throw my hands up, exasperated.

The moron at the window knocks on the glass, licks it, and laughs.

Problem is, I know the guy.

"You don't think I invited him here, do you?" I ask.

Vauxhall shrugs.

"You gotta be kidding me."

The retard outside yells my name. He yells it over and over. So loud.

Vauxhall's eyes bug out. "Just one night, Ade. Why is that so hard?"

I huff and stand up and throw my napkin on the table all dramatically and walk out of the restaurant. What's funny is that I'm kind of excited to be out of there. The guy at the window, the cretin, is Jeremiah. One half of the Pandora Crew.

Once I get outside he jumps up on me like a dog in heat.

"Holy shit, Ade! Wait til you see what we have planned for tonight!"

I push him off, look back at Vauxhall through the window.

Slowly I say, "Dude. You're interrupting my Date Night with Vaux. This isn't cool. You're getting me in some major trouble here."

Jeremiah waves to Vauxhall. Says, "Look across the street."

Vaux waves back. Disgusted.

Jeremiah says, "Corner of Third and York. Check it, bro."

I check it. There's a gnarly van with smoked windows idling at the corner. This van, it has a pastoral scene airbrushed on the side. Waterfalls and lily pads. A unicorn with a rainbow sprouting from its back. The rainbow was in shades of gray. The unicorn, the thing, has fangs.

Jeremiah says, "The Shriek."

"Nice name," I say. Looking close at the van I notice the dude behind the wheel is none other than Gordon, the better half of the Pandora Crew. Only he's rocking a fake mustache and massive mirrored sunglasses.

Jeremiah says, "Kiss Vaux good-bye for the night, player. Wait til you see what's inside that bad boy."

Still looking at the van, I say, "No can do. She'd kill me."

Jeremiah goes, "Please. Don't be such a pushover. You're not even eighteen."

I look back at Vauxhall. She's paying the check, ignoring me.

Jeremiah says, "Give her a kiss and come out and play."

I dutifully go inside and walk up to Vaux and kiss her on the forehead. She wipes my kiss away and gives me the finger. She says, "I'm beginning to understand why Paige hates you half the time."

"Please, baby. I didn't think this—"

"You never think anymore, Ade. Just forget it and go. Go on."

And I give her a half smile before I bail.

THREE

This whole Pandora Crew thing all started about three weeks ago.

I met them the way I seem to meet a lot of people: by vision.

I was at the Blue Bird after this one show and bumped into Gordon. Literally bumped into him on the sidewalk outside.

This has happened a whole lot.

With these newly enhanced abilities, I find I'm bumping into people all the time and flashing out into their future. Ninety-two percent of the time it's boring as all hell. Ninety-two percent of the time it's just watching someone get old and slow down.

But not Gordon.

Nah, with him I saw . . . Well, I can't even describe exactly what it was.

I've never dropped acid. Never done shrooms.

But Gordon's future was what I imagine I'd see if I ever did. It was all swirling colors and branching shapes that seemed to push and pull their way out from the background static. Really, can't explain it.

So I stopped him.

No point in beating around the bush, I just came out and said it. "You've got a crazy future. Not like anything I've ever seen."

He didn't look at me like I was drunk.

He didn't freak out.

That was the first sign.

"It's not a future," he said. "It's the other side of reality. Like the flip side of this life. You know how you can kind of see through the pages of an old comic book, stuff printed on newssheet? Well, that's what it is. It's the other life bleeding through."

I didn't know how to take that. Looked at Vaux and she shrugged.

I could tell even then that she didn't like Gordon.

She saw the danger in him.

We exchanged numbers and the next night, we hung out.

That's when the switch was flipped.

I was at Gordon's house and we drank and watched movies and didn't talk about anything. Really. I didn't ask him about his background and he didn't ask mine. We didn't talk school. We didn't talk girlfriends. We didn't talk.

There was just this knowing between us.

This simple understanding.

Kind of like the way little kids, kids who can't talk, play together.

And then, somehow, we wound up in the backyard.

We smoked a few cigarettes. I coughed through all of them. And then Gordon motioned to the garage. He said, "You're not going to believe the idea I just had."

First thing I promised Vauxhall: I won't jump off anything.

There really hasn't been a reason for me to jump off anything because there hasn't been a reason for me to knock myself out. No Buzz. No need.

This, however, was different.

This was about living.

Gordon said, "If ever there was a time to test the old hypothesis that teenagers think they're invincible, it's right now."

We climbed up onto his roof and he pointed to a big fir tree across the yard, like a decent thirty feet away.

Gordon said, "We're going to jump it. Land in the branches."

"That tree is on the other side of the yard, dude."

"That's what makes it challenging. Yes."

And he backed up, all the way across the roof to the far side, counted to fifteen, and then he booked, like he was running track, going for the freaking gold, and hit the gutter and, wham, he flew. Flew clear across the gap between the roof and the tree like in some slowed-down scene from an action movie.

He flew right into the fir tree.

It wasn't pretty but he made it.

After he'd climbed down, his face all scratched up from fir needles, he stood on the lawn below me and said, "Show me what you got."

"Nah, I think I'll pass."

"What?"

"Looks stupid."

"Oh no you didn't. You didn't just call it stupid. Stupid is you not doing this because you're afraid or you're worried about . . . I don't know. What's your problem, Ade?"

"I'm recovering."

"Worst word in the English language. Recovering. Ade, you jump onto that tree and then we'll talk. There's something I need you to understand."

I shook my head. "You're an idiot."

"Am I? Jump and find out."

So I backed up, dug my heels in, and . . . paused.

Here's the crazy part: It'd been five months since I jumped off anything higher than a sidewalk. And, as expected, I got this nutty kind of thrill just thinking about jumping. I was only seconds away from sending myself into the air and my heart was pounding in my chest like I was going to kiss Vauxhall for the first time in months. The Delirium. This feeling, the Buzz reaching back out from whatever dark recess I'd stuffed it down into. It was calling me. Pulling me back. What made it different, though, was that it felt different. This rush, honestly, it made me feel guilty.

Worse, I liked it.

And I ran, jumped, cleared the edge of the roof and crashed into the fir tree. The impact made the tree sway hard to the right. It cracked and threatened to break. I hung on, my skin being pinched by a thousand needles, and then climbed down.

Gordon gave me a pat on the back and then he pulled out a penlight and put it in my face, stared hard and long at my eyes. Then he laughed.

"You've got the bug."

"Bug?"

"How does it make you feel? When your pupils get all blasted out like that? When your heart is rushing and your skin is crawling with pleasure? It's a high, isn't it?"

"I don't have a—"

"No. I can tell. Have a look, brother."

And Gordon turned the light on himself. His eyes like blown-open craters in his head. The dude had the Buzz, hard. I'd never seen my pupils as big as his were. Thing is, he wasn't shaking from it. He wasn't sleepy. He didn't seem doped up.

Not like me.

Not like how crazy and crackheaded I felt.

"You and me are cut from the same cloth," Gordon said. "We're freaks of the same brood, dude. You've got the bug. Tell me what happens with you, how it works."

And so I told him. I told him how it used to work. I told him how I stopped. I said, "Nowadays, the Buzz is gone. I can touch someone and see. It's simple."

"But you miss the glory days, right?"

I didn't want to tell him about this new sensation.

I didn't want to tell him that the Buzz was back and a hundred times heavier.

Standing there, his penlight lighting up his jack-o'-lantern face, Gordon nodded knowingly. Sagely. It was obvious that he'd been waiting for this moment, his big reveal, for a very long time.

I pushed him on it. "How long have you known about me?"

"Couple months."

"How's it work for you?"

Gordon smiled. "Exactly the same."

Back on the roof, with a bottle of Gordon's mother's wine, he lit up a cigarette and leaned back and laid it all out in a word. "Chaos. You see, for me it's the amount of chaos present in the system at any given time. You up the chaos and the Thrill grows."

"How? I don't get—"

"I'm not like a physicist or anything but I've read some books. Talked to a few people. But the deal is simple: If everything's chill, then I'm getting nothing. But the more I shake things up, the more revolutionary, more rebellious, I get, then the Thrill just goes through the roof. Especially if I'm the one creating the chaos. And lately, I've realized something massive. My whole show, it's leading to one super big realization. The Ultimate Thrill."

"And what's that? What do you see?"

"You'll find out later. But nah, I don't see."

"Then what?"

Gordon snickered. "I'm not like you, Ade. Not like the others, those Diviner idiots. I'm just in this for the kicks, there is nothing else. Thrill or be Thrilled, amigo."

"The Thrill? That's what you call the high?"

"Yeah."

"I called it the Buzz."

I don't mention the new sensation. The Delirium. The Buzz turned up to eleven.

"Why'd you quit? What happened?"

"I changed. My abilities, they got stronger. More powerful."

Gordon chewed on that. "What'cha doing Tuesday?"

Second thing I promised Vaux was that I wouldn't crash anything again.

Not a car, not a bike, not a skateboard, not even a toy car.

And that was cool. I didn't miss it. Didn't miss that destructive impulse, that was, until the next Tuesday at two in the morning when I met up again with Gordon at a construction site in Westminster behind the old mall.

I found Gordon leaning back on his car like some action-movie star. He was seriously wearing leather pants and a vest.

Really. A vest. He was smoking again and he slicked his hair back when he saw me.

"What's on tap tonight?" I asked, getting out of my car. "More jumping?"

I couldn't tell why I was psyched to be there but I was. The adrenaline was starting to flow. I was practically salivating at the thought of doing something crazy. Something wrong.

Gordon slapped a hand down on my shoulder. Pointed at a bulldozer.

"Joyride."

"What? In that?!"

"Of course."

"Dude, that's stupid. What're we going to do? Dig a ditch? Roll some crops?"

Gordon was disappointed. "You have a lot to learn, Ade. Thankfully I'm here to teach you a few things. Come on."

I didn't know you could hot-wire a bulldozer but Gordon could and did.

As I watched I could feel the Delirium soaring in my bloodstream.

Started to twitch like a damn junkie.

When the thing was running, chugging along so loud I was sure it would wake up the entire city, Gordon motioned for me to climb aboard. He turned on the lights and jerked the bulldozer into motion.

I had to yell over the rumbling of the engine. Loud. "What are we doing?"

Gordon, all grins, was like, "We're liberating some toads."

"What?"

"Toads. Liberating."

I just went with it and we took the bulldozer down a small neighborhood street, lights flicking on inside the houses as we went as though the bulldozer were magic. It was a bumpy ride. I'm guessing driving a bulldozer is difficult and Gordon wasn't very good. He was spirited however. He was beaming, time-of-his-life smile plastered on his face.

Took almost fifteen minutes to get to the end of the street.

This is mostly because the bulldozer was going a top speed of six miles an hour.

The street dead-ended at a fence. Rickety old wooden fence. And beyond it was darkness. Just straight up matte-black darkness. A few pinholes of light in the sky from stars and a few passing cars on the interstate like a mile to the east.

Gordon pushed the dozer as fast as it would go though I didn't notice any significant change in the speed. He shouted, "You might want to buckle up, dude!"

Of course there were no seat belts.

I just grabbed on to what I could. Pushed my ass as far back in the seat as it would go and I also half closed my eyelids, bracing for what I saw coming.

Gordon was going to take the fence.

It wasn't like in an action movie where there's some ridiculous chase scene and the main character drives a wonky construction truck through a wall and all sorts of shit goes flying into the air, atomized instantaneously. No, going through the fence in the bulldozer was like pushing over a clay wall. No drama. No action. The fence sort of buckled at first and then it just gave. Went down flat. No even a sound over the roar of the engine.

Halfway over the fence and Gordon shuts off the headlights.

"Seriously?!" I yelled in his ear.

Gordon said, "Prepare to dive!"

The Delirium sang like something out of Wagner.

And we dove. Actually, the bulldozer dove. Straight off what felt like a fifty-foot cliff but turned out to be a four-foot drop onto the slope of a hill. The bulldozer kicked up a ton of dust and I had thorny weeds springing up at me along with clods of beady dirt. The shock of the fall shook the dozer's cab so heavily that I bit through my bottom lip. The metallic taste of blood filled my mouth as the dozer started to plow down the slope. Gordon turned the lights back on just in time for me to see the shovel front end of the bulldozer collide with a small retaining wall around a pond.

The impact sent me flying out of the cab.

Actually it was more like gliding for the few seconds I was airborne.

Behind me, somehow still in the cab, Gordon was cheering. Shouting.

Those few seconds in the air were blissful. The night was warm and there were crickets just going nuts in the bushes and I even recall the hum of dragonfly wings over the water. Also the moon was as full as I'd ever seen it. Just squatting there over the earth like the biggest, brightest smile you'd ever seen.

Incredible.

And then I landed in about two feet of pond water atop two feet of pond muck.

I skidded to a stop in a wicked stand of cattails. The smell, a summer's worth of leaves rotting underwater, was the first thing I noticed. And then the silence. The bulldozer was finished. Engine kaput. I could see it wedged up against the retaining wall and Gordon was sitting, smoking inside the wreck of it.

He had a gash on his forehead, blood running down to his mouth, and he was just taking in the full extent of the destruction he'd caused. I couldn't see it, but I was sure his pupils were dilated out the size of hubcaps.

I pulled myself up from the grime and stepped out of the weeds.

So many times the Buzz had me woozy but this, the Delirium, it made me feel like I'd downed a whole Costco-size bag of Peeps. Or I'd mainlined some Sour Patch candies. Crazy. Sickeningly good.

Gordon extricated himself from the wreckage, tossed his smoke, and then walked over to me, holding something fat and flabby in his hands. It was a toad. Big, brown, warty, with googly eyes and a grin. He put it down in the water in front of me and it just sat there, staring up glassy-eyed at the moon.

The water in the pond was going down. Every second another inch of it disappeared. And I noticed more toads. Tons more toads. They were everywhere, hopping all over my feet. Hopping all over the wrecked treads of the bulldozer.

"Liberated," Gordon said, all bloody faced.

"What was the point of that?" I asked.

"Of which? Freeing the toads from their cement cells or wrecking the dozer?"

"Both."

Gordon tapped the side of his head, universal sign for thinking incredibly deep thoughts, and said, "There is no point. It was purely action and reaction. It was a thrill."

"So, that's it? We're going to just wreck things? Break stuff?"

The thought of it had me quivering with anticipation.

Such a junkie.

"For starters," Gordon said.

"And then?"

Gordon winked. "Remember I told you I was going to teach you a few things?"

"Yeah."

"Well, I'm almost done. Soon we'll bring in the big guns."

"Big guns?"

"My partner in crime, of course. He doesn't just meet with anybody."

Enter Jeremiah.

We met him at a rock concert, some jam band, in Boulder.

My ears were still ringing when Gordon brought him over to me. Guy was sweaty and stank of pot. His eyes were the reddest I'd ever seen. We went to a Village Inn and I had coffee while Jeremiah ate chicken-fried steak and eggs over easy and pancakes.

I assumed Jeremiah was the ringleader.

But when he ate like a wild man it was clear he wasn't. Gordon was just setting me up again. Creating expectations that couldn't be met. Twisting reality. His game. The same way a dictator says the people really rule.

Jeremiah belched and leaned back.

"Gordon tells me you're like us," he said.

"Yeah, I guess."

"You are. I can see it in you."

"What can you see?"

"You crave the insanity of living for the moment. Of throwing everything out."

"Okay."

And that was it. He nodded to Gordon. They got up, threw down three dollars, and walked out of the restaurant. Left me with the bill.

I was super pissed but let it go.

See, already I was hooked.

The Delirium in my soul.

Bitten.

FOUR

Tonight, on the way from the steak house, Gordon takes the highway south to Centennial and he swerves between cars, crosses lanes, like he's on some European racetrack.

I'm in the back of the van and, well, it's freaking incredible.

Gordon and Jeremiah have a couch in here. A black leather couch. Also there's a disco ball and the whole thing is lit up by like fifteen black-light strips and on the blacked-out windows are old-school rock 'n' roll psychedelic posters. Oh and there's a bubble machine churning out a steady stream of bubbles that catch the purple light. Makes the whole tableau look like something in the deep ocean.

Jeremiah and I are sharing a joint.

He's telling me about our plans for the evening. They sound complicated.

". . . is when we hit the ramp at Lincoln and the shit will go flying."

"You mean literally flying, right?" I ask.

Jeremiah takes this long drag, the burning red tip of the joint contrasting crazily with the purple light playing over his furry face. He says, being surprisingly serious, "I always mean it literally, bro. All these things we're doing, it's not like they're just games for the sake of killing time. We're a crew, dog. Pandora Crew. We're opening up the lid of something that can't never be closed."

He hands me back the joint. Nods.

He says, "When I say flying, I mean flying."

Gordon whips the van back and forth and back and forth. Up front he's banging his head to something by Black Sabbath and then AC/DC. He hits the padded ceiling of the van with his fist. He barks like a drill sergeant.

In between drags of the joint I see Vauxhall's disappointed face.

I imagine her driving home cursing my name. I imagine her lying in bed listening to really depressing music and writing and then crossing out my name in a journal like a thousand times.

I can't get her out of my head.

Jeremiah cashes the joint and right when he drops the blackened stub into a half-finished can of Sprite, the van stops.

Gordon jumps out with a big pack on his back and swings open the doors.

He grins and shouts like he's gone deaf, "Tiger's in the bush, boys!"

Jeremiah throws me a black ski mask. I look at it in my hands, confused. He laughs and Gordon laughs and then Jeremiah says, "Dude, that whole plan I just told you about was all code. Don't you ever read the texts we send you?"

"Uh . . ."

"Well." Jeremiah looks to Gordon. "This'll be twice as thrilling then."

I scoot myself out of the van and pull the hood down over my face and have a look at where we were at. It's the Park Meadows Mall. Just this vast parking lot surrounding an outcropping of bland retail. And it's late. The mall closed like two hours ago and the empty parking lot is pretty much a sea of lonely sodium lights. Whole empty solar systems of suburban space.

Jeremiah pulls binoculars out of nowhere and holds them up to his eyes. He scans the lot and then points. I follow the line of his finger to see a white speck moving across the lot about half a mile away.

Jeremiah says, "Security."

Then he asks, "Gordon, what's a 10-66?"

"Suspicious person," Gordon says, reciting from memory.

Jeremiah asks, "10-70?"

"Prowler."

"11-54?"

Gordon says, "Suspicious vehicle."

"10-79?"

Gordon says, "Bomb threat."

I ask, "So . . . We're spying on the security guards on an empty lot because . . ."

Jeremiah pulls a heavy-duty walkie-talkie out of nowhere and flicks it on. Static and then voices. The security guards, maybe even the one in the speck of a golf cart across the lot, talk to each other. They aren't talking in codes. Mostly they're talking about how much their jobs suck.

Jeremiah looks to me. Smiles. "Get ready for business."

"Business?"

Gordon says, "B and E, brother. B and E."

And that's when he pulls out the gun.

FIVE

I haven't seen many guns.

This one is big. Ugly. Snub-nosed.

I don't even know what to say.

Gordon smiles, says, "You probably shouldn't have let us in your house, bro."

He's talking about last week. When I let them meet my mom.

See my place.

Honestly, they just showed up last Thursday after swim practice.

Totally unannounced.

Both super high.

I had just gotten home and was tossing my towel into the laundry basket at the bottom of the stairs when the doorbell rang. Mom was in the kitchen, making dinner, and she yelled out that she'd get it.

Then she was like, "Uh, I think it's for you."

Seeing them on my porch was like seeing ghosts.

I didn't want to invite them in. Didn't want to go where I knew they were likely to take it. And at the same time, something in me wanted to destroy stuff again. Something in me was excited about the thought of chaos. Craziness.

And let them in.

Despite herself, my mom made them finger sandwiches and gave them a purple-colored fruit drink that came from a big plastic gallon thing in the fridge that had a piece of blue painter tape on the front of it that said FRUIT DRINK.

These dudes both stank of pot. Gordon had leaves in his hair. Like hip hoboes.

Gordon was the first to ask for a tour.

After he burped.

My mom obliged, showing Gordon and Jeremiah around my house and pointing out everything Jesus about it—the Jesus wall clock she got in Taos, the velvet Jesus on the pantry door, the ceramic Jesus holding sheep by her bed—but by the time she got to her bedroom, they were only interested in one thing.

"Holy shit," Gordon said, seeing the wall of index cards. "I mean, sorry, holy cow. Is this what I think it is?"

My mom gave him a confused, sad look. "Ade," she said, looking at Gordon but talking to me, "would you like to get your friend here a bar of soap to wash his mouth out?"

Jeremiah cracked up at that.

The scene was tense. Not good.

I did this uncomfortable laugh. "Gordon just comes from a bad family is all, Mom. He's just not used to polite company and he'll be sure to watch his language."

Gordon chimed in, half snickering, "I'll bite my tongue."

"Good," Mom said. "Proverbs 21:23."

Then she looked to me, as if I should explain the walls.

"Uh," I started, "this is basically where my mom recorded all of, uh, my—"

Mom cut in, elbowed me. "Don't be shy."

And then, stepping in with her eyes bright and her mouth all smiles, she told Gordon and Jeremiah all about the visions I had. She told them that the wall was my future and that it recorded everything I would do for the next seventy-plus years. She said, tussling my hair, "Ade can speak to Baby Jesus."

Jeremiah took a seat on the edge of my mom's bed, leaned in, the expression on his face mocking and yet fascinated. The way he looked was the way you look at someone who's really, extraordinarily stupid. "Is that so, Ade? Can you talk to the Good Lord?"

I shot him a look. My look told him to fuck off.

He backed down. Retorted, "Awesome."

Gordon was standing next to Mom, looking over the index cards and squinting down hard to make out all the fine print. I could tell right away he was totally stunned.

He pointed to a card dated May 14, 2054 and asked, "What's the number for?"

That card, No. 39 in the 2054 series, was labeled VACATION TIME and the note on the card said, "Went to the mountains. Skied. Fairly relaxing. Boring even. Until collision with tree just after lunch. Rushed to ER, admitted to hospital but climbed out window before MRIs."

Mom explained, "The number refers to the vision. That's vision thirty-nine for that year."

"He's had thirty-nine visions of that single year?"

"No." Mom pointed to the card as if it would clarify for Gordon. "See, in 2054 he has thirty-nine visions. Thirty-nine concussions."

Then she looked at me and smiled. Her boy.

Gordon walked around, eyeing all of the cards, taking it all in. Then he turned to me and said, "Do you know what this means?"

"No," I said. "What?"

"Leapfrog."

"Huh?"

Jeremiah joined in. "Huh?"

He didn't say anything more until after Mom had gone to bed and Gordon and Jeremiah and I were on the back porch staring up at the moon and watching Gordon blow smoke rings around it. His rings were pretty good; the moon looked like it was wearing a smoke coat for the few seconds before the smoke became clouds and the clouds vanished.

We were waiting for Gordon to tell us what his idea was.

What leapfrog meant.

He dragged it out.

"We're going to see just how far Ade can go," Gordon finally said. "You think your mom's asleep yet?"

I shrugged. "Probably. Why?"

"Hang on a sec."

He got up, pulled his lighter from his pocket, flicked it a few times, and then said, "I'll be back in just a minute."

He wasn't back in just one minute.

Jeremiah and I waited, the two of us just staring up at the now naked moon. Both of us sitting there wondering just what the hell was happening and probably Jeremiah sitting there wondering why I wasn't in the house checking up.

"He's not stealing anything, is he?" I asked, my voice kind of cracking.

Jeremiah shrugged.

"He better not be stealing anything."

"Probably he's lighting something on fire," Jeremiah said.

"What?!"

"Yeah. He's a total firebug."

I jumped up when Gordon came walking back out. Whistling. He sat between Jeremiah and me and then spread out five index cards on the grass in front of him and then lit his lighter to show us.

In the grass: five of my visions. All from different future years. All of them occurring on the very same future day.

Gordon pointed to the first one. "Monday, March twenty-sixth and you're twenty-seven. You ride a motorcycle across a salt flat into the side of a mountain."

Gordon pointed to the second one: "Saturday, March twenty-sixth and you're thirty-three. This one you jump off a bridge into, uh, it says . . ." He held the lighter closer. "Oh, right, dangerously shallow water."

He pointed to the third one. "Thursday, March twenty-sixth. You're fifty-six. You're downtown and you decide to crash your Land Rover into a street lamp."

The fourth one, the flame guttering, making crazy shadows on the card. "Wednesday, March twenty-sixth. Seventy-one. You roll your wheelchair down the stairs."

And last. "Monday, March twenty-sixth. You are eighty-six years old and you're old, got bad Alzheimer's, and you actually hit yourself over the head with another nursing home resident's bowling trophy. Nice move."

Gordon let the flame go out. We were sucked back into the darkness.

Our eyes adjusting to the light, Gordon asked, "What day is next Thursday?"

Jeremiah didn't get that Gordon was being rhetorical and said, "The twenty-sixth."

Gordon lit a clove cigarette and leaned back on the porch and then blew out a big ring of smoke and said, "These things all happen on the same day just separated by like decades. The thing is, if Ade is able to focus enough to kind of match up all the times. You know, an afternoon here, a morning there. If he can push down hard and pull the timelines together, I'm guessing you can piggyback all those concussions, dude."

"I thought you said leapfrog?" I asked.

Gordon smiled. "Right. You're going to piggyback these concussions together so that you go from one to the next and then you're going to leapfrog into what comes next. You'll jump from the future you see in one vision to the future you see in the next. Get it?"

Jeremiah didn't get it. "Huh?"

"Simple physics, bro." Gordon blew some smoke at Jeremiah and said, "It's like those things you see on the desks of businessmen. You know, the things with the little silver balls that knock back and forth and back and forth. The motion of one gets the others moving, right?"

Jeremiah was still lost. "Just explain it is all."

"Our next big project is Ade. We're going to help our buddy here go where no one has gone before and come back to talk about it."

I got a queasy feeling. Told myself I didn't want to hear where Gordon was going. I told myself that whatever he was planning, I really didn't have to participate in it. I said to myself, just kick these guys out, go back in the house, curl up in bed, and dream about Vaux. Only I don't do it. Only I don't move an inch.

Gordon blew another fucking ring and said, "Ade's going to die."

"Hell no I'm not," I said, shaking my head violently. "Not a chance."

Gordon chuckled. "The high, dude, it'll pretty much be better than anything you have ever experienced."

"And how would you even know that, Gordon?"

Gordon stubbed his cigarette out on the porch. "Because I know someone who's done it."

He let that sink in before he added, "What happens next is the culmination of everything, Ade. You'll put the last puzzle piece in the big picture. You're the one who's going to make the ultimate thrill really mean something. I'm about to show you the wizard behind the curtain, bro."

He added, "The ball starts rolling this instant."

Tonight, staring at the gun in his hand, I almost think I know what he meant.

He can tell.

Gordon's good at noticing the little things.

He said, "You laid out the path, Ade. This is what happens next."

I told him I'm not down with it. Not anymore.

"Not much of a choice at this point, bro." Gordon smiled.

"That's pretty much like you asking God or whatever not to push the button and start the Big Bang. You can't rewind yourself out of this. And the point is simple: Once you start something rolling, it never stops. Not even if you stop it."

And he cocked the gun.

SIX

That click tells me everything.

The hammer of the gun going back, it's surprisingly loud. And it lets me know that this has officially gotten out of control. This is officially fucked.

I look all confused at Jeremiah.

"I just help him work the magic," he says.

"Well, this is sucky ass magic."

Gordon laughs and looks at his cell. "We've got twenty-three minutes."

"I'm not shooting anything," I say.

"Neither am I," Gordon adds. "Lighten up, Mr. Grouchy."

Gordon gives a thumbs-up and away we go. I don't know why I follow them. Could just turn around and run the other way. Could but I don't.

Too late.

Already the adrenaline is rushing.

The Delirium coming around the bend.

Hiking up the mountain toward me.

We run down a little embankment and through the parking lot weaving between the cars as though we're soldiers. More like children playing soldier. Only Gordon does have a gun so maybe it's children playing maniacs.

We barrel over bushes by the entrance to Macy's and hole up against the stone wall there, crouching like bums, Gordon leans on his backpack, his walkie-talkie all fired up with static though none of the mall cops're talking about three kids in ski masks.

Gordon gives the old three fingers . . .

Two fingers . . .

One finger . . .

And then he whispers, "Go."

Jeremiah jumps up first and runs over to the door to Macy's and whips a little handheld gizmo out. He waves it around the front doors, pushes a few buttons on the thing's keypad.

Still crouched beside me, Gordon whispers, "He got it off eBay."

I just nod.

"It unlocks the doors, some sort of cat-burglar technology developed in Europe."

Again, I just nod.

"Pretty sweet stuff, he's been dying to use it."

"What are we doing, Gordon?"

"I'm not even going to answer that."

And then the doors of the store click and Jeremiah pushes them open and gives us a thumbs-up. Gordon jumps up first and again I follow. We dash inside, no alarms going off, and play the running, weaving game among the headless mannequins.

Then we reach the next set of doors.

Jeremiah waves his magic thief box and I stomp my feet impatiently. "Okay, so we didn't come to the mall to steal popular summer wear. What exactly are we doing?"

Gordon puts a hand on Jeremiah's shoulder and whispers something to him.

Jeremiah laughs. "Totally, dude."

And then the next set of doors click and we're in the mall.

Gordon's walkie-talkie's blowing up. The conversations are hard to hear but one of the mall cops totally loves fried chicken and the other mall cop really prefers it baked. With southwestern-style corn.

We make our way down to the Urban Outfitters first.

Jeremiah pulls out his black box deal and starts his work but he isn't at it long before there's a tremendous bang and the glass doors of the place just shatter, huge chunks of glass falling like frozen waterfalls, and the alarm starts wailing.

Gordon stands behind us, gun smoking in his hands.

"We now have twelve minutes."

"For what?!" I shout back in his face. My ears ringing.

His walkie-talkie isn't squawking about food anymore. They heard the shot.

Gordon says nothing, just walks into the store and walks back out with two pairs of rubber leggings. In my mind I'm thinking: Seriously?

He points with the gun at the escalator.

"Up," he says.

We go up.

On the second floor we race down to the food court.

Behind us, the alarm's still screaming and we can hear the crash of boots, the mall cops on the case. My heart's racing. Just pounding away. And that's when the surge of adrenaline hits me.

It's like everything just sped up.

My vision gets shaky. The Delirium in full force.

My hands twitching like a tweaker.

This massive smile breaks out across my face.

Damn, why does this feel so right?

We're about fifty feet from the entrance to the food court and I'm going to explode in some sort of wild dance, just that much energy running through my body, when we see the first mall cop.

He's young, maybe twenty, and he's standing there with his hands out, palms up, and his hat pulled down low over his eyes like a cowboy.

"Stop there!" he shouts.

And we do.

Then Gordon shows the dude the gun and the dude drops to the floor. Hands over his head, he's shouting into the carpet. "Don't! Please. Please. Please."

Gordon smiles, says, "Don't stress, homes. It's all good."

The guy looks up, lips quivering.

Gordon says, "We're not here to kill anyone. Won't even get a scratch. Just keep your ass on the floor and make sure you get all the glass out of your hair."

"The glass?" the guy asks.

And that's when Gordon opens up with the gun. He shoots out the windows of the atrium above us and the glass comes raining down into the artificial pond below like flat icicles falling from a fake sky.

Kid mall cop screams.

The glass makes the sound of one of those rainsticks and when it's over there are at least five more alarms blaring in the mall like the chirps of crickets from hell. Down on the first level we can see five more mall cops running. All of them with tasers drawn.

"Why the hell'd you do that?" I ask Gordon.

Gordon, all grins, says, "Because none of this is real."

My heart has pretty much gotten a dose of nitro by this point.

It's racing so fast that it's practically unbuckling from the tendons or whatever that hold it in my rib cage. I can see Jeremiah has the same thing going. Only Gordon is cool-headed. He motions us to follow him into the food court.

We run past the McDonald's and he shoots the sign on that.

"Not real," he says.

Also he blasts a hole in the deep fryer at the one Mexican place.

"Not real."

And takes out a chunk of the ceiling in the smoothie joint.

"Totally fake."

Then he runs us down the hallway to the bathroom. And as we pass one of those AEDs, those automatic defibrillator things you see on hospital shows that restart someone's heart, Gordon doesn't even slow, just reaches out and rips it off the wall and throws it under his arm like he's a running back going for the touchdown.

In the bathroom, he closes the door behind us and takes off his backpack.

Then he throws it down on the floor and pulls out this massive magnet. Not the kind you see in the cartoons that are horseshoe-shaped and have red ends but just this thing the size of a dictionary and dusty black.

"Every bit of success is planning," he says. "Even chaos needs to be scheduled."

He brings the giant magnet up near the door and the magnet flies out of his hands onto the metal lining the knob and the doorframe. The sound it makes is best described as cacophonous. Car-accident loud.

"We're locked in, boys," Gordon says.

Then he looks down at his cell and smiles. "And we have two minutes to spare."

I'm almost jumping out of my skin with chemical excitement.

"That was insane!" I shout. "What the hell are we doing next?"

Jeremiah laughs.

Gordon looks at himself in a mirror, splashes some water on his face.

"So here's the big idea, boys: There are scientists who study reality. Kind of like physicists but more philosophical. They think that in the future it'll be possible to totally re-create reality inside a computer. You know, make a world that you can't distinguish from this one. A digital world that seems totally real. Like on Star Trek."

Gordon pauses, checks his teeth. Then: "Thing is, they say that if such a creation is possible then the most logical next thought is that we're living in a re-creation right now. This world isn't real but just a digital copy. What they say is that right now we're in the future and this, this is all an illusion."

Then he turns around to both me and Jeremiah, the two of us giddy like preschoolers hopped up on sugar dust, and says, "J-dogg, you're going to test the hypothesis first. And Ade, you're going to take it to the next level with your skills."

Jeremiah immediately takes his shirt off and sits down on the tile floor.

Gordon pulls his own pants off and pulls on the rubber leggings. They're tight and not a good sight. He sits down on the floor across from Jeremiah with his rubber legs crossed. Then looks over at me and says, "Get me the AED."

I hand him the case.

He opens it, starts attaching electrodes to Jeremiah's hairy chest.

"The rubber leggings keep me from getting as zapped," he says.

"That will kill him, you know," I say, almost too matter of factly.

"Of course it will. That's the point," Gordon says. "But it will also bring him back to life. Amazing how technology works these days, right? Besides, everything we've done, everything the Pandora Crew stands for is leading up to this very moment. We're testing the fabric of reality here, man. We're all dying tonight."

My jaw drops open, my heart starts to slow.

Gordon, sensing it, picks up the gun and points it at me.

My heart races again.

The Delirium the only thing keeping me sane right now.

He says, "You need to keep those endorphins flowing. That adrenaline pumping. Otherwise this isn't going to work."

Jeremiah chimes in, "Dude. The rush is key."

And that's when Gordon presses the button on the front of the AED and it starts to charge up and Jeremiah begins panting like some foul monkey at the zoo and then the AED beeps that it's ready and says something, in an electro voice, about getting clear of the machine and I back way the hell up and then Gordon pushes the button.

And Jeremiah dies.

Right in front of me.

SEVEN

So here we are.

This very microsecond between me being alive and me being dead.

Gordon, gun still in his hand, turns to me and says, "Now it's your turn, brother."

I tell him to go to hell.

But really, the Delirium wants me to say right on. Let's do this.

He laughs. Chambers a round in the gun. He says, "You have jumped off roofs, you've crashed cars, you've been beaten up like a thousand times. This is no different. Only this time, you're out for a little bit longer."

The AED beeps, telling us it's ready.

Gordon says, "You have thirty seconds to get your ass on the floor here or you're going to miss out on the most amazing experience you'll ever have."

And, amazingly, I sit.

The Delirium holding me in place.

It has me panting like a dog.

Gordon looks at his cell counting down and the AED wired up and ready to go. His finger hovers over the button.

And then he nods his head, says, "Enjoy the ride."

And he presses the button.

What I feel is brief, maybe only a tenth of a second, but it seems to last an entire afternoon. I think the best way to describe it is being roasted alive over a gas fireplace. The metallic taste in my mouth is like I've eaten an entire cutlery set and my fingernails are blackening, charring. And right when I think I can't take it any longer, wham! I find myself spinning down the outer-space tunnel into the future.

The pain is gone.

The searing has stopped.

I open my eyes and I'm maybe in my late twenties.

And I'm on a motorcycle cruising across a desert. Maybe this is still Colorado or maybe it's Utah or Nevada but it's desolate. It's barren. Just the wide blue sky and the hard pale ground and me on the bike.

I'm wearing leathers and I've got a helmet on. Gloves even.

I kick it up a gear and we're really zooming.

Odometer says I'm doing something like sixty.

And that's when I notice the rock. It's like this pyramidal thing sticking out of the crusted top of the sand a few hundred yards away. I'm headed straight for it, speeding up to seventy miles an hour.

The rock is the only thing out here. I'm guessing it was put there by someone, maybe me. And it doesn't take a brain surgeon to realize that I'm going to hit it. It will, however, probably take a brain surgeon to put my brain back in my head after I do. Colliding with this thing, at this speed, it's going to be nasty.

I speed up even more, now doing seventy-five.

From here I can see the surface of the rock. It's all pockmarked and weathered and it looks like it's been collided with many times over. Thing is jacked.

Also there is an X painted in red on the top half of it.

I know why that is there.

Closer and closer, the bike raging under me, busting up the silence of this place, I look down at my wrist at a high-tech watch that I'm wearing. Despite the pretty colors and the fact that the thing is as thin as a piece of paper, it's doing your standard countdown. It's at twenty.

Then nineteen.

And that rock is getting bigger and bigger the closer I'm getting to it.

The bike is at eighty miles an hour.

The plume of dust behind me is a freaking thunderstorm it's so huge.

What's weird is the countdown's started too early. Even at this speed, even from this close distance, I can tell the watch'll hit zero before the front wheel even comes within an inch of the rock.

So that means something else is happening.

The watch is at ten when I realize what it is.

Eighty-seven miles an hour.

The rock only fifty feet away.

And, both my hands snapping down hard like the jaws of sharks, I hit the brakes. This doesn't slow down the motorcycle so much as it just fucks it up completely. I go flying off, over the handlebar. The bike flips. It tumbles. I see parts of it, a wheel here, muffler there, spinning out into the sky. It's breaking apart.

I shoot forward, straight at the rock.

Before I close my eyes, I see the X getting bigger and bigger.

The rock is as large as the side of a bus and then it's a mountain, and right before I crash into it, head on, I hear the watch on my wrist beeping.

Time's up.

Smash and I'm out, spinning again into space.

Down the tunnel through time like speeding through a city on a rocket.

And then black.

When the black clears up, I'm downtown.

And this time: I'm fifty-something years old. Being in an older body, I can immediately feel the difference. The weight on my bones distributes differently and I can feel myself breathing. Every breath. In and out. This is new.

I'm downtown and it's Denver and I'm on the 16th Street Mall.

I'm wearing a suit. Nothing flashy. It's navy and has gold buttons and I've even got an ascot on. All I can think is it's Date Night with Vauxhall but this isn't a costume. This is seriously me dressed up to do something.

It's late afternoon; the shadows off the buildings are long.

There is a cold wind blowing through the city and it's got to be a Sunday in the fall because the tourists aren't stomping around and there are no businesspeople talking loudly and sipping from coffee cups.

I'm standing on a corner, watching cars pass, then lean out and look to my right and seem really psyched to see a bus coming. It's a mall bus. Doesn't go very fast and stops at every intersection but it's coming.

This massive smile breaks across my face.

I look down at my wrist and there's another watch there.

This one is even more high-tech than the last one. It's so thin it's practically part of my skin, maybe even embedded in it, and the display is 3-D. Just hovering there over my wrist and spinning around. It says 5 SECONDS.

The bus is only a block away.

I crack my neck.

Roll up my sleeves.

The rush of adrenaline going through my body tells me that it's been a while since I've done anything really exciting. It's been a while since I've let my body loose like this.

And the watch sings this little electro song.

That's the signal.

The bus is only ten feet from me when I close my eyes and step off the corner right in front of it. The driver slams on the horn. I can only imagine the expression on her face. Here it is Sunday and she's thinking she's killing an older dude just before her shift is over. What a thing.

The bus hits me. Slams me.

This old body of mine, it gets tossed like a rag doll. I purposely let my limbs go limp. Purposely just let myself fall wherever. I don't even open my eyes when my head bounces off the pavement.

This is because I'm already concussed.

I'm already in the outer-space tunnel.

The lights flash.

The tunnel closes in.

And when I open my eyes this time I'm in a wheelchair.

It's not like the last time I saw myself in a wheelchair. I'm not a drooling mental case this time. I'm not looking at myself in the mirror. I'm not seeing Jimi and Vauxhall making out outside my window.

No, this time, I'm just a super-old dude.

Just looking down at my wrinkled hands, the veins all distended and purple and running under the skin like the roots of some sickly tree, I'm guessing I'm like eighty-nine years old. Maybe even older.

I'm sitting in this chair at the top of a staircase.

I'm wearing a patchwork quilt over my legs. Each square, each patch, is a photograph printed on the fabric of it. The photo that's closest are of people in their fifties. I'm guessing my kids because I'm in the pictures too. Two women. Vauxhall is there. We seem such the big happy family. And in the other photos, farther out down where my knees start, are pictures of young people. Twenty-somethings first. Probably the grandkids. Three women and three men. And then, almost disappearing at my feet, the very edge of my old-man vision, I can see photos of great-grandchildren. Like ten of them. I can't even make out the sexes but just see bursts of blond hair and smiles and rosy cheeks. Almost like something you'd see in a really cheeseball Christmas postcard.

This is me at the end of the line.

I wonder where Vauxhall is?

And then, with my hands shaking, I wheel myself right to the edge of the top step.

This time I don't have to look down at my wrist to see the countdown. I just think about the time, just think about numbers, and they appear right there in my line of vision. A little off center, to the left, and totally see-through. Like the numbers are made out of glass. Another win for technology.

What I see now is THREE SECONDS.

And then, probably the very last time I'll give a huge grin, I push myself down the stairs. It's about as ugly a scene as you can imagine. I get all caught up in the wheels. The chair slams me every other step. On step three I dislocate my shoulder. Step five I fracture one of my hips. Finally, step seven, right when the pain is reaching its I-want-to-scream-my-freaking-head-off limit, I hit my skull, hear a crack like a bite into a stuffed taco, and I'm out.

Again with the space tunnel.

Again with the endless stream of lights.

Only this time, when I open my eyes, I'm not anywhere.

Like honestly not in any place. I'm in a void. Just blackness.

And in this no-place I feel incredibly comfortable. Fact is: The comfort I'm feeling here is exactly the same as a memory of comfort from my childhood. It was when I was six, lying in bed by the hot-air vent, and only half awake. Winter, and I had my long underwear on. I was buried under blankets but the window was open. Outside it was snowing and the moon was sitting low on the horizon, so motherly. That feeling, me under those covers and snug with the cold wind whistling against my face, is exactly how I feel here. Calm. Peaceful. Not too hot. Not too cold.

Pretty obvious it's death.

Pretty obvious this is what happens next. The eventual.

I'm just cuddled up in this blackness when I feel the water. There isn't just darkness here but warm water all around me. I'm lying on my back in black water and it's moving slowly. Waves breaking the surface in stop-motion and me just drifting on the surface.

The lights appear next.

They're tiny. Like stars twinkling above me. But not nearly as distant. These stars are maybe only a few inches away from my face. If I wanted to, I could probably grab them. But I don't want to. Somehow, I know that I shouldn't. The lights are colored. There is a red one, very faint, to my right. A blue one behind it. Green. Yellow. Purple. All these little Xmas lights above this dark molasses sea.

In this place, nothing else matters.

It's pure, animal. I'm only alive. Not thinking. Not worrying. Damn, does it feel good.

I don't want to think about Gordon. About whether this is reality or a re-creation of something. Of course it's real. It has to be. But still I'm doubting.

What if it isn't real?

What if nothing is?

The lights hovering closer to my face seem to grow slowly, larger and larger. They lose their focus the same way like when you zoom a camera in on distant lights. Just become these pixelated blobs. The lights sit right on top of my eyes, indistinct and heavy with color. And I want to let the boundaries of myself go.

Drift particle by particle into the shallow sea.

Become one with it.

Become one with the lights that—

And just like that, like being pushed out of a womb at a million pulsing miles an hour, I am back in the outer-space tunnel bombarded with bright white light. Going backward for the very first time, it feels like falling up into the sky. Like gravity losing its hold.

Then searing pain.

Being burned with an entire pack of cigarettes.

It gets so intense I open my eyes and scream.

Wouldn't you know it, I'm back in the bathroom, sitting straight up like a zombie sprung back to life, and Jeremiah is clapping like one of those toy monkeys in the corner and Gordon is just grinning ear to ear.

On my chest, the electrodes from the AED.

My singed chest hair sends off little curlicues of smoke.

The cops are battering down the door.

The Delirium is rampaging through me like a Viking berserker.

Sirens are screaming. People are shouting. Chaos basically.

The Delirium is singing a rock opera in my head.

Thank God Vauxhall isn't here to see the fact that I'm laughing like a child. That is until I notice that Gordon and Jeremiah are gone.

The Delirium has me shaking in fits.

It's slapping me silly like a bad parent.

It's cracking me over the head with a clown's rubber hammer.

And I'm alone with probably a million furious cops charging into the room in about ten seconds.

EIGHT

Here's the freakiest part.

When the cops come busting in with all of their guns out and mouths open in rage, I don't back down. I actually stand up, shirt-

PAST CONTINUOUS | 51

less and probably still steaming, and say words that make no sense coming out of my mouth.

I say, "What's your problem, pigs?"

This is the Delirium speaking.

It's using me like a ventriloquist's dummy.

The cops shout for me to get down.

Hands behind my head.

On my knees.

I don't budge. The Delirium has taken my voice, it's kicked my personality into a corner and come out all blustery and chest puffed up. It's acting like a goddamned maniac.

"Do you mind?!" I shout to the officers. "I'm doing something here."

They don't see the humor in it.

Calmly, one of the cops repeats himself.

Hands behind my head.

On my knees.

For a split second I'm able to get past the Delirium, squeeze past it, and in a totally weak and ineffectual child voice I say, "It's not me. Help me."

Yup. Instant psych ward stuff.

I've been there once when they thought the concussions had done me in. When they assumed my healing abilities, however unguided they are, weren't going to pull me through. It wasn't fun.

The cops move closer.

Guns not shaking in their hands.

Mouths not closing.

Eyes getting narrower and narrower.

The one who spoke to me before tells me that this is the very last time. He repeats his steely-toned mantra about me getting my hands behind my head and getting down on the floor. And he adds a useful nugget about something bad happening if I don't.

The usual me trapped behind the Delirium.

I can't figure out what's going on.

Don't know how to explain it.

And right before the cops taser me while I fight them off with all my strength, shouting horrible things that only the Delirium would say, I think: It's not just that I'm being possessed. I'm being taken over.

That or I've lost my mind.

NINE

She is, of course, the first to visit me in jail.

The way Vauxhall walks in, I've seen this sort of thing in movies. Her head all hung and it's like she's embarrassed to see me. Like she's embarrassed to be seen visiting me. This failed boyfriend of hers. This newly minted reprobate.

This isn't a movie and I'm not in maximum security so there's no big to-do with guards taking Vaux through like ten levels of security, all the doors whooshing open and the gates locking behind her. Also we don't talk on cheap telephones through a bulletproof plastic window.

No. Vaux and I meet in a cheerily decorated lounge. There are copies of *Newsweek* and *Tiger Beat* and *ESPN* that are eighteen months old. The furniture is all donated. All of it covered with various shades of cat hair.

I sit in a plastic chair and Vaux sits across from me on a pleather couch.

The guard, Stan, is outside the door. He's fat but he's got a rad mustache.

"Paige told me you're being charged as a terrorist," Vaux says.

"What?"

"A terrorist."

"Seriously?"

"That's what Paige says."

"Jesus. That's not even—"

Vaux has a notebook on her lap. She reminds me of my mom when she opens it up and starts taking notes. Looks up at me every few seconds. Takes a few more notes.

"Can't you at least give me a kiss?" I ask from my plastic chair. I even lean in.

Vaux rolls her eyes, gets up off the couch, walks over to me, and matter-of-factly kisses me on the forehead, totally avoiding my already pursed lips.

Then she goes and sits back down.

And then she goes and writes again in her notebook.

"Seriously?" I ask, crossing my arms.

"What?" Vaux looks up, feigning like she didn't hear me.

"Do you think I'm a terrorist or something?"

"Or something."

I make a noise that I've heard girls make when they're in fights. A noise that's like something a mammal that normally lives underwater makes. All irritated. All bitchy.

Vaux writes in her notebook.

"Will you chill for a minute with the freaking notebook? Christ. What are you writing in there anyway?"

Vauxhall gets up off the couch and walks over to me and opens the notebook.

I take it from her and she stands, waiting.

It's drawings of me. This sort of comic book of me. And what's crazy is how good the thing looks for her having only finished thirty seconds ago.

Panel one, drawn in this sort of funky locker room, Fantagraphics style is me sitting across from her and I've got fangs and devil horns and I'm cradling a severed human head in my lap.

Panel two, this one has me carrying all sorts of out-of-control weapons and blowing up buildings left and right. I'm a one-man army and I've even got Stallone-style biceps.

Panel three, last one, shows Vauxhall—she looks all cute and anime style—kneeling and crying in front of a gravestone that reads: HERE LIES ADE PATIENCE. DUDE, DID HE MESS HIS LIFE UP AND RUIN EVERYTHING HE HAD WITH THE BEST GIRL EVER.

I close the notebook and look up at Vaux and say, "I love you."

Then she leans over and gives me a kiss.

A real kiss.

A passionate kiss.

And then she goes back to her seat with her notebook.

"Are Gordon and Jeremiah here?"

Vaux shakes her head.

"Seriously! Damn."

"What happened, Ade? The doctors said you were burned."

I take a deep breath, then I tell her how the evening started. I tell her about the Pandora Crew's crazy scheme and about how it all seemed so nonsensical at first. Then I say, "But it was all planned out. The whole thing was for me to push beyond, well, beyond everything."

For the first time this evening Vauxhall actually seems interested in what I'm telling her. She can see the fascination in my eyes.

"What do you mean?"

And I get up and spread my arms all dramatic. "He had this thing figured out in order to let me see beyond my own lifetime. It was all timed down to the second. When the shock hit, I went into the future but then piggybacked those visions and kind of leapfrogged into the . . ."

"Into the what?"

"Into death."

"What are you saying, Ade? Are you okay?"

I sit down next to her. My eyes say it all. But still I continue. "I saw myself as a old dude. An ancient dude. And even then, like seventy years from now, I'm pushing myself down a flight of stairs to the future."

"Not the Buzz?"

"No. No. That wasn't part of it at all. This is different."

"So why, then?"

I can't bring myself to tell her about the Delirium.

I just can't.

Instead I say, "I don't know. But after I went down the stairs and hit my head, I leapt into this place that was incredible. It was amazing, Vaux. It was just darkness but there was water too. And these lights. These little pops of color. So beautiful, it was the most amazing thing I've ever seen. And I think it was real!"

Vauxhall doesn't know what to make of it.

The look on her face tells me she's freaked out. Scared.

"What do you—"

"I saw into heaven. Or the afterlife. Whatever you want to call it, Vaux."

"You died?"

I swallow hard. Nod.

With that she stands up. She's already crying, tears rushing down her face, and she says nothing to me when she knocks on the door. The guard outside opens it, lets her out. Locks it behind her. She doesn't even wave good-bye.

I sit back down and grab a ten-month-old copy of *Us* magazine.

But I don't really read it. I don't even fake-read it. I flip through the mag, look through the photos though what I'm really seeing is Vauxhall. Every word on the magazine's pages is about how Vauxhall no longer trusts me. Everything I'm thinking is splashed out on the pages. Seems like every headline starts with "Distrust" or "Gone Crazy."

Late last night I broke into a mall, ran around with a guy with a gun.

Shots were fired.

Property was destroyed.

I died. Saw into the future.

The whole time my body was on fire with the Delirium.

And it's only now that I'm locked up, kept alone, my chest

still burning, that I realize what I've done. I throw the magazine down and run my fingers through my hair.

What am I doing?

What does it mean?

Why?

CHAPTER TWO

ONE

Dear Judge Klein—

My lawyer suggested that I write you. He didn't need to; I was planning on doing it anyway. Fact is: I'm totally ashamed of my behavior. I thought long and hard about trying to explain it all to you in detail. Just flesh it out in some massive letter. But it would be twenty pages easy and it probably wouldn't have made a lick of sense.

Past six months have been something of a blur to me. This isn't because of drugs or because of some weird teen thing that I'm thinking or doing. I know you talked to Dr. Borgo, he told me some of the conversation you had, and that's all good. What he's told you is the truth as far as everyone is concerned.

Only, I'm not crazy. Not in the way you must think. Not like the people who come into your courtroom babbling about lizard aliens and remote control devices in their teeth. What I did was crazy. What I did makes no sense. But I did it because my life has been such a roller coaster of emotions. I've lived more in the past two years than I think I will the rest of my life. And only just now is it catching up with me.

Anyway, this is just rambling but really I wanted to write you and thank you for letting me off easy. Dr. Borgo explained my mental situation and I know sometimes the medical stuff doesn't make sense but thank you for trusting me. That means a lot. Maybe when you're not busy and I'm of legal drinking age, I'll buy you a beer and we can talk about what happened. Just man to man.

I've got a lot of work to do to repair this situation.

Thanks again.

Regards,

Ade Patience

P.S. This won't mean anything to you right now but we bumped into each other in the hall outside your courtroom and I thought I should tell you that when you go to Mexico for your wife's sixtieth, don't eat the oysters.

TWO

My dad burps the second I enter his room.

My coma dad in his hospital bed.

In his permanent sleep here.

I actually startle hearing him belch.

Like he might wake up any second.

I say, "Dad?"

Of course, he has no reaction.

He's not here.

He's in his fantasy world.

Part of me thinks that maybe, him being able to move around in people's minds and all, he knows exactly what he's doing. But that's probably not true. My dad lives on an entirely separate plane now. What happens here, in this life, means nothing to him unless I let him in on it. Let him inside my head to see it.

These days, with my abilities honed and focused the way they are, I don't have to have a vision or a dream to let my dad in. There isn't any of the hide-and-seek garbage that we were doing before.

No, pretty much it's a direct connection now.

Like psychic DSL.

This morning, I close the door to my dad's room and then plop down on the end of his bed and using just one finger I touch his hand.

The effect is instantaneous.

I have no idea how it works. Not exactly. My dad tried to explain it once. He said that it was more due to him doing something than it was to me, but still the deal is freaky. I'm in the hospital, the here and now, one second, and the next I'm whisked off to whatever place my dad wants to meet up in. Never the same place and never a place I would have chosen or thought of.

Today, it's some tropical jungle.

It's green and hot and there is this constant sound of water like maybe there's a waterfall just beyond the nearest impenetrable stand of tropical trees. I'm standing under two massive trees, curlicues of ferns all wrapped around my legs. Bugs in the millions scuttling through the undergrowth. Birds shrieking. Monkeys swinging.

"Hey, buddy."

I look up at the tree to my right and there's Pops. He's sitting in a recliner on a platform in the tree about twenty feet above me. There's a blond woman with him. She's wearing like some sort of Tarzan getup, a monkey fur bra or something. He waves her away and she just vanishes.

"Come on up," Dad says, and automatically a ladder made of bamboo tied together with vines drops down out of nowhere.

I climb up, the ladder creaking with every step.

"It's safe," Dad says. "Everything here is safe."

I get up to the platform and a second recliner has materialized there.

So I take a seat next to my dad and look him over. He's maybe mid-thirties in this reality and he's got a beard and long hair held back in a sloppy ponytail. He's bronzed tan and he's wearing what you'd expect: jungle-explorer khakis and a sweat-soaked T-shirt.

"Want a beer?"

I shrug. "Sure."

Two beers appear on the platform between us. Bottled import stuff.

Dad hands me a bottle opener and I pry the lid loose, have a sip. It's good. Gives me shudders how cold it is going down my throat in this heat. Dad sees the shudder and he laughs. Probably thinking I'm a wuss. That kind of laugh.

"Who was that woman?" I ask him, jabbing back.

"Her name is Lola."

"Of course it is."

"What's that supposed to mean?"

I look away. "It's your world. Just figured maybe, I don't know, you'd have created a version of Mom or something."

Dad groans. "If I brought your mom into this, it wouldn't be my world anymore."

I put my beer down and look out into the trees. The sun has started setting and the jungle is getting louder. All sorts of things tumbling out of the trees to sing their songs.

"Look, Pops," I say, still staring at the trees, watching a particularly large centipede scuttle across a branch. "We need to talk about something."

He looks over at me. For some reason I don't want to make eye contact.

"The thing is," I start, "I'm not thinking right anymore. And that's strange but really I haven't been thinking right or clearly since eighth grade. But this is new. This is me thinking like someone else. And . . . Well, I don't know what but I'm hoping you can help me."

And that's when I look over at him.

He gets how important this is right away and suddenly, almost like he hit some sort of dimmer switch, the jungle noises start to go way down and all the scaly and armored things that have been scuttling out from the ground turn right around and go back. He basically turns this green inferno off.

Suddenly it's not nearly as hot.

The sun just drops away and we're left with this magic hour

lighting. It's where the sky is light and pale but the sun is totally gone. No moon either. Just empty sky that feels heavy like it could fall on us.

"Tell me," Dad says.

"Mostly I've been doing crazy stuff. Not crazy like before but stuff that doesn't just hurt me. Things I feel guilty about doing but that when I was doing them seemed just incredible. Like having the Buzz again but sloppy. Like too sugary. Too out of control. I call it the Delirium but really it's basically like psychic meth."

"Okay."

"And it all kind of culminated when this guy, this other diviner dude, killed me."

"Killed you?" Dad screws up his face.

"Yeah. But listen, when my heart stopped I jumped into the future and just kept on jumping. Years over years over years. And then, I stopped at this place where it was just darkness and these beautiful lights and the most soothing . . . I can't even really describe it but I'm pretty sure it was being dead. Then my friend brought me back."

"I've never seen that."

"Well, that was my first question. I was wondering if . . . Well, if it was real."

"I doubt it." Dad shakes his head. A bat flies by slowly like it's underwater. "When the accident happened, I only felt pain. Just a burn. And out into the nothing. Like really nothing. No soothing. No lights."

I think on it, then say, "I guess that maybe that's a good thing because I can't stop thinking about that place. If you'd have been there, you wouldn't be able to either. But if it's not real, then . . ."

I don't like the thought of the alternative so I push the idea away.

"Dad, Vauxhall is super worried about me. I'm worried. Something has changed and I don't like the feeling that's inside of me right now. It's not me. There've been a few times when I'd hit my head and then after I came to, my hand or one of my feet would be asleep. Like totally not feeling anything. And I'd look down at it and it would seem like it wasn't mine. Like it was someone else's hand or leg on my body. Wouldn't last long but it was freaky. Now, right now, that's how my whole body feels. That's how my mind feels."

Dad holds on to that for a minute.

A full minute.

Then he nods and says, "You want me to go in and take a look?"

"Would you mind?"

"No. If you want me to I'll do it."

I nod.

And because this is his world, because really I'm not in a jungle but sitting on the edge of his hospital bed just blanking out, he doesn't have to do anything funky to get inside my skull. He doesn't even have to touch me. I'm in his mind, he can just dive in.

Dad closes his eyes and I watch the jungle.

Nothing moves. It's on pause now. There are birds caught in midair. Little dashes of light that turn out to be fireflies stuck in the sky. And it's so silent that my breathing sounds like a hurricane moving back and forth and back and forth across a shore.

Dad opens his eyes and I can already tell it's bad.

Something terrible.

He's shaking.

He reaches over and puts his hand on my shoulder and says, "You have to go see Dr. Borgo. He'll know what to do. Say that it's like Render again."

"What?"

"Render. He'll know what that means."

"Tell me what's happening, Dad. What did you see?"

"I can't. Just go talk to him. I'm sorry."

And then Dad just unplugs me. Like that I wake up in the hospital room, Dad back to his coma self. Sunlight blazing in through the blinds and stirring up all these motes of dust. Dude just totally kicked me out of his personal heaven.

I stand up and give a big huff.

"You're so lame," I say, and then flick my dad off.

THREE

Vauxhall's wrong. Paige doesn't hate me, she just has this new girlfriend, Veronica, and Veronica has massive boobs.

Lets everyone know it too. Like she's wearing billboards.

Veronica looks like Paige only she's sexy. Like the weird pin-up version.

Paige has never been sexy. At least not to me. She's got all the requisite parts, only she doesn't use them in any of the ways that guys consider sexually stimulating. For Paige, it's more the living-in-the-moment, the one-of-the-guys kind of über-comfortable thing. I wouldn't say relaxed 'cause Paige tells me that's too lesbian, but it's close. It's like, well, a girly dude thing. Sort of.

Anyway, Veronica has long dyed black hair with bangs, wears sweaters or shirts, tights, and black thigh-high leather boots, and struts around like she's made of some different element than the rest of us. And also she's always got cleavage.

Always.

If you can't see the half orbs of her boobs, then it's not Veronica.

V-neck sweaters equal cleavage.

Dresses equal cleavage.

Suits equal cleavage (with a tie down the middle).

It's nuts.

And Paige loves it. And Dr. Borgo clearly also loves it.

We're in his office. Paige and Veronica have given me a ride, and even though Dr. Borgo's kind of stressed at having two other people, extra people, in the room, he's grooving on the cleavage.

It's like Veronica's always carrying around a rainbow.

I'm not in the doctor mood so Paige gets things started.

"He's not himself," she says, pointing at me. Me, the thing.

Borgo starts in with the psychobabble immediately. "Ade is a complicated person. He's been through a lot. I'm not at all surprised that he'd act out of sorts every now and then. You know, experiencing significant trauma can cause severe, though often not lasting, personality changes. It isn't—"

"No," Paige goes. "No, he's actually not himself."

Dr. Borgo chews on the arms of his glasses, looks me over.

"And?" he asks.

I nod. "Pretty much," I say. "There's something . . . possessing me."

I don't get into the whole is-this-reality-real-or-not, the did-I-actually-die-and-see-heaven thing.

Dr. Borgo asks, "How do you mean?"

I lean in, eyes locked on Borgo's. "Like someone else is in here." And I punctuate that by pointing at my forehead. Tapping my forehead with my index finger.

Tap. Tap.

Clearly Borgo isn't going to give me anything new so I bust out what my dad told me. I say, "It's Render again."

Dr. Borgo goes all quizzical.

"That's what my dad told me to tell you. He went inside my head and checked it out and when he came out he was shaking and said Render again."

My shrink leans back in his chair. "Do you know what that means?"

"No. He wouldn't tell me. But I Googled it. Got nothing."

"That's because it's a secret."

"—"

Paige rubs her hands together. "This is getting good," she says.

I shoot her a nasty look and Veronica shushes Paige.

Dr. Borgo gets up and goes to a file cabinet behind him. He pulls out the bottom drawer and digs around for a second. Then, without turning around, he says, "Uh, Paige and Veronica, it's better if you step out for a few minutes. What I have to tell Ade is confidential."

Paige looks at me all shocked. Raises her hands, pleading for me to say something. Veronica stands and pulls Paige up with her to the door.

"I'll let you know when you can come back," Borgo says. Then: "Actually, it'd probably be better if you just waited out in the lobby for a while. Or go and get some lunch. We might be a while."

The girls leave.

The good doctor pulls a box out from the bottom of the file cabinet, turns around, and then walks over to me with it. He places the box in my lap and says, "Have a look."

I open the box and inside is a stack of photos and a video-cassette.

I look at the photos first. They're old and faded. Bent. The first photo I pick up is a close-up of a boy's face, he's maybe ten years old and has blond hair and gray eyes and looks distracted. The writing on the photo under his face says RENDER FETE. Next photo is similar. Another close-up of a face. Another boy with very similar features. Almost the same boy but he's got different-colored eyes, dark brown this time, and he's smiling. Really big. Written on this photo is JERRY FETE.

"Okay and . . ." I say to Borgo, not knowing why he's show-ing me these.

"Keep looking."

I go to the next photo and that's when my jaw drops. These two kids, Render and Jerry, they share the same body. Render's head is on the right and Jerry's is on the left. In this photo they're sitting on an exam table. Two little heads and scrawny necks on the same little kid body. Two arms. Two legs. My eyes are blown out of my head.

Borgo says, reading my expression, "Siamese twins. Born in France in the late seventies. They were wonderful children."

"It's crazy . . . How did . . . ?"

Borgo says, "Couldn't be separated. They shared an intestinal tract as well as a heart. And honestly, they were quite healthy. The early estimates predicted that they'd live for around fifty years. It wasn't uncommon, before the surgical advances of to-day, for Siamese twins to live long and healthy lives. Even marry and have children of their own."

"Wow," I say. Not even wanting to think about that.

I put the photos back. "What's the deal with them?"

"Gifted. Had prognostication skills like your father's."

"You showed him this stuff?"

"Yes. It was part of the therapy I tried."

"And why are you showing me?"

Borgo takes the box from me. He takes out the videocassette and then puts the box down on his desk. He's got a cheap TV/VCR combo set up on a wheeling cart in the corner and he wheels it over, flicks it on. Then he puts the video in.

"It's hard to forget what I'm about to show you," he says.

"I don't know if I really want to then."

"You do."

"Why?"

"Because your father has seen inside your head, Ade. He says that what happened to Render Fete is exactly what's happening to you right now. I can try and explain it to you, talk you through it, but I honestly think it's just better if you see for yourself."

And with that he presses play on the VCR and sits down on the edge of his desk.

The first ten seconds of the video are just static. Then come the familiar color bar things that you see when you're watching public access at like three in the morning. This is followed by a digital countdown, looks very '80s.

Then: The Fete twins are sitting in a high-backed chair. They look older than in the pictures and they look all sleep-deprived. Bags under their eyes, thinner, sunken even. The boys are talking into the camera, slowly like they're reading from a prompter, but they're speaking in French.

"What are they saying?"

Dr. Borgo says, "Just the date and the time and how long they've been at the facility. This was filmed in a mental institution by a colleague of mine in Montreal. He was studying Render in particular."

And as if on cue the camera zooms in on Render as he recites.

"What happened to them?" I ask, not wanting to see more. Worried about where this is headed.

"You'll see."

Not the answer I want.

I prod, "Maybe we can just fast-forward."

Dr. Borgo looks over at me sympathetically. "Ade, I've known you for how many years now? You never shied away from crashing your car into a wall or fighting with bikers. If you want to know what could happen, then you need to just watch this. If you truly are as concerned as I think you probably should be, this is essential."

"Scared straight, huh?"

"Pretty much."

The camera zooms back out. The two boys are handed a toy.

It's like one of those puzzles where you slide the pieces inside a box. They work on it together. Jerry seems particularly interested. Render just kind of looks back and forth from the game to Jerry.

"What sorts of abilities did they have again?" I ask Borgo. Don't like the silence.

"Telekinesis but on a much deeper level than most researchers have seen. Like your father they could get into other people's heads. Other prognosticators' visions as well. But Render, his skill went beyond just the run-of-the-mill mind reading. He was able to utilize a strange form of psonic plasticizing and—"

"Wait. What?"

Borgo keeps his eyes on the flickering screen. "He could change matter with his mind. Manipulate physical spaces. He could also affect the organic makeup of living tissue."

"Sounds nasty."

"It is."

Someone off camera asks the boys another question. Jerry keeps on playing with the game, not bothering to look up. He answers. Render stares at whoever is asking the questions. Seems royally pissed off. Then he looks back to Jerry.

"Here," Dr. Borgo says. "This is where it begins."

And against my better judgment I lean in closer to see. Another question comes from whoever's behind the camera and Render gets really mad. He shouts something. Shouts loud enough that the camera shakes. Either it shakes because the person holding it is freaked out or it actually shakes because of the shout.

Reading my mind, Borgo says, "He made the camera shake."

There's more. Render makes this face, like he's taken a bite out of something made of salt and lemons and glass shards, and the camera just starts quivering. Whoever is behind the camera yells, high-pitched like they're scared to death. And then, the camera still shuddering, Render, almost barely contained by the frame, looks over at Jerry, who's still distracted with the game.

Render closes his eyes. Tight.

And that's when Jerry starts to shake. His head just starts to bob. Jerry turns to his attached brother all confused. He looks hurt. Like he's being betrayed.

"I don't think this is necessary," I say to Borgo.

Borgo says, "Watch."

I do. I see Render staring at his brother. The screen is just crazy shaking now like whoever has the camera is running in place with it. Every third second the shot is lost, bouncing up to show the ceiling tiles or down to show the carpeted floor. But when Render and Jerry are in frame, what I see is so strange that I don't get it. It makes no sense.

Jerry is getting smaller.

And smaller.

Render is staring him down the way you'd stare down a bad dog.

Jerry is freaking out. His face this mask of fear and sadness.

It's heartbreaking.

And still his head is getting smaller. It's about half the size of Render's. Even more, it's actually getting younger. Like one of those nature films where they show a flower bust out of the ground and bloom all sped up, this is the reverse. We're watching

Jerry's hair get pulled back into his head. His eyes get bigger. His head just smaller and smaller.

The shaking is almost too much now.

I'm getting motion sickness watching this.

Borgo says, "Almost . . ."

I lean in even closer to see what's happening. Render's face so evil-looking. His eyes just beaming out this hate. And Jerry's baby eyes are all innocent and vanishing. Soon, his head is so small there's no room for eyes so his eyes get sucked back into his head. And the same with his nose. His ears also.

There's just a mouth in a fleshy ball.

And then the mouth, no noise coming out of it, starts to shrink. It's the size of an ear and then it's a belly button and then it's just a freckle before it's gone. Render screaming down at it, throwing daggers with his eyes at the thing that was his brother but is now just a big cyst on his shoulder.

The shaking calms down a bit.

The camera isn't going up and down and up and down.

Render seems to calm as the lump on his shoulder turns into just a patch of pale skin and then that patch of skin peeking out from the stretched neck of the XXXL shirt the boys were wearing slowly blends in.

The camera is totally stable.

Render looks downright peaceful.

His brother is gone. Absorbed into him. Vanished.

The camera lingers on Render's face, zooms into his tranquil eyes, and holds there for a few beats before the television screen goes back to static. The hiss and rush of it is jarring and I fall back in my chair.

Look over at Borgo. He's somber. Nods to me slowly.

"What the hell was that?" I ask. "What did my dad see inside my head?"

Borgo turns the television off.

Then he sits down all professional behind his desk. Considers. Then says, "Reason you're acting differently. Reason you don't feel like yourself is because there is a war going on inside you. A war for your very identity."

"What are you talking about . . . ?"

The Delirium. I already know this . . .

"Jimi. He didn't succeed. He wanted to completely switch your childhoods but it didn't work. You stopped it midway. And now you're stuck with half of his childhood. I suspect in his case it's actually worked out to his advantage. Your good memories, the childhood that afforded you the personality you had until now, has tempered his bad ones. Unfortunately, you haven't been able to take on his childhood without bad side effects. It's the same as when you transplant a kidney or a liver. If that transplant organ has, let's say, cancer, then the rest of the system will be infected."

"You're saying I have cancer?"

Borgo gives this little doctorly laugh. "No. Not the kind you're thinking of. You have been infected with Jimi's past. And it's destroying you much in the same way that Render destroyed his brother, subsumed him."

Pretty much I'm feeling like he just told me I do have cancer. Worse. I have this crazy flash of Jimi's head erupting from my shoulder and slowly shrinking mine.

"And so—?" At this point I stand up. Panicked. "What does that do to me? Like what effects?"

"Change in personality. Hallucinations. Strange sensations of—"

"Seeing things?"

"Yes, that's possible."

I think of the blackness at the end of time. The lights. A hallucination?

"So, what do I do about it?" I ask.

He says, "You need to have it removed."

"How?"

"At first I thought it might be the same way you had it put in, via some sort of transference. An ability like Jimi's. But I realized it was unlikely that it would work. No, you're going to need to do something radical."

"Radical?"

Borgo motions for me to sit down.

I do.

"In many cases, a cancer needs to be cut out and then the surrounding tissues and nodes as well. We need to have that past cut out of your personal history. Delete it."

I laugh. It's all the pressure of the past few minutes coming out. I just totally let loose with this torrent of crazy-man laughter.

My shrink doesn't mind. He gets it.

He gets me.

Well, he thinks he does.

I pull myself together. "So, what next? Don't tell me there's some dude out there that can do this."

Borgo is silent.

I know what that means. There is a dude.

"Who is he?"

"I've only heard stories. Rumors. He showed up a while ago and is as underground as you get. Basically, you can't find this guy but if you're looking for him, he can find you. What he does is surgical. He takes out the bad pieces of your history. Fractures and resets the past."

"Sounds dangerous."

"Well." Dr. Borgo stands up and walks over and puts a hand on my shoulder. "We're talking about uncharted territory here, Ade. This is as dangerous as it gets. If you do this you'll be messing with the very fabric of the universe. Seeing the future is one thing. Changing it another. Think of that as algebra. The past? That's the most advanced, PhD-level mathematics you can imagine. Or can't. What you do to the past, it's irreversible. Make the changes and who knows what could happen. Risky. Risky."

"Like what could happen?"

Borgo rubs his chin. "You could die. You could be born all over again. You could kill everyone on the planet. You could mess up the course of human history. Ade, everything in the future that you've ever seen will be changed. Undoubtedly. The future you see now is the one that comes from the you that exists now. If the you changes, everything changes."

"I'm not totally following but I get the drift. Maybe there's something else?"

"Doubtful."

Never one to pause before jumping in, I say, "Doesn't sound like I have a choice."

"You don't. If you want to stay who you are, you have to do it."

"Messing with the very fabric of the universe, huh?"

"Pretty much."

"And you're cool with that? What if what I do changes who you are? Erases you or makes you a child or turns the world inside out?"

"I wouldn't know. That's the thing about messing with the fabric of the universe, whatever you do instantly becomes ancient history. Any changes you make are changes that have always existed."

"Now you're making no sense."

"I'm just telling you not to worry about anyone else but yourself, Ade. Truth is: If this guy is real and he's doing this stuff, he's already changed the past countless times. And yet, Hitler's still in the history books. There still was a slave trade. The Broncos still lost to the Steelers in oh-five. Do what you need to, Ade."

"So who do I talk to first?"

"I don't know, but I think *you* do."

FOUR

Whole drive home Paige is silent.

She doesn't need to ask me what happened. She can read it in my face. Maybe not the details, but she knows it's heavy-duty shit. Like Borgo, Paige just knows me.

Well, she thinks she does.

Boob girl Veronica clearly doesn't.

"Come on," she says. "At least tell us some of it."

This is the third time she's asked in two blocks.

I pull the car over, shoot Paige a look. "Are you guys serious?"

"What do you mean?" Paige asks.

"Yeah," Veronica chimes in.

"I mean, are you two like a thing? Soul mates?"

"Why?" Paige asks.

"Because if I'm going to tell her even part of this, I need to know that you're not going to have a nasty breakup next week and all my personal shit is going to be on a blog somewhere as retribution."

"I would never do that," Veronica says. And she huffs.

"She would never do that," Paige confirms.

I say, "So answer my question."

Paige looks back at Veronica. She smiles, nods.

"I think we're in this for a while," Paige says, still staring into Veronica's eyes. "But we're in high school, Ade. And neither of us has crazy superpowers. We're just lesbians and Veronica has a nice smile, some witty jokes, and a beautiful rack."

I say, "That'll do."

I drive in silence to this really nice Thai place on 8th and then pull over.

Cars zipping by us on Colorado Boulevard, I tell them exactly what it felt like to watch that freak-show movie. I tell them how Dr. Borgo laid this mission out as being honestly the most dangerous thing I could possibly do. I pull out my wallet and fish out a fifty and hand it to Veronica and say, "I want you two to have a nice dinner on me. If anything goes nuts and I mess the whole space-time continuum thingy up, at least you had some excellent pad thai and got to stare into each other's eyes."

Paige wants to smack me. "Are you serious?"

"About what?"

"About doing this."

"Yes."

"Why don't you just get therapy, Ade? Maybe some time in jail would do you good. Get your head straight. You don't have to change the course of human history just because you've got a psych problem."

"Paige, I'm literally turning into someone else."

"Yeah. So. You should see Veronica when she has her period."

Veronica slaps the back of Paige's head. Paige nods her apologies.

"I'm just saying," Paige says. "You should really consider the rest of humanity, you know, all two billion or whatever of us, before you go and fuck with creation and turn us all back into fish."

"I don't think the changes are going to be that dramatic."

"But there could be changes, right?"

"Could be."

"And? Don't you think maybe you should sleep on it? Maybe sit down and have a chat with a focus group first? Do a poll? This is insane, Ade."

"It is. You're right."

"And you don't feel bad about it?"

"Not really."

Paige throws her hands up, exasperated. "I hope this is just a joke."

Veronica is quiet.

I say, "The old me would take all that into consideration for sure."

"And the new you?"

"No. The new me's going to do this regardless of the costs."

Veronica, bottom lip trembling, asks, "Why?"

"Because I'll be lost if I don't. I want this changed before Vaux-hall sees me. Before it gets worse and she freaks out or worse. What if . . . what if the bad side of me comes back and does something to her? Does something I regret?"

"Romantic but still batshit insane," Paige says.

I unlock the doors. "You two have a nice dinner."

They get out and don't bother to wave good-bye. To them, I just pushed the big red button on the computer that'll launch the nukes. To them, I just doomed us all.

Before I leave, I roll down the window and say, "It won't be that bad. I promise. Everyone's always just a pessimist when it comes to changing things. How about thinking that if anything happens, the results will make everything sweeter?"

That's when Paige leans in, stares as deep into my eyes as humanly possible, and says, "Are you even worried that what you're about to do just might destroy the very thing you want to save?"

FIVE

And so I go to the Diviners.

They've moved from the old place by Paris on the Platte.

I don't know if after my showdown with Grandpa Razor business suddenly picked up, but now they're in a penthouse by the railroad. This magnificent gleaming glass building that shines like a stained-glass window floating over the city. Can't say it's their lair anymore. This, this is their empire.

Walk in the lobby and it's modern art central.

All these glass things, probably hand-blown, hanging off the walls like they're squids and octopuses pinned up there by alien fishermen. Seeing them, the new me wants to smash them. Not good.

I make my way to this circular desk in the middle of the room.

Guy there is wearing a hotel suit that makes him look like a solider from some way-in-the-past European war. He nods to me slowly. Asks, "To see?"

"Uh, Gilberto."

"Gilberto who?"

Weirdly enough I'm blanking on the name so I just spit out, "The Diviners."

That gets through and the security guy picks up a phone— it's a rotary phone to maintain the hip edge of the place—and dials. He eyes me while he waits for someone to pick up. Then: "Yeah, I've got a . . ."

I'm supposed to answer. I say, "Patience."

Security dude screws up his face but says, "Got a Patience here."

Then he nods. Hangs up.

"Top floor," he says. "Exit the elevator left."

The elevator is all brushed silver and there's a flat-screen television on one wall. On the screen is this really soothing video of a babbling brook probably somewhere back east. Ferns surround it, rocks piled up and moss-covered on the sides. Very nice.

Whole ride up I'm kind of entranced by the brook.

I hardly notice when the elevator stops.

It dings.

Doors swoosh open and I step out into a hallway. Head left.

The walls are lined with portraits of people I know nothing about. People I don't recognize from anywhere. There's a man with a goatee, shaved head, thick-framed glasses. He's wearing a hoodie and on this little placard under his photo it says, J. TILLER, ONOMANCER, NYC. Another portrait has this young girl, maybe seven and blond. Her placard says, H. SELLER, GYROMANCER, DES MOINES. And there are more. Old women and frail men with mustaches. There are placards about capnomancy and tyromancy.

The hallway ends at a large oak door.

It is, of course, cracked open.

I push it all the way open and step inside and I'm not surprised to find the place looks like something you see in a perfume commercial. The walls are white. The furniture—all of it from the couches to the lounge chairs to the lamps to the bookcases— are white. The curtains are white. I'm guessing the white fridge in the kitchen is filled with milk.

Place seems empty.

I walk over to these picture windows and from up here can see the whole city. I-25 is just rows and rows of red lights like smokers all lined up and inhaling together. I'm standing there, thinking back over what Paige told me, when my cell rings.

Got this kickass ringtone that sounds very '80s.

It's Vaux.

"Hey," I answer, still staring out at the city.

"Paige came by. Actually, she and Veronica are still here."

"Okay. Cool."

There is radio silence for about ten seconds.

Then Vauxhall says, "Come over. Please."

"Can't, babe. If Paige told you everything, then you know I can't."

"This isn't a joke, Ade. Please."

"I know. I don't think it's a joke. I want to be myself again and I want to be myself with you and I'm willing to do anything to have that."

"Anything?"

"Yes."

"Then come over. Stay with me. Don't go out tonight."

Watching the cars leaving the city, I say, "I'm already out, Vaux. Trust me on this. Whatever happens, I'm doing this for you. I can't change myself without taking a risk. If I have to, I'll change the world, change human history, to be with you."

And that's when I hang up.

Take a deep breath.

And that's when I turn back around and notice there are now three people sitting on one of the white couches. It's Gilberto wearing a white suit with the shirt halfway unbuttoned and his tan skin shining through. And it's Belle sitting next to him in a sleek white dress with her hair dyed purple. And it's, well, someone I've never seen before. This guy is young, is wearing a white T-shirt and black slacks, and has a ponytail. Thing is I can't see his face because he's wearing a gas mask. Yeah.

Gilberto is the first to speak. He says, chuckling despite himself, "Ade, been a few months. What brings you here?"

"Just catching up."

Belle laughs. Guy in the gas mask makes no noise.

Gilberto leans forward, pulls out a cigar. He's moving up in the world for sure. He lights it, takes his time puffing away on it. Then he says, "The guy you're looking for is downtown. He's quite expensive."

"That's it, huh?"

Belle says, "I've been really bummed that I haven't seen you in like forever." She gets up off the couch and walks over to me and gives me this massive, tight hug. Then she smiles. Something's up.

"What's up?" I ask her, watching the guy with the gas mask over her shoulder. "Who is this weirdo?"

Belle hugs me again. Whispers, "You don't want to know."

Then she peels away and sits back down. Gilberto crosses his legs, cigar balanced nicely, and blows a ring of smoke. He says, "His name is the Glove. Well, technically that's not his name, but that's what everyone calls him."

"And he can do, uh, what I'm looking for?"

"Yeah," Gilberto says. "He's the magic man."

"And when you say he's expensive?"

"I meant it." Gilberto smiles. "Dude is super pricey. No set fee. He'll determine the charge based on what you're asking to do."

"You've used him before?"

"Several times."

That has me smiling. I relax a bit. "And the universe seems the same to me."

Gilberto just nods. Slowly. Then he stands up and walks over to me and puts an arm around my shoulder. He turns me to face the window again. I can see the trail of red lights in my own reflection. Gilberto's reflection very grim.

"We're living in very interesting times. It seems as though the world changes faster than any of us can comprehend. Tell me about Vauxhall."

"What do you mean?"

"She's the love of your life. What are you doing here?"

I turn and stare at Gilberto. Try to read him through his eyes. Not getting much.

"Tell me about the cat in the mask."

Gilberto shakes his head. "Can't tell you."

"Why?"

"He likes to be mysterious."

I chew my bottom lip. Need to get this show on the road. And I'm not comfortable with the scene here. Something very bad under the surface.

"Tell me where to find the Glove."

Gilberto gives this little laugh that tells me he thinks he's in control. That this here is his show. He says, "We need to make a deal first."

"A deal? For what?"

"Well, I can point you in the right direction but you need to do something for the Diviners. You need to be a team player for the first time in your life, my man. It's simple really. Only thing I know is that you need what the Glove can supply. Other details don't matter. You find him, you just tell him one thing for me, okay?"

"One thing?"

"Yup. When you're comfortable, in his abode, you tell him that I haven't forgotten the deal we made. That's it. You be careful, Ade. You're moving up to the big leagues now."

We turn back around together. I notice the guy with the gas

mask is now leaning back, hands behind his head. Looking awful comfy. And even though I can't see his eyes, I know he's looking at me. Staring deep into me.

Belle waves. Blows me a kiss.

She says, "I'll call you next week. We need to have lunch."

And then Gilberto walks me to the door. Gas mask stays on the couch, head turned to follow us all creepy like he's half robot.

At the door, Gilberto says, "He's at Muddy's most nights. Only thing you need to know about the guy is that he's ugly. Really ugly. Don't forget what I asked. Do it and we're good."

"When haven't we been good?"

Gilberto smiles.

He says, "Have fun out there, bro."

SIX

It's been months since I've been to Muddy's.

It's a coffee joint on the west side.

Mostly where the hippies and the dirties hang.

Just walking into the place I feel jittery. Wired. I'm scanning the place, looking at every table. Good thing the café is actually pretty much empty.

There's this one dude with a big beard, sipping a foamy mocha thing in the back corner and a group of girls, college girls, with books cracked open on their tables, talking quietly. Sighing a lot.

And by the bar, reading *Naked Lunch,* is the Glove.

I can tell it's him immediately. The guy is hideous. Not in the monster-in-the-closet way or the mauled-by-rabid-pitbulls way, but he just exudes this creepiness that's like a cloud hanging over him. I haven't felt anything like it since my first meetings with Grandpa Razor and I'm hesitant.

The Glove must sense that 'cause he looks up from his book and smiles.

If you could take the skinniest, grossest junkie on Colfax and dress him in a too-tight spandex shirt, throw a licey black cap on his head, and give him a spattering of facial hair that's not at all symmetrical, that's what the Glove looks like.

I walk up, sit down next to him, ask, "Glove?"

"Who's asking?"

"My name's Ade. Diviners sent me over. I have a question."

"Ade?"

"Yeah."

He laughs. Hard. The air rattling around in his chest like bones. Then he calms down and wipes his mouth with the back of his hand. That same hand, he puts it out to shake. Against my better judgment I take his hand, shake.

And I get like this static jolt from it.

That gets the Glove laughing all over again.

"Let me guess," he says. His teeth are gray. "You want to try and fix something in the past. Go back and make it, um, not what it is now."

"Yes."

"And you want to do this because you think it'll help. Help now."

"Right."

"Let me tell you, guy." He leans in close, his eyes are bloodshot.

"Messing around with the past isn't like any of those other pastimes that the Diviners get their kicks from. This, this is serious business. You jerk around with the future and no one notices. Why would they? But the past. Nah, the past is something special."

"Can you do it?"

"Sure. I can do it. I've done it four times with you already."

And he smiles.

"What the hell's that supposed to mean?" I ask.

"A joke," he says.

The Glove takes a long sip of his coffee then wipes his nose, looks over at me. There's something about his eyes that remind me of my dad. Something distant. Something lost. Forgotten. It makes me sad looking at him so I turn away.

"How much?" I ask. "Heard you're pricey."

The Glove says, "I'll do it for free."

Wow. Color me shocked.

"Why's that?"

"Because I can tell you've got a problem."

"You can?"

"Uh-huh."

"So, how does it work? What do you need to do?"

The Glove puts a hand on my shoulder. The shock again, only this time I don't jump from it. He tells me that the how of it isn't something he can explain. He tells me that he didn't even know he had the ability until he used it. He says, "First time I did it, the results were dramatic."

"Dramatic how?"

"Dramatic in the worst possible way. You've got to really,

really want to do this, Ade. I can't guarantee you anything. Actually, there is one thing I can guarantee: You won't be the same after."

"That's the point," I say, a bit frustrated. "I don't want to be the same."

"How this is going to work is you come to my apartment and you bring me some Mad Dog. Also you bring me an eight-piece dinner from Kentucky Fried Chicken and you don't skimp on the biscuits. I will additionally require a ball-peen hammer."

"Ball peen?"

"A hammer for cracking open rocks. Like geodes."

"Okay. I can get you most of that."

The Glove puts his head on his fist and stares at me hard.

"Fine," he says after a moment. "Just bring me some Mad Dog."

"Okay."

"Good. I want it cool. I like it cool."

"Chilled, sure. When should I, uh?"

"That's up to you, Ade. Depends on how soon you want to change the past. If I were you, I wouldn't rush into this. Go back home. Think it over for a few weeks. You know, take this slow. You still want to do it after that, then you know where to find me."

"I don't want to wait weeks."

"Rushed?"

"Sort of."

"Tell me."

"I don't think you'd understand, man. No offense but it's super complicated."

The Glove laughs about that. He really give his deepest skeleton-dance chuckle over that and then settles back into his seat and says, "Why don't we just head back to my place now, then? We'll pick up what I need on the way."

SEVEN

On the way means walking three blocks south, under the interstate and past the homeless shelter with the red neon cross that flashes LORD and then SAVES. LORD. SAVES.

The night is crisp.

Crisp enough that I can actually see my breath.

And the stars have apparently multiplied because there are so many more thousands of them that I have never seen before. The sky is deep and crowded with all their blinking and spinning.

The Glove isn't much for small talk during our jaunt.

Despite his seemingly fragile nature, the dude is a fast walker. It's like he's speeding back home to get me alone. And when we walk down a particularly dark block where the streetlights have all burned out, I consider turning and running.

Maybe he picks up on my stress 'cause he slows down. Walks beside me.

"How is Grandpa doing these days?"

"Razor?"

That gets a laugh. "Who else would I mean?"

"—"

"So how is he?"

"He's fine, I think. You know, he and I aren't on the best of terms."

"Hmmm."

"What's that supposed to mean?"

The Glove considers, skips a curb, kicks at a stone lying in the street, and then stops, turns to me, and says, "Look me in the eye."

I do. His eyes are jaundiced. Yellow. Bloodshot.

"What do you see, Ade?"

"Nothing. What am I supposed to see?"

He shrugs. And starts walking again. Even faster than before.

His apartment complex is only half a block farther. The place is basically the brick-and-mortar manifestation of the Glove himself. It's two stories, maybe ten apartments. Scarred. It's dark. All the lights out. Dingy. Ugly. And it smells. Just looking at it, I can already smell the rotting garbage that is surely piled up inside.

He stands at the front door, fiddles with a key, and turns and smiles.

"Coming in?"

I say, "Yeah. Just give me a sec, need to make a call."

The Glove unlocks the door, reaches inside, and flicks on a light that must be like two watts 'cause it's almost even darker now. He stands there a second longer and then holds up three skeletal fingers. "Three B," he says.

And then he turns and leaves. The door still open.

And that's when I take my first breath in like ten minutes.

I flick my phone out, dial up Vauxhall.

It rings twice before she picks up.

"Where are you?"

"Downtown. There's something I need to do, to make me my-self again."

"I know."

"Seriously, babe," I say. "Everything will be fine. I'll see you soon."

"Ade. Please. Don't do this to me. I just stopped crying fifteen minutes ago."

"I'm sorry."

I let the night sink back in. Look up at the apartment building, let my eyes travel to the sky again and the endless array of super-novas and white holes spitting out matter.

Then, into the phone, I say, "I just wanted to tell you I love you. You know, in case I come back totally different."

Vaux says, "I thought that was the whole point."

EIGHT

I walk into the apartment complex, make my way up the creaki-est stairs imaginable, and try to avoid all the spots on the carpet-ing that could still be fresh piss.

Second floor and 3B is right there, top of the stairs.

The door is open a crack but the amount of light flooding out of the room is what I imagine it looks like when you open up the Ark of the Covenant. Or get abducted by aliens.

I push the door open and peer inside. My eyes adjust quick.

And then, cautiously, I step in.

The place is huge. It's a studio but probably wasn't when the

Glove moved in. The only vertical lines are the weight-bearing beams left from the demo and the floor has been stripped bare, down to the original, water-stained hardwood.

Giant room is practically bare. I see a futon mattress and a squat black mini fridge. There are clothes in a pile in one corner of the room but little else to suggest someone truly lives here. The one thing I'm not mentioning yet, only 'cause I'm still trying to get my head around it, is the massive black ball in the center of the room.

This black ball, it's easily the size of a car and six feet high.

It's tethered to the floor by cables and wires like it might float off if it weren't.

The Glove pops up out of the shadows behind this metal orb and walks over to me, stands next to me like he's admiring the thing himself. He says, "There's a ladder on the far side. You climb in through a submarine hatch on the top."

"What's it for?"

He scoffs. "It's for what you want to do, of course."

"How's it work?"

"Complicated."

"Try me."

The Glove likes my tenaciousness. I can tell. He walks toward the sphere, motions for me to follow him. The floor creaks and squeaks and sounds as though it's going to just come apart.

"This is a sensory deprivation tank. I got it secondhand but it was originally used for experiments that some neuro folks were doing at Harvard in the early eighties. Taking all sorts of mind-altering mushrooms and climbing in here and just letting their minds go. You are going to drink a concoction I give you, then you'll climb inside and float in the solution. I will stand outside and watch."

"And I'm drinking what?"

"Mushrooms. While those Harvard nerds had their drugs and were able to tap into some really gnarly places in the mind, they couldn't do much else. What they were missing was what I like to call the twisted middle."

"And that is?"

"Too complicated to explain without you taking some physics courses. But I will tell you that my ability is very similar to yours. Kind of just the reverse. And stronger. You can see the future but not manipulate it. Me, that's what I can do."

I look over at the black ball sitting there like it dropped from space.

"Sounds relatively painless."

The Glove laughs. "It's not."

Then he traipses over to the mini fridge and pulls out a glass bottle of sick-looking liquid, all yellow and chunky. He pours some of it into a chipped coffee mug. While he's doing this, I ask, "What about the Mad Dog? Want me to get that now?"

The Glove looks up at me and shrugs. "You can get it for me after."

That's when I bring up the worry. "Some people have told me that doing this, going back and erasing Jimi's childhood, well, what's become my childhood—"

"That's what you're doing, huh?" the Glove interrupts. "You said it was super-complicated but that doesn't sound very complicated to me. You were told that doing something like that might have serious ramifications for the rest of us, right? Change the world, right?"

"Yeah."

The Glove pads over to me with the drink in his hand. He gives it to me. Then he says, "You walking over here tonight changed the world. Changed the future. Every single action you take, it leads to some random different effect. You are constantly changing the world. Every step you take."

"So there isn't anything to worry about?"

The Glove smiles. "No, there's a lot to worry about. Tons. But I can tell by the way you walked into this place, by your eyes this very moment, that you're going to do this no matter what."

The he says, "Have a sip."

I do.

Shit tastes hideous. Like drinking forgotten milk that turned into green yogurt at the back of a fridge months ago. I cough and sputter but push the rest of it down.

"Takes a few minutes before you'll feel anything," the Glove says.

Then, like some showman, he motions to the black ball.

"You're going to want to take off your clothing. Works better that way."

I try not to think about how freaky this is and I slip out of my clothes but leave my boxers on. The Glove rolls this old-school staircase ladder, the kind you see in ancient libraries, over to the side of the ball. He climbs up and unlocks the submarine door lid at the top.

And then I climb up.

Already I can feel a strange tingling in my fingertips.

It's like my hands starting to fall asleep.

I stand at the entrance to the tank and peer in. The water inside is dark but seems clear. I put a foot in. It's warm and must be the exact same temperature as my body because it feels like stepping into nothing.

"This is just water, right?" I ask the Glove.

He's standing just over my shoulder.

He says, "And salt for buoyancy. A lot of salt."

I remember what Gilberto told me. "Oh, Gilberto says he didn't forget the deal you two have."

"What deal?"

"The one he didn't forget."

The Glove is silent.

I'm starting to see colors at the edges of my vision. Little flickerings of light. Tiny rainbows just outside of my view. I remember the other things the Glove asked for. "What about the KFC and the little hammer you wanted?"

The Glove, behind me, chuckles. "You can get the chicken later."

"What was the Mad Dog for?"

"For me, dumbass. Takes away the, uh, hardness of life. I don't need it to help you do what you want to."

"And the, uh, ball hammer?"

"Ball peen. No, I've got one."

I turn around and he's holding this itty bitty hammer in his left hand. It's raised up. Kind of like he's going to try and knock me with it. He says, "I couldn't pass up the opportunity to miss this moment. This, Ade, is where it all began."

And then he hits me on the forehead with the hammer.

I'm shocked at how hard he hits me. Square in the forehead. The ball-peen hammer is so tiny, so lightweight, but the way he hits me it's like he's shot me. I can practically feel my brains spinning out of the back of my head.

He's right. This isn't painless.

And so I fall into the black-ball tank.

Splash for sure but don't even feel it.

My vision has gone so wonky I see only jagged snags of color flashing and bursting out all around me like some carnival electrical storm. And in the middle of this Technicolor freak-out, I see the Glove smiling and waving good-bye to me.

NINE

What happens next is nearly impossible to describe.

It's not the going-down-the-light tunnel like usual.

It's not spinning out into outer space.

It's kind of the reverse.

Light seems to be dragged out of me. Like all the particles that make up my body are being ripped from me at light speed. Basically it's what you see in the old sci-fi movies when the captain yells out for them to hit hyper speed or warp speed or whatever. Points of light become lines. Really, it looks like neon lines being shot like Las Vegas arrows out of my body.

And then black.

Black and a heartbeat.

It's because I've got my eyes closed. And I'm afraid to open them.

I wait a few seconds.

Just take comfort in the ticktock of my heart.

Finally I take a deep breath and open my eyes and I see:

The inside of the tank. I'm floating in the liquid and the hatch is open and I can see the ceiling of the Glove's apartment. Everything is shockingly quiet. I can hear the lapping of the water and for the first time I can feel that I'm bouncing, floating.

I try to sit up and find it's surprisingly easy to do.

There's so much salt in this tank that it's practically pushing me out of the water.

There's also enough light coming in the hatch that I can see my hands and feet. Nothing changed. Nothing different.

Did anything even happen?

I clear my throat, taste salt, and then yell, "Hey! Hey, I don't think anything happened!"

There is no response. Just the soft splash of the water.

"Hey, Mr. Glove! I'm in here."

No answer.

And so I try to get out but getting out of the tank is harder than I thought.

Even though I'm floating on top of the water, the hatch is so high above me that I can't just reach up and get the edge of it. So I try moving back and forth and back and forth to make a wave in the tank.

At first it works great, I get higher and higher, enough that I can just graze the edge of the submarine hatch.

But it's not enough.

I kick the side of the tank and it makes a low rumbling noise.

I yell, "Get me out of here!"

Nothing.

So I come up with a new plan. I think about how when I was a kid we went to a friend's house and they had this backyard pool that was kind of up on stilts. It was small but deep. Maybe five people could fit in it comfortably.

My cousin Rick and I would rock the pool. Kicking back and forth and we could actually feel it threatening to fall. The wooden supports creaking like they were going to break. We imagined how much fun it would be to have the thing topple over and we'd ride this chlorine wave out onto the lawn, maybe even down the hill through the neighbor's backyard.

That thought has me going.

This thing is a ball. I rock it enough and maybe it'll roll.

So I kick.

And kick and kick and back and forth and back and forth.

The black tank starts to rock.

Hard work and I'm sweating in this warm water. The salt is starting to sting my skin. And I just keep kicking and pushing, rocking the ball.

I hear the floor creaking.

The boards of the hardwood cracking.

Water splashes up out of the hatch in great waves.

And then the ball rolls!

It falls forward and I move with the water, see the hatch like a moon arcing over to my feet, and soon I'm upside down and the water is in my mouth and my nose and my ears. And the ball rolls, the hatch moving past and under me.

It crosses the apartment and crashes into a wall.

Bricks groan and crumble.

But it stops.

The water is sloshing out all over the floor because the tank is on its side now. I get up, bruised and sore, and push my way out of the hatch. Crawling loose from it like I'm crawling loose from a womb.

And then I'm out, lying on the hardwood in a puddle of salt-water.

Freezing.

The Glove isn't here. The apartment is empty.

I get up and run over to my clothes, piled where I left them. I pull them on over my wet, sticky limbs, and then check my cell. No phone calls.

Then I leave.

As soon as I'm outside the apartment, I call Vaux.

She doesn't answer.

I leave a rambling message. I tell her that it's over and chances are pretty good nothing happened. I tell her that it was probably a fluke. I say, "Good thing I didn't pay for any of it. I'm coming over. I want to see you."

The night looks the same.

The city looks exactly the way it did when I went into the Glove's apartment.

Nothing happened.

Nothing changed.

But I do feel different. There's something missing. That energy. That Jimi energy isn't in my body any longer. The thrill I got with the Pandora Crew, I can't even imagine what it felt like now. The idea of risking my life is frightening.

The Delirium is gone.

Because the idea of breaking something, of tearing up the night, doesn't make me happy. The thought of running wild and just going nuts in the city doesn't excite me anymore.

I stop and look up at the sky. The same stars that have always been there.

The same moon.

And I let out a big sigh.

I call Paige.

She answers on the second ring. "So?" she asks. Her voice full of worry.

"I think it worked."

"Do you feel—"

"Yeah. Totally different. Totally like myself again. It's gone."

Paige is elated. She sounds like she's going to cry.

"Are you coming over?" she asks.

"Yeah. You still with Veronica? I mean, is anything changed."

"Yes. Nothing's changed. You did it, Ade."

"Hell yes," I say, and even more of the tension melts away. "I don't know how but it worked. The cancer is gone. I'm free. Look, I'm going to stop by Vauxhall's place first and see her. I just really need to see her first. Then I'll be over."

There is a pause.

Then Paige says, "Who's Vauxhall?"

What a joker.

CHAPTER THREE

ONE

Dear Jimi—

I know we haven't talked in a while and I'm sure you'll think it's odd that I'm sending you a letter instead of just giving you a call or coming by the pool to see you this weekend (how's the lifeguarding thing going anyway? Always wanted to try that). Anyway, I'm a letter writer, it's in my nature.

I just wanted to let you know that I've done it. That your past— your mom and all the horrible things she did to you—are now truly buried. Well, more than buried, they're all gone. Erased. Never happened. At least for me.

I'm not sure if you've noticed anything different. If your childhood memories, the ones that were left after, well, I guess we don't need to get into that again. Just curious is all. I'd love to know how you're doing. Give me a call.

I'm going to be busy the next week or so.

A few things that I need to do.

Laters,

Ade

TWO

I went to Vauxhall's place and it was quiet.

Dark.

No one inside. The place was deserted.

It was only after I'd banged on the door twenty times and gone around the house and stared in every window that I realized the place was empty.

She didn't live there anymore.

No one did.

At first I thought it was possible that maybe she'd moved while I was at the Glove's but that didn't make sense unless she was hustled into the witness protection program. I considered that too but then ditched the idea.

I called her cell phone at least one hundred times.

Her voice mail just the same as always.

Left just as many messages.

It's been two hours since I've come out of the tank and I've stopped by home but Mom was asleep and I didn't want to wake her so I wrote my letter to Jimi and then took off. Amazingly, even though my body is choking on the stress right now, my mind is trying its damnedest to be practical.

To be rational.

I'm walking up to Paige's place now.

I don't know what she's going to tell me when she opens the door.

My heart is beating so fast I'm worried it's going to jump the rails.

My body continuing its war against this world.

This isn't happening, is what I'm telling myself.

It isn't.

I'm sure, totally hoping to be sure, that I'm still in the tank. That I'm still in the Glove's apartment. Whatever happens next, regardless of how bad it is, how emotionally devastating it is, I don't want to believe it's real.

For me right now this is either a fantasy. A hallucination.

Or I'm sure of nothing.

This has to be fake.

Paige swings open the door and jumps on me. Hugs me tight. She doesn't look different at all. She's wearing the same pj's she's always had. And as I step into her house I notice that it looks the same too. Her room. Exactly the same.

Paige is jumping up and down in place.

Her hair bouncing.

Her smile bouncing.

I take a seat on the edge of her bed and the dam in her mouth bursts.

"So? Did it work?"

"Yeah. I feel different. Good."

"And it's all gone? Like removed?"

I nod. "Yeah."

"That must be freaking strange. Like when you think back to your childhood is it just a blank or something?"

I try. It's a blank. I nod.

Paige seems relieved. Then she changes gears. "I can't tell you how stressed I've been. You haven't done anything this crazy in months. I haven't been that mad at you since last summer. This has been so like emotionally insane and the past few hours have . . . Wait, why's your forehead bleeding?"

"Vauxhall's gone," I interrupt.

The look on my face should tell her everything she needs to know.

"Yeah. Okay. You said that name before. Who's that?"

"Stop messing around, Paige. I'm serious."

Her smile fades. She screws up her face. "Yeah. Fine. Who's Vauxhall?"

That pisses me off and I stand up ready to storm out of the room. "I can't believe you're doing this to me, Paige. So not cool. I went to her house and it was empty. She's moved and she's not answering her cell. I'm in a panic!"

"Okay. Okay. I'm sorry. Please, sit down."

I wait a beat and then sit again.

"Look, I'll help you find her. Is there any place she hangs out?"

"Yeah. With me. I don't know . . ."

"And where did you meet her?"

I groan. "Stop it, Paige!"

"Ade." She slams her hands down at her sides. "What is your

problem?! I don't know who the hell you're talking about, this Vauxhall chick, but it's starting to really freak me out. And you look like you're on drugs. Are you?"

"Yeah," I say, remembering the mushroom drink. "But I'm not screwing around."

"I knew it." Paige sits in the chair at her desk and shakes her head. "Why don't you go home and sleep it off. Did the dude you saw give you drugs?"

I stand up. This isn't working.

"I'll call you later, babe."

And I march out of the house with Paige behind me rubbing my shoulders.

"I'm just glad everything worked out. That it's over and nothing went totally—"

"I just wish you could be serious for once."

I step outside. Turn around.

Paige just shrugs her shoulders and says, "I'm sorry you're so out of it."

I roll my eyes.

"Here," Paige says. "Let me at least get you a Band-Aid."

THREE

I go back to the Diviners.

Band-Aid and all.

On my way there I call everyone I can think of. Everyone programmed in my phone. None of the people I wake up have ever heard of Vauxhall. Not Borgo. Not Heinz. Not anyone. All of them sleepy and mumbling, they say, "Never heard of her. Why are you calling me in the middle of the night about this?"

I try Vauxhall's cell number again and again.

Her voice mail is the same. It's her voice. It's unchanged.

By why doesn't anyone remember her?

Why isn't she here?

At the Diviners, I walk through the lobby and find I like the art.

I don't want to break the sculptures.

I make my way to the front desk. Dude is still there. He eyes me.

I say, "Penthouse. They'll be expecting me."

He still calls up. Says, "Same guy back again."

Then he hangs up.

He frowns at me and says, "You know where the elevator is."

And I take it. The video screen is not of a babbling brook but of a wheat field with wind whipping through it. Clouds on the horizon. Thunder rattling in the distance. It is a window to another world. And it is not the least bit soothing.

The ding happens.

The door whooshes open.

I walk past the portraits and they are all the same.

The door, as before, is opened a crack.

I step inside and the room isn't white anymore. It's black.

Black couches. Black curtains. Black fridge. And on one of the black couches is Gilberto. He's sitting with the guy wearing the gas mask. Both of them are wearing all black.

Gilberto stands and claps his hands. "Good work," he says. "How do you feel?"

"Fine. It worked. But . . . tell me about Vauxhall."

Gilberto cocks his head to the side. Looks at the guy with the gas mask on.

Gas mask guy shrugs.

Gilberto says, "I'm not familiar with that name."

I try not to let my surprise show. The shock hits hard though. A block of ice lodged into my heart.

"Why don't you know that name?" I ask.

"Just not familiar." Gilberto shrugs. "Is this person someone I should know?"

"Yes."

"Well, then. You'll have to introduce me to, uh . . ."

"Her."

"Right. That all you came back here for? To ask me about this Vauxhall girl?"

I walk over to the window and look down at the city, at the highway. The order has reversed. Now the other lane is filled. Cars all coming toward me. Strings of white lights.

"I told the Glove what you wanted me to. He had no idea what you were talking about," I say.

Gilberto says, "Yes. He told me."

I spin around. "You've seen him. Can I talk to him?"

"Of course." Gilberto smiles. Then he turns to the dude in the gas mask.

Gas mask guy stands up, undoes the straps on the back of the mask, and lets the thing slide off into his hands. Then he looks at me. The Glove.

I want to scream in his face.

What, I don't know. But I know I want it to be loud.

"I told you it wouldn't be painless."

And I punch him. Straight in the dude's wheezy stomach.

He folds like a lawn chair and gasps and coughs and then laughs. Yeah, laughs. Laughing like maniac. Pulling himself together he says, "When you realize what's going on, you're going to lose it. Again."

I pull the guy up by his shirt. Me, suddenly the bully.

The thug.

"What did you do to me?"

"Nothing you didn't already do to yourself."

I'm tired of the riddles. The bullshit. I just want an answer that makes sense.

"Where is Vauxhall?"

"Downtown . . . Purple Lounge . . . with a friend."

I let the Glove drop to the floor and pull myself back together. Actually sigh.

"See, that wasn't so hard," I say to the entire room.

Gilberto just stares at me. Eyes burrowing beneath my skin.

The Glove picks himself up, dusts off, and then sits back down beside Gilberto. They actually do a little fist bump, which is not only totally strange for Gilberto but it tells me this whole thing is a charade. Both of them are screwing with me completely.

"When I come back here, I'm kicking both of your asses," I say.

It's only when I slam the door behind me and I'm in the elevator headed down to the first floor and the night and my lover, that I realize I didn't get a flash of the future when I touched the Glove.

I saw nothing.

I shake it off as a fluke.

FOUR

The Purple Lounge is this '50s-style diner.

It's got everything done up in shades of purple. The servers all cruise around on roller skates and the food is pretty much chicken-fried only. As in chicken-fried steak. Chicken-fried chicken. Chicken-fried fries. Oh, and the mascot is this fat, purple chicken. Usually you see the poor schlub in the costume on the corner throwing feather-shaped coupons at scared passersby. One of those places.

I don't bother with my car.

The Purple Lounge isn't far from the Diviners' new loft so I just book it across town. I run down Larimer and then take the 16th Street Mall up to Wazee. I'm surprised at how warm the weather's suddenly gotten. It's like ten degrees warmer suddenly.

Gotta love Denver.

The chicken guy is on his corner and as I run past him he throws coupons in my face and makes his clucking sounds.

I make a mental note to kick him in the balls sometime.

I push through the line at the entrance and then walk into the restaurant casually, trying to maintain some semblance of cool. I don't know who Vaux is here with. Who the friend is. Maybe if she's cheating on me I want to sneak up on them. Though just the thought of that has my stomach in knots.

It looks like the Purple Lounge has become the spot to be seen in. Place is crawling with teens.

I make a second mental note to take Vauxhall here on the next Date Night.

I'm rounding a corner near the bathrooms when I spot her. She's wearing a '50s-style dress with big black-and-red polka dots and has this big red bow in her hair. She looks amazing, bright red lipstick on, and her eyes just gleaming.

Seeing her melts away all of the anxiety.

It just floods out of my muscles and then dissipates like it's evaporating off the surface of my skin. Seeing her sitting there, talking, it's like diving into a cool pool after wandering in a desert. The release, the relaxation, is instant.

I actually laugh to myself. How could I have gotten so freaked out?

How did I let Paige and Gilberto and the Glove twist me up into knots like this?

I shake it off, take a deep breath, and then notice the guy Vauxhall's at dinner with.

He's tall and thin and he's . . . ME.

Yeah, me.

Not the me that I am right now. He's dressed super preppy and he doesn't have the haircut I have. Doesn't hold himself the way I do. He doesn't speak with his hands like everyone says I do. But the guy is me. He has my face.

He is Ade Patience. Only different.

I stand frozen, staring at him.

Could I be losing my mind?

It's like there's this funhouse mirror across from Vauxhall

and I'm seeing myself reflected in it. Like she's batting her eyes at a reflection of me that's off.

The guy, this other me, he senses something's up and turns around and actually stares at me and the feeling is like having a laser beam shot through my heart.

It's like staring into a cold sun.

I'm losing my mind.

Then the clone smiles. Even his smile is mine.

I'm not sure what to do. Vauxhall leans in and asks the guy about me. She's looking at me like she doesn't know me and pointing at me and asking this guy who's supposed to be me who *I* am. If that makes any sense at all.

For a second I think maybe I somehow switched bodies. Maybe that is me sitting and having dinner with Vauxhall. I turn and look at my reflection in a window. I look the same. So who the hell is this other guy?

I'm losing my mind, sure of it.

So I walk over.

And as I approach the table, the copy of me leans back in his chair. The expression on his face, which is exactly the expression I'd have on my face if some dude who looked an awful lot like me walked over to interrupt my dinner with Vauxhall, communicates his displeasure. Intense displeasure.

Already I can tell that me and my clone aren't going to get along at all.

Walking that distance, maybe thirty feet, dodging other tables and passing diners, I keep my eyes on Vauxhall. It's only been a day since I saw her last but it feels like years have passed. Decades. Centuries. The world has turned to dust in her absence.

When I reach the table the first to speak is the dude.

"What's up?" he asks. Pissed.

He even raises one eyebrow the same as me when I'm annoyed.

I ignore him. "Can I talk to you, Vaux?" I ask.

She screws up her face. Looks to the dude, confused.

Then, to me: "Do I know you?"

"It's me. Ade."

She shakes her head. My face not registering.

My voice shaking, I say, "Ade. Ade Patience. I need to talk to you."

She looks uncomfortable.

The other me says, "You need to back the hell up, bro."

The way he talks is nothing like I talk. The guy's a douche.

He stands up, gets in my face. Puffs out his chest like he's going to fight me.

"I don't know who you are," he says, trying to control the timbre of his voice, trying to keep it down so as not to disturb all the Purple Lounge patrons. "But you don't know her and you don't know me. I suggest you turn back around and leave before this gets crazy."

"Crazy?" I don't budge. I don't even blink. "Please don't play games with me, Vauxhall. This has been the worst night of my life already. Please don't—"

Vauxhall shakes her head. "I don't know you."

"You're freaking her out," the dude says.

Looking into this guy's face is like floating under my own reflection.

The differences are there. Obvious. He's got acne scars on his cheeks that I don't have. He's got stubble that I've never been able to grow. His pupils are a lighter shade. Other than that, though, he's a replica.

I say, "Don't you find it funny that we look exactly the same?"

Dude looks to Vauxhall. She shrugs.

"Listen, tweaker," he says. "You need to back the eff up."

I turn to Vauxhall.

"Don't you recognize me?" I ask. "Don't you see that we're the same person?"

She honestly looks like she's going to lose her shit. This is bad.

To the guy she says, "Let's just leave, Karl."

The me named Karl says, "No. This punk needs to leave."

And he pushes me just to get the point across.

Being pushed by your mirror image is a strange thing. Feeling your own hands push you backward is like being disembodied. The push doesn't do much to convince me. If anything, it backfires. Now I want to talk to Vauxhall even more.

"Vauxhall," I say. "Please, just give me one minute."

Karl is fuming. He raises a fist.

But Vauxhall stands up. Says, "Okay. Fine. One minute."

I look at Karl and nod and then turn and walk with Vauxhall across the restaurant to the windows near the entrance. As we pass by, all the other diners watch us. Everyone staring. Whispering to each other. I follow Vaux, lost in the scent of her hair. Her perfume washing over me. Already I've forgotten about Karl.

We sit next to each other, Vauxhall at least five feet away from me, arms crossed, on a long couch next to the hostess. The hostess smiles at us, all uncomfortable.

I don't like being this far away from Vaux. Feels terrible.

I must be sick. I'm sure this is like a fever dream.

I'm sure that I'll wake up in a few minutes and this whole thing will be a dream.

Vauxhall says, "So?"

I collect myself. "I don't know why you're doing this to me. I know things got a little nuts the last few weeks but—"

Her blank expression tells me my worst fears are real.

She doesn't know me.

She's not joking around.

This is a nightmare.

I start over. "Okay, look, I don't understand what's going on here but you and I know each other. We've known each other for a long time. I, uh, I've known you before I even met you. That sounds crazy but it—"

"Totally crazy. I've never seen you before."

"But I look just like that Karl asshole," I say, gesturing back to the other me who is glaring at us from the table. Grinding ice cubes with his molars.

"Why do you think you know me?"

"We're the same, Vaux. I have abilities like you do. The Buzz."

"What?"

"Remember Jimi? The Diviners?"

"No. What is this about?"

"It's about us."

Vauxhall looks down at her feet and says, "Listen, I think you've got me confused with someone else. Maybe I look like someone you know or something. Maybe you're just really messed up. But I don't know you. I don't want to know you. And if you don't leave me alone right now, Karl is going to hurt you. Bad."

I lean in and try to take Vauxhall's hand. She moves it away fast.

Like I'm poisonous.

"I know what you can do," I say. "What you can see in the heads of the guys you're with. What that feels like. How you liberate them from their nightmares. Even the ones they never knew they had. I understand it . . ."

And for the first time, even as brief as it is, a flash of recognition sparks in Vauxhall's eyes. She narrows her eyes, whispers, "How do you know about that?"

"Because I'm like you. I was like you."

"But—"

I say, "We beat it together. We conquered our addictions and it made us incredible. Like superheroes. But things went bad for me. It's complicated but I'm here now, I'm back, and I need you to be with me."

Tears start to form in the corners of Vauxhall's eyes.

She's shaking.

We've made a breakthrough. Whatever is going on here, I'm changing it.

And that's when Karl punches me across the jaw.

His knuckles scrape across my face. Like instant rug burn. And I go flying backward, my head bouncing off the windows with a hollow thud. My ears ringing, I stand up, all wobbly and ready for a fight.

But there won't be a fight tonight.

Vauxhall runs to Karl, hugs him. He stares at me over her shoulders.

His face nestled in her hair. He mouths the words: *You're.*
Dead.

And then he flicks me off.

And they leave.

And my heart breaks.

I just lost the love of my life to a bad version of myself.

FIVE

I'm walking out of the Purple Lounge, hanging my head, grinding my teeth, when a car narrowly avoids smashing into me.

When I say narrowly, I actually mean it did hit me. Just not as bad as it could have been. Just kind of sideswipes me. Spins me around. Knocks me flat.

Then it skids into a mailbox. Letters explode into the night air as the car keeps rolling, collides with the side of a building, and just accordions in, steam pouring out of the busted radiator.

I brush myself off and check out my sore left side.

A big bruise is spreading out under the skin.

I hobble over to the car and pull the driver out.

Dude's laughing even though there's blood streaming down his face.

Dude's laughing 'cause he's got the Buzz. His pupils blown wide open.

Dude's laughing 'cause this guy, this loser who almost ran me over, is also me.

Just like Karl.

Only this me, this other version, has scars all over his face. He looks like me back in the depths of my Buzz-addiction days if I didn't have the crazy-fast healing and non-scarring thing that I do. But under all the scars I can see myself.

He, however, doesn't seem to notice.

Just all blissed out and enjoying the Buzz, he lets me put him down on the sidewalk while sirens start blaring and the gawkers pile up around us.

I lean down and get in his face.

"What's going on?" I ask him. "This doesn't make any sense."

"Uh . . ."

He smiles again. Missing all sorts of teeth.

I pull him up by his collar. Second time I've done that this evening. "Who are you? Tell me where you came from."

"Name's Adam. I, uh, I . . . grew up here, man."

I pull him closer, stare deep into those Buzzed-out pupils.

"Do you notice anything about me?" I ask.

"No."

"What's your last name?"

"Constant."

"Adam Constant? That's rich."

I look back at the car. Thing is totally wrecked. How is he getting home?

"Why did you crash?"

He doesn't answer. So I shake him.

"Why did you crash?" I ask again.

"To see."

And that makes total sense. What doesn't make sense is that

I'm touching him. My skin on his skin and I'm not seeing anything. Second time tonight that's happened.

"What did you see?" I ask. "How far out?"

Adam smiles. Grins his dentally challenged smile and says, "You're one of us too. Aren't you? Are you a Diviner?"

"No. What'd you see?"

"Not far out. Not far enough. I saw myself in this big tank. Like an aquarium. And I'm trying to get out of it but I can't. It's filled with water and I'm floating in this thing and it's totally nuts but I can't get out. Crazy, right?"

Adam chuckles.

And then, maybe because the Buzz is slipping away or maybe it's because he can see through the haze enough to really, honestly see what's happening, this look of recognition washes over his face.

"Wait . . . How do you know about this?"

I haul his ass up and ask him if he's hungry.

He nods. "Sure."

"My mom's a great cook," I say, and we head to my car.

Me and my jacked-up twin.

I'm going to figure this out. Chances are this is a dream. Chances are that this is a hallucination. Maybe I'm still in the Glove's tank. Maybe I'm unconscious somewhere. If this were a movie, and we were near the end, I'd wake up on the tiled floor of the mall bathroom with the AED leads strapped to my chest and the whole thing, this whole nightmare of Vauxhall not knowing me and these other me's running around, would just have been some weird delusion brought on by dying.

I'm kind of counting on that so I don't take it all too seriously.

If you're sure it's not real, there's nothing wrong with having some fun.

SIX

When we walk into the house, the lights are dim.

Mom's on the computer in the kitchen. She's got her glasses off and is sitting far too close to the monitor. It's buzzing right up in her face, bathing her in this vibrating blue glow.

She says, "Casserole's in the oven." And doesn't turn around.

I clear my throat.

"Mom, we have a dinner guest."

Mom spins around, throws her glasses on her head.

This moment is something of a test. I want to see what Mom's reaction is. The fact that no one but me can see that Adam and Karl are total duplicates of me is bizarre. It's the one thing really freaking me out.

I'm expecting her to just smile and introduce herself.

Just nod and say something along the "nice to meet you" lines.

Instead she goes pale and almost drops out of her seat.

She's shaking and I'm worried she's going to have a heart attack.

Adam looks to me all worried.

I lean in, take my mom by her arm, and steady her. "What's wrong, Mom?"

Her voice is rattling around inside her throat. She just points to Adam.

"Do you see it?" I ask.

She nods. Then says, "Your double."

I break into a big smile and hug my mom hard. Super hard.

Adam looks a little uncomfortable, the Buzz dying down inside him. The thrill wearing off and he's realizing that this is weird. At some random dude's home. Some random dude's mom staring at him, tears welling up in her eyes.

My mom pulls the casserole from the oven and Adam and I have a seat at the kitchen table. He looks totally out of place.

I can see him eyeing the edge of the kitchen table.

The machinery behind his eyes telling him that if he hits the corner at just such an angle, at just such a velocity, he can knock himself out. Get the Buzz back.

I interrupt him before the process goes any further.

"I know what you can do because I've done it," I say.

And I tell him all about my jumps from the roof of Mantlo High School, all the fights, all the car crashes, all the accidents. I tell him about the Buzz and how it felt. I say, "It's an amazing feeling. But it destroys you."

He shrugs. Shovels steaming casserole into his mouth.

My mom doesn't eat. Just watches this strange twin of mine.

Her eyes dart from mine to Adam's. Mine to Adam's.

I say, "I've been in the future you saw."

"What future?" Adam asks, mouth dripping marinara.

"The one where you're trapped in the aquarium. I just came back from there."

"Weird."

"Yeah. It's weird."

"So? Uh, did I get out?"

"Yes. You did."

"Sweet."

He just nods and shovels more food.

"Aren't you curious about me? About how I know?"

Adam chews what's in his mouth before leaning back in his chair and downing the glass of whole milk he asked my mom for. I don't drink milk so it was an odd moment.

Then he sighs and asks, "Honestly?"

"Yeah," I say, leaning in on my elbows.

He shrugs, like whatever, and starts in. "So here's the deal. I don't actually care. I mean, I think it's kind of funny that you seem to know me and it's kooky that you understand the whole high thing. And, yeah, there's something definitely weird going on between us, but I don't care. All I care about is knocking myself out. That's it. I can see the future and in the future I'm just doing the same thing. Knocking myself out. It's like this everlasting loop thing. You know like when you draw that one symbol—"

"Infinity symbol?"

"Right. Yeah. Like that. Knocking myself out is all I do. And I'm so totally fine with that. You can tell me anything you like, it won't change an inch of it. Won't make me even pause for more than a few seconds. See, that's the beautiful thing about my life. Nothing shocks me. Nothing surprises me. I have no expectations. Really, I'm like a child and it's the most amazing thing ever."

Then he pushes back from the table, wipes his mouth with the back of his hand.

"If you'll excuse me, I'll just use the bathroom."

My mom points to the right. "Down the hall, on the left."

"Thanks," Adam says. "I'll only be a minute."

He stomps off down the hall.

We hear the bathroom door close.

We hear the water run.

And we hear him slam his skull against the side of the toilet.

My mom jumps up, ready to run in there.

"Wait," I say. She sits back down. Looks anxious.

"He's fine," I add. "He's doing what he wants."

My mom toys with her napkin in her lap. Finally she asks, "Where did you meet him?"

"Downtown."

"And?"

"And there is another one. Looks just like me. The other guy, he's not like Adam. He's clean-cut and put together. His name is Karl."

"With a *k*?"

"Yeah, why?"

My mom nods to herself. The she says, "That was what we were going to name you. Karl Felix Patience. What happened? How are there two?"

"I don't know, Mom. But it gets even worse. Vauxhall doesn't know who I am. She was on a date with the Karl guy when I found her. No one can see what you and me can. No one can tell that we're all twins. Or doubles. Or clones. Whatever. Something changed in the world. Like reality shifted over or—"

"What did you do?"

"I . . . I just tried to save myself."

My mom gets up from the table and walks over to the fridge and pulls down the big leather-bound Bible she keeps on top of it. She got the book from a Greek Orthodox friend and it weighs a few tons.

She clears a place on the table and then plops it down.

Then, her hands folded on the cover, she looks at me all gravely.

"Who did you talk to, Ade?"

"A man called the Glove."

"Where?"

"At his place."

"And what did he tell you he could do?"

"Change the past. Change my past."

She shakes her head. Opens the book and flips to Matthew. Then she slides the book over to me and points out a few lines. "Satan showed Jesus all the kingdoms, every one from here until eternity. That's time travel."

"Are you telling me it was Satan?"

She nods.

"It wasn't. It was a man. A man with abilities like mine."

She closes the book.

"When he did what he did, that's when all this changed?"

"Yes. It worked. The problems I was having were gone. Instantly. But after, well, as soon as I got out of his place, I noticed that everything else was different. He didn't change me but changed the world around me."

"And the doubles appeared?"

"Yes."

Then, for the first time in a very long time, for the first time in nearly forever, I ask my mom if she can help me. I say, "Tell me what to do, Mom."

She smiles.

Then she reaches over and takes my hand, says, "I don't know but we'll figure it out. I'm here for you. Get some sleep."

I kiss her on the forehead.

Then I go down the hall and open the bathroom door.

Adam isn't there, only a puddle of congealing blood.

Weird.

So I look around the house, my heart beating a little faster with every room I check, and don't find him. Where the hell did he go?

I look in my room last and of course that's where he is, head all busted up and blood just pouring down his face. Big smile. Eyes all blown out. He says, "You won't believe what I saw."

CHAPTER FOUR

ONE

Dear Vauxhall—

I don't have your address. Don't know where you live now.

But I'm going to send it to the only Rodolfo in the phone book and hope it gets there.

You need to read it. You need to remember me.

I'm sorry to come across like some sketchy stalker but you do know me. Deep down, you've always known me. I realize that it's going to take a while to get you to see that but I'm willing to do it.

I need you to remember: Our time in the car watching the planes land at the airport. When we went to the movies. Dinners with my mom and Paige. Our coffee after the reservoir when I changed the future. And Date Nights. I need you to remember how much fun you had with me on Date Nights.

My number's at the bottom of this letter.

My address and my e-mail too.
Take your time. Think it through.
Remember me, Vauxhall.
I love you.

Ade

TWO

Adam sleeps on the couch.

I sit across from him in my mom's favorite puffy chair just staring at him.

He doesn't sleep nicely.

He coughs and gags in his sleep like he's swallowing tons of phlegm. And he talks. Nothing I can understand but the mumbling comes in bursts and starts and sometimes he even gestures with his hands. Doesn't last long.

The more I watch him the more weirded out I am at the thought of him existing.

The longer I stare at him the more freaked out I get.

I sit in that for a while. Don't panic. Don't jump up and call Paige. She wouldn't understand anyway. She'd just try to talk me down off the ledge. But I need to be here. I need this panic to help me navigate what's coming next.

Two clones.

Adam: the version of me who's let the Buzz take total control. The version of me that I only just barely avoided becoming. The version Paige was seeing all the time last summer.

And Karl. Who the hell is Karl? Must be the asshole version of me. The one I didn't know anything about. Maybe the one lurking inside. I have to think on it more.

I try to rationalize it.

And that helps. The freak-out subsides and is replaced by this strange calm. I'm sure it's what dudes on the battlefield feel when the chaos of the war just gets too much. When there are grenades exploding and bombs falling and bodies being blown apart and the whole earth just raging on fire and the soldier finds that eye of the cyclone to lose himself in. I'm totally there.

Watching my duplicate sleep. All jacked up.

I actually start to smile.

Whatever is happening, I have this.

I totally got this.

And then my phone rings.

I look at the time before I answer it and I'm not surprised to see it's nearly five.

An unknown caller. The number isn't even displayed.

For a split second I consider what'll happen if I don't answer.

Chances are good this is a fluke call.

Chances are also good they'll just call right the hell back.

I answer. Don't even bother with the hello part.

"Yeah?" I say, eyes on Adam.

"Been a while, cowboy."

The voice on the other end sounds like it's being beamed to me from the other end of a particularly disgusting vacuum cleaner tube. Only one voice sounds this badly diseased, this wretchedly unhealthy. Grandpa Razor.

"You know what time it is?" I ask.

"Of course. I set an alarm just to wake up and call you."

"That was nice."

"You're not sleeping, of course."

"Of course."

Grandpa Razor clears his filthy throat. Then: "You've been very, very busy. Wasn't but a few months ago that you broke the Rules and humiliated me. Ruined that poor boy, your only sibling, that I was trying to help."

"He almost killed me. So did you."

"Well, that was then. Let's talk about now. Right now."

"What do you know?"

He laughs. It's a lawn mower starting underwater.

He says, "I know that you went further than anyone imagined you ever could. You don't think it's strange that Gilberto, master of nothing, would be able to direct you so effortlessly to our charming acquaintance, the Glove, do you?"

"I actually thought he might."

"No. Not our Gilberto. I'll be honest with you, Ade, I noticed you back on my radar screen a few weeks ago. Those nutty Pandora boys. When they got you roped in on their antics, well, it only made sense. Now that Jimi's gone good and soaked up your privileged background, I have to turn to you, even in the shadows, to have a decent amount of entertainment."

I ask, "Why are you calling?"

Adam groans in his sleep. Rolls over and scratches at his balls.

"Because I want to help you."

"Help me? Why?"

"You've messed things up pretty royally. I don't think you even have the slightest idea how much. I'm not going to bullshit you. I kind of pride myself on being the guy pulling the strings. The whole wizard behind the curtain role seems to suit me perfectly. It was what I was born to do. What my ability is meant for. You and I have had a rough go of things and I'm not going to deny that. I'll admit I kind of tried to make you disappear—"

"Kind of?"

Adam tosses and turns. Mumbles something lewd.

"More than kind of. Listen, if you accept my apologies, I want to offer you a helping hand. You scratch my back and I'll scratch yours."

I let my silence do the talking for me.

Grandpa Razor chuckles, more to himself than me, then he says, "You don't trust me. That's understandable. I wouldn't trust me either. Not the way I treated you. But this is different. I'm not saying we need to be friends. I'm not saying that I'm suddenly your best pal and your only shoulder to lean on. Far from it. But we both have a horse, so to speak, in this race, and I want to ensure that whatever you do next—and believe me you're going to be doing a lot of things next—I come out on the winning side. The surviving side. What do you say?"

"I say it sounds like you need me more than I need you."

Adam coughs at the same time Grandpa Razor does.

The echo effect is startling.

"It would seem that way, wouldn't it." Grandpa Razor waits a beat and then he delivers the whole reason he made this phone call in the first place, the whole reason he's subjected me to his hideous voice and all the memories that come with it. He says, "It's true that I can't offer you my divination services, they wouldn't be of much help in your situation. And my knowledge of your association with the Pandora boys isn't much of a benefit either. What I can offer you, however, is the one thing you want most in life: Vauxhall."

Hearing him say her name, even though he corrupts it with his tongue, I stop breathing. Even my heart stops beating. I'm hanging on his every breath.

He knows it too.

He relishes it. I can imagine him licking his cheese-encrusted lips.

Grandpa Razor says, "That's the beautiful thing about changing the past. Everything you do has crazy ramifications that can't be anticipated. Can't be guessed at. As you already know, some people see the changes, others don't. Some people, like your beloved, are changed in subtle ways, others are changed a bit more dramatically. Even more, there's no going back. You have to deal with what you've done."

I'm getting tired of Razor's diatribe. "Cut the shit," I say. "Tell me about her."

"She has no idea who you are and yet she's in love with you. Another you. That's harsh. Even more harsh, she's got abilities like before but they're different. And that is where I come in."

"Spit it out!" I shout into the phone.

It's loud enough that Adam's eyes snap open. He looks at me a bit confused, then smiles. He stretches, sits up, and listens in. Nothing I can do about it.

Grandpa Razor says, "Not going to be that easy, Ade. Even you should know that by now. Despite my teaming up with you, I'm not going to make it easy. It'll still be deliciously painful.

Speaking of . . . Well, we'll get to that soon enough. Come to my place and bring breakfast and we'll talk."

"You suck."

"Ha," he laughs. Then adds, "You only have two days to make everything better. The Glove didn't tell you that bit."

The line goes dead.

Adam clears his throat, says, "I know that voice."

I say, "Guy's such an asshole."

"No doubt. What did he call you about?"

"Not important."

Adam cracks his knuckles and says, "Did I tell you what I saw? The vision I had after I hit myself on the toilet in your bathroom?"

"No."

He leans forward and says, "I saw you kill me, dude."

THREE

I drag Adam out with me.

We head over to this egg place. It's got some punny name like Egg-ceptional or Egg-zactly. Stupid. But they make eggs with brown sugar and milk and they're grub.

Over a plate of sausages and scraps of toast, Adam tells me the details.

"It's kind of sad, really," he says. "Not some big blowout. Not some super-sweet action scene. You kind of apologize and act all disappointed and then you put your hand in my stomach. Not like gory. Not like some zombie thing with intestines being all pulled out and all this blood but—"

And he demonstrates by sticking his hand out into midair. He makes a whoosh.

"—like that. And it's totally not painful but the Buzz, wow, the Buzz is killer."

"And that kills you?"

"Not really kills. More like I start to come apart. Again, not in any gory way but like my particles and shit just fold up on themselves and suddenly I'm fading away."

He messes around with the egg yolk still left on his plate.

Then he looks up and says, "But you're going to change it, right?"

"Change it?"

"Stop it. You're not going to kill me. I heard you on the phone with Grandpa Razor, he said you changed it before. You can do that."

I dismiss it. "Yeah. Yeah . . . No, totally. I won't kill you."

"Cool, man. Cool."

Adam says, "So I also heard you've got some majorly jacked-up stuff going on. I don't think I get any of it but if you need my help that's cool. I mean, I've got nothing going on and I know a few people around town. Like Grandpa."

"How do you know him?"

"He tried to get me involved in his little gang."

"The Diviners."

"Yeah. But I wasn't down. Not at all. Those suckers are lame. Besides, all they wanted was for me to help them look into the future and get stock numbers. Just hustlers is all. Especially that one Gilberto dude."

"Definitely."

Sitting there, my kinda clone across from me, hearing him talk with my own voice, it's like talking to the brother I never had. This guy, despite his goofiness and his reminding me of the worst aspects of myself, I kind of like him.

"Who else do you know?"

"Uh . . . I know that Vauxhall girl too. The one you mentioned on the call."

"How?"

"She's freaking hot, man. I've been crushing on her hard for years. She used to go to my school and we were friends for a little bit but, well, she kind of got sick of my craziness and bailed."

That makes sense. But I don't tell Adam that.

"And that Karl guy?"

"Asshole, right? Yeah, he went to my school too. I hate the guy, mostly because he's a dick, but also because he's totally getting it on with Vauxhall but I also kind of respect him. For the same reasons and because he has this crazy thing he can do."

Adam motions for me to lean in closer so no one hears.

There is only one other person in the egg place and she's probably eighty-five years old and has headphones on. Whatever, I lean in.

Adam, all secretive, says, "He's got the Buzz thing too, only it doesn't overwhelm him. It's like he's got a leash on it. He can get the high and just make it last all day."

"How's he do it? Concussion?"

Adam shakes his head. He does it so vigorously that he gets a bloody nose. Little splashes of red that fall out of his left nostril down onto his plate. Tiny red paint splotches. He doesn't even know it.

"He's a vampire."

"What?" I'm starting to doubt Adam's even limited consciousness.

"Not like blood-drinking," he says, noticing the bloody nose he has and grabbing a napkin to stuff up into his left nostril. "No. No. He's like an energy vampire. He can drain it off people. Like suck away their life force or something."

Adam can tell by the way I'm looking at him that I don't buy it.

"I'm not kidding, man! He can touch you and then you just feel like you've run a marathon. Listen to this story: There was this one guy at school, this football player dude with one blue eye and one brown eye—"

"Yeah," I interrupt. "I've met him."

"—well, not recently you haven't 'cause of what Karl did to him. It was at this pizza joint on Colfax at lunch. Karl was there with his best friend, this girl with pink hair named Penny who's like a total freak, and that football player was making fun of her. Just being so rude. Karl sat back, being his asshole self and just watching for a few minutes, before he stood up and walked over to the guy and just put his hand on the football dude's forehead. Instantly, the dude froze. Like in that game of freeze when the music stops, you know? Anyway, Karl had his hand on the guy's head for maybe two minutes when it started happening. The guy got all gray, like the color was just washing out of him, and I swear, though no one else there believes it, they all thought it was a gag, that the football player dude suddenly got really, really old. Like all wrinkled and bent over. He's in a nursing home now, bro."

"That's ridiculous," I say. Not even sure why considering everything I've seen.

Adam, napkin turning red in his nose, raises his hand. "Scout's honor. True story. Everyone else there just thought it was like a practical joke with makeup. But I was close up and saw it go down. Wasn't faked. Besides, if it was, where did that football player go? He wasn't at school the next day and my buddy Bill said he saw the dude at a nursing home when he was there visiting his grandma."

Adam pulls the napkin from his nose. Has a look at it.

Bleeding's stopped.

Then he says, "I wouldn't mess with Karl."

I just nod. "I'll take that into account. Look, you can come with me but I think it's probably better if you just stay in the background. Cool? This is important stuff and it's complicated but I think it might be good if you come along."

"As backup, right?"

"Sure. As backup."

We order some eggs for Grandpa Razor. I make sure to douse them in habanero sauce before we leave. Just an extra treat. See what the old man does.

As we're leaving Adam says, "I need to just hit the restroom, okay?"

I tell him fine though I know what he's going to do.

Whole time we were eating, talking, I could see him eyeing different surfaces, the edge of the table, the corner of the counter near the register, the steps outside. The guy is a total addict. I let him feed the addiction, though as he walks to the bathroom I make sure to grab a whole pile of napkins for the inevitable clean-up.

I give him three minutes but hear the bang in two.

The woman working the register looks over at the bathroom, concerned. Then she looks to me as if to suggest, it's your friend, why don't you figure out what he just did. I shrug. And then head to the men's room.

I knock first. "Yo, Adam. It's me."

No reply.

I try the door and it's unlocked. I peek inside and see blood. Blood on the side of the sink but no Adam. He's not here. Another disappearing trick.

Being the good original version of myself, I dutifully clean up the mess.

And then outside. Nod to the woman at the register.

Adam is, of course, waiting for me in the car, enjoying his Buzz. He's all relaxed, with a bloody lip and his black-hole pupils, and nods to me. I have to unlock the car to get in and as I slide into the driver's seat, I ask, "How the hell'd you get in here?"

He laughs his drugged-out laugh.

"Dude," he says. "I didn't tell you?"

"No. Tell me what?"

"That I can teleport, bro. Shit. That's old news."

FOUR

We're zooming down Speer, past the mall and all its scarf ladies, past the high-end boutiques and all the young, wealthy mother shops, past the place where there used to be an amazing bookstore but now there's a sickeningly dull Pilates gym, and Adam tells me about teleportation.

This is new.

This is major.

And as he talks, the more I begin to think that maybe I didn't change my past, didn't erase it, but that maybe I changed the world around me. Maybe I'm the same as always and I slipped sidelong into another world. One where people look like me and Vauxhall has no idea I exist and an idiot can teleport.

Adam lays it down for me. "It's when I've got the high, you know. I'm all tripping out after the concussion and if I close my eyes, focus down hard on someplace, I can—pop!—just move over to it. Clothes and all. Pretty sweet, right?"

I don't know what to say. Adam can tell. He just keeps motoring.

"First time I did it, I kind of freaked out. I jumped off the roof of this one bowling alley downtown, you know the one at the Pavilions, and landed on the walkway there and as soon as the Buzz set in I was grooving and thinking about tacos and wham! I was inside that taco joint on Park Avenue. Ha!"

He laughs hard thinking on it.

"What was crazy was that it was closed and getting out I set off the alarm. Anyway, after that I just kind of did some fun shit with it. Snuck into a girl's closet while she was getting changed, even. That was gnarly."

My response, cold but simple: "I think you might come in handy, Adam."

We get to Grandpa Razor's place and first thing is it's no longer a giant crack house. Whatever I changed in my own history, it changed this place too. Getting out of the car I'm not struck by a wall of piss stink. Walking across the lot I'm not stepping on crack vials or syringes. And when we walk inside, I'm floored by the fact that the lobby is not only clean but downright fashionable.

There's a zen thing going on. All black and white and mid-century styled.

Sweet Jesus, what did I do?

We take the elevator to the penthouse and inside the brushed-steel lift Adam says, "God, I hate the design of this place. Chilly. Makes me just claustrophobic."

When the doors spring open we find ourselves standing in a lobby festooned with plants and mahogany furniture. The bookshelves are stacked with leather-bound tomes. The light is dim but comfortable. For the first time, the name Grandpa actually seems to make sense.

Even that doesn't prepare me for what we see when the door to the penthouse opens.

Grandpa Razor is wearing a smoking jacket.

He's easily a hundred pounds thinner than his previous incarnation. His being thin makes him look even taller than before and he's even wearing loafers. Loafers! Then there's his formerly disgusting beard that, today, right now in his spacious penthouse, is neatly trimmed and streaked with aristocratic gray.

Too bad his voice is so monstrous.

"Hello, Ade. Hello, Adam," he says. "Come on in."

We do.

His place is even more incredible inside. As we walk toward the patio I see a grand piano, a giant fish tank with what I think are eels swimming around in it, a bust of Mozart, two potted ferns, and, weirdly, a manservant.

Razor notices me noticing the butler-looking dude and says, "That's Ralph."

Ralph nods slowly at me.

Then we're outside on the patio and drinks, lemonade, await.

I sit in a lounge chair while Adam takes a seat on a barstool and Grandpa Razor sits back in an all-weather armchair. He pulls a cigar from his breast pocket and lights it slowly, rolling it around in his mouth.

Adam is guzzling lemonade and rocking out to a song only he can hear.

Grandpa Razor, looking over at Adam, says, "Remarkable."

"You don't look like I remember," I say.

Grandpa Razor says, "I figured."

"Tell me what's going on, if you know."

Adam interrupts, "Where's the bathroom, bro?"

Grandpa Razor doesn't even have to clap, Ralph just shows up next to him and motions for Adam to follow. Adam jumps up, looks at me, says, "How badass is this butler?"

"Badass," I say.

He leaves, literally skipping into the apartment.

"His head might leave a mark," I say to Razor.

The newly cleaned up, almost dashing Grandpa says, "Ralph will clean it up."

I sit up in my seat, narrow my eyes. Cleaned up or not, I don't trust this guy.

"Tell me what's going on," I demand.

Grandpa Razor blows a smoke ring and clears his throat. "I'm going to make this very simple: You erased half of your lifetime from history and in doing so, you fractured the reality you're currently living in. Fractured it, I might add, in five places."

"Five? That couldn't sound more random. Stop bullshitting me."

"I'm not. Not at all." He takes another drag. Blows it out, says, "The physics are all way above my pay grade but the basic concept shouldn't be new to you. That is if the science teachers in the public schools are doing their jobs these days. Always difficult to say." He pauses, reads my annoyance, then: "For every fork in the proverbial road there are two or more options, each option leads to a separate reality. It's all very carefully balanced, a perfect God-operated machine, and when you go and mess with it, let's say pull out a gear or a lever or two, then the whole thing starts acting, well, funky. By erasing your past, you erased those forks but the realities behind them already existed. So, there are orphaned choices. Orphaned versions of you. Five of them are now in this reality and only people aware of the erasure, aware on a cosmic scale, can see the resemblance."

"Okay. And if that's true, if Adam and Karl are two, where are the other three?"

"You'll meet them soon enough."

"How about you? How many of you are there?"

Grandpa Razor grins at that. Teeth shining in his beard. "There were five, just like you. But I, being somewhat familiar with this sort of thing before, dealt with them."

"Dealt with them?"

"Yes, much in the same way you will have to. That's the crux of the next thirty-six-odd hours, Ade. You need to deal with each and every one of your multiples or the fabric of the universe will heal itself and you'll be stuck like this . . . a mess."

"How do you deal with them?"

"You battle them. You overcome them. You consume them."

I make a face. It's obvious what I'm thinking.

Grandpa likes the discomfort he's causing. "Not like cannibalism. No, it's a matter of two objects occupying the same space. They can't. Matter and anti-matter. You need to delete your multiples from this plane of reality. The only way is to consume them. Absorb them as your own. There are many benefits, in fact."

"Like?"

"For me, it's been quite obvious. Each of my duplicates reflected a different aspect of my being. Some more balanced than others. As I consumed them, I took on their abilities, their aspects. Resulting in . . . the new me."

He stands up. Turns himself around.

There's something very old-school Jimi in the display.

Then he sits back down and says, "You're going to have to do the same and, if you're successful, you'll be rewarded with their gifts. Like Adam in there. Wouldn't it be nice to be able to do what he can? And if you aren't successful, your duplicates may actually absorb you. I'm not sure exactly what happens then but it won't be pretty. And it wouldn't—"

"Wait, how come there were five of you? There aren't five Vauxhalls. Or anyone else."

Grandpa Razor taps his temple. Giving me the old aren't-you-the-clever-one.

He says, "Because we're bound up, Ade. Like I said, I'd met

the Glove. You and me have a history that is intertwined. You change yours and it changes mine."

"What about Vauxhall?"

"Just one of her. But she doesn't know you because, while the two of you are intertwined, it's not in the past but in the future. Your erasing history changed that. You can get her back."

"How do you know?"

"She and I have talked. She came to me seeking answers. I gave her a few."

I move forward, inching closer and closer to the new and improved Razor.

Through gritted teeth I ask, "What answers?"

Grandpa Razor laughs and laughs and laughs. And then he wipes all the phlegm off his chin with a handkerchief. Then he goes, "I'm going to keep that secret. Back pocket, for now. I can't tell you everything, can I?"

"Yes. You can."

"Ha. What I need from you now is some reciprocal motion. I've explained most everything you asked and given you the tools to take on what's coming. Now, it's your turn to do the favors. I didn't come by this information on my own. And I didn't learn it entirely from the Glove. There is another."

"Here we go again with the vagaries. What other?"

"A world you haven't encountered yet, Ade. A whole stratum of ability that exists beneath the familiar one you know. This person usually watches from the sidelines, he doesn't often meddle in our affairs, at least not in ways we can see. But he's messing now, now that you went and changed things. And I want you to kill him."

I sit blank faced. I'm not trying to be a badass. Not putting on some stoic face. It's more that my mind is seizing up. Information overload. Nothing really making clear sense.

"What?!" I manage to ask.

"Calls himself the Enigma. I can't tell you where to find him but I can tell you that everything you've seen, all the powers you are aware of, pales in comparison to his. The Enigma is the next evolutionary step in divination. Gilberto, Anka, even the Metal Sisters aren't aware of his existence. He's the secret of the secrets. Dream wrapped within a dream. The mission is very simple: Absorb your duplicates, kill the baddie, and get the girl. Congratulations, Ade, you've just—whether by accident or design—moved yourself up to the next level. What you do in the next few days won't just change the past or the future, it will change everything."

"I'm not killing anyone."

"Oh, you'll kill him alright. When the time comes, you won't hesitate."

"Tell me what Vauxhall has to do with all this?"

Grandpa Razor frowns. "You're so impatient."

"Tell me!"

"No. 'Cause I don't want you to rush in blindly, ruin this."

And with that, as if to put an exclamation point on it, Razor stands.

He turns to head back inside when Adam suddenly teleports back onto the patio, knocking over the stool he was sitting on. Glasses tumble. Shatter. Adam just grins through it all, bloody-mouthed. He's missing teeth.

I stand up and catch Grandpa Razor by the tailored sleeve.

"Where do I start?" I ask him.

"Oh, I've planned that out for you. Get ready to rumble, Ade. I invited one of your duplicates over. I believe he's that part of you transferred over from Jimi originally. The angry, furious part. It'll be your first test and he should be here any—"

He's interrupted by the sound of the doorbell. It's like an electronic gong.

Grandpa Razor raises an eyebrow. "Well, I'll send him out."

FIVE

Adam and I wait in silence.

Well, I wait in silence.

Adam pretty much belches and bleeds all over the patio.

Between burps he says, "What's going on exactly, bro? I'm confused."

"Don't stress," I say. "I got this."

But of course I don't. I'm stressed. Stressed deep.

The wait is interminable.

Grandpa Razor's swank pad is silent. But my heartbeat is pounding in my ears over it all. This terrible boom-boom-boom like one of those drummers on a Viking ship. And as every second passes, the sound of it gets louder. Louder.

I replay all my past fights.

All the ones I have memories of. Or think I have memories of.

The smackdown under the bridge on Broadway. The melee

with the skinheads at Monaco Lanes. The two times I knocked Garrett, the rapist asshole from Mantlo, senseless. And from each one of them, like some sort of mental ninja, I pull particular fight moves. I categorize them in my mind. Each punch. Each pull. Each kick. Each throw.

Beat. Beat. Beat.

And then, he walks out onto the patio.

Just like me, same as Adam, the dude has my features and my build. But this guy is doing something entirely different with it all. First, his head's shaved. He's got a nose ring and a spattering of facial hair like he rolled around in someone else's shavings. And tattoos, up and down his arms and even on his neck.

The guy is wearing sunglasses and really long shorts.

No shoes. But tats on his feet.

Grandpa Razor hovers like a well-dressed ghost over the guy's shoulder. He says, "Ade, I'd like to introduce you to Tad. Tad's here to avenge the brutal beating and subsequent arrest of a close friend of his. A, uh—"

Tad says, "Garrett."

"Right. Garrett. I believe you are familiar with the gentleman?"

Tad glares at me. Even with sunglasses on I can tell.

It's freaky having someone use my own eyes to burn a proverbial hole in my own head. Freaky seeing my own hate reflected back on me.

Grandpa Razor continues setting it up. Playing up the drama. "Tad's a member of the 49th Street Bend Sinisters, a local, well, how did you phrase it once, Tad?"

Tad says, "Street squad."

"Right, it's a professional organization. They are well respected and equally feared. Anyway, Tad was detained, very much illegally, several months ago and shared a cell with Garrett. They got on swimmingly and Garrett hired Tad here to make several legal adjustments. Basically, Tad's been hired to kick your ass. Severely impair you, if possible."

Tad adds, "Totally possible."

Grandpa Razor smiles.

Adam scoots out of his chair, heads for the door. "Dude, I've got your back and all, but this . . ." he says. "This is a bit too gnarly even for me. Good luck, man."

Razor grabs hold of Adam's shirt. Holds him.

"Oh, you've got a dog in this fight too, Adam."

And he pushes Adam back out onto the patio.

Tad cracks his knuckles, then his neck. Then he removes his sunglasses. Unlike me, this duplicate has cold, blue eyes. Looks good, honestly.

Staring into those eyes, I say, "I'm not here for this."

Tad scoffs. "But I am."

And with that he lunges, swings.

I'm slow. Even with all the moves rattling around in my head. Even with my years of experience, I'm not fast enough to avoid Tad's fist. Well, maybe it's 'cause it's my fist.

He hits me just above the left eye.

Something cracks. Cartilage rips.

And I go flying back onto one of the patio chairs, toppling it.

Adam is like, "Dude!"

But he doesn't rush to my aid. Really he just curls up behind the big armchair.

I pick myself up, squinting. Say, "Garrett's an asshole."

Tad growls. No kidding.

He steps closer, fists raised.

I say, "I'm guessing you're an asshole too."

And he lunges again. This time I'm ready. I don't swing. I keep my arms back, my fists out of the way. It's a psych-out trick. Make him think he's got the momentum. And that's exactly what I'm using when I throw my right foot in front of his. Catch him off balance.

He stumbles. Fists circling wildly.

Lands one in my ribs, nearly knocks my breath out. But I've got him wobbly and use it, bring a fist down on the back of his neck and he sputters. He falls.

I back away quick while Adam cheers.

"Nice, brother!"

Grandpa Razor nods from the door.

Tad is up within seconds. And he wastes no time in barreling over the furniture and slamming into me. The two of us go tumbling into a potted plant, sending mulch sky high. He pummels me as we roll. Fist and fist in my face. My chest.

And with every hit there's a weird twinge. An electrical shock.

Not only am I getting my ass kicked by my mirror reflection but it also feels like he's got tasers for fingers. Nails embedded in his knuckles.

Tad senses it too. Makes him hit harder.

Adam yells, "Come on, Ade! Do something."

But I'm stuck, trapped under the barrage.

I can feel the skin on my left cheek starting to snap under the strain. The bones beneath are bruised. My teeth are rattling loose. And my eardrums are swollen to bursting.

Probably only ten seconds from passing out.

Eight seconds from having my optic nerves stretched to breaking.

Five seconds from having my heart misfire.

Despite the pressure on my ears and the constant thud of Tad's assault, I do manage to hear a rather loud knock and then, almost before the sound is gone, Adam suddenly teleports between Tad and me. Like a Tad, Adam, and Ade sandwich.

His bloody face dripping only centimeters from mine, Adam smiles.

Says, "I'm buying you some time, homes."

And then he's ripped away, Tad tossing him to the concrete like a sock.

Adam knocks his head on the railing. Hard.

He's knocked completely out.

But his move does buy me time.

Time enough to get my hands around the leg of the stool.

I'm up quick, already shaking off the beating, and as Tad turns back around to me, ready to go again, I bring the stool down on his head. The sound is glorious.

I kind of wish it was being filmed because it would have looked so sweet in super-slow motion. Chunks of the stool, splinters, flying off like insects from a kicked bush.

And it's quick, shocking enough to knock Tad on his ass.

I'm in his face faster.

And I hit him in his throat. It's a nasty move. One that I've been subjected to at least a dozen times and I know it sucks more than being kicked in the balls or smashed over the head with a bowling ball. A lot more. But it's effective in keeping a guy down. Keeping him out of sorts enough to not have to worry for at least thirty seconds.

Tad, coughing and sputtering just the same as I did, rolls away.

I have my thirty seconds and turn back to Grandpa Razor.

He's clapping slowly.

He says, "Now. You're going to put your hand into his chest. Visualize it like you're placing your hand and arm through a window. See what happens."

I roll Tad onto his back, sit on his arms, and put my hand over his chest.

Try pressing.

Nothing.

Tad is still choking but his eyes are raging.

"Not flat," Razor says. "Like a karate chop. Slow."

I turn my palm vertical and with the tips of my nails push my hand into Tad's chest. Where skin would be there is this shimmering light, like on the surface of a lake.

"Good," Grandpa extols. "Excellent."

With my hand pretty much buried inside his chest cavity, I can actually feel Tad's heart beating. There is no blood. Just the reflective, glittery light.

Tad starts to shake. Not like he's being electrocuted but as though he's slipping out of the frame. Like in a movie when the picture gets messed up. Or in a video where the lines start overlapping and the image gets all over-processed. Digitally blurred.

The light gets brighter and brighter.

Tad's face seems farther and farther away.

And then, with an explosion of brilliance, Tad's gone.

Just my hand in midair and all around us this white, curling smoke.

I stand up, turn back to Grandpa Razor. "So, what next?" I ask him.

He says, "Now you open your Christmas present. Look inside; see what ability you just gained. From what I've heard, it's a doozy."

I close my eyes and try to relax and already it's clear. Like second nature. Like I was born with it. Instead of the concussions, instead of the future, I find something amazing. I open my eyes and to Grandpa Razor, I say, "Get me some of the nasty, illegal cheese of yours. To go."

He nods knowingly, then says, "You taking your friend?"

Adam is just coming to. All wonky.

He asks, "What'd I miss?"

SIX

I get back home and my mom nearly faints seeing my face.

Adam comes in stumbling after me.

First thing Mom does is call Paige.

I crash for a few hours and when I wake up I hear a ruckus. I stretch, sore like I've been run over, and make my way into the kitchen where I find Adam and my mom sitting across from Paige. They're all eating sugar cereal.

I go to the fridge and pull out a silver bowl with tinfoil on top.

Then I sit at the table and take the tinfoil off. The hit-you-in-the-face smell of the cheese is as immediate as a ballistic missile. Paige jumps up and dashes to the other side of the room, as far away as possible from the sickening cheese that's crawling in the dish.

Clearing my throat, I tell them all how it will go down. I tell them how I'll eat a spoonful of this stuff and chew it slowly and by doing that I'll be able to move my mind outside my body. I say, "This right here is the first step in saving the world."

"Seriously," Paige says. "If you eat that, I'm going to puke."

My mom, a slather of Vick's VapoRub on her upper lip, says, "How do you even know this will work? I mean, it sounds awfully like a scam, Ade. Like a charlatan pulling your strings. I don't like it at all."

Adam is actually eating a cold slice of pizza he found in the fridge.

I told him I didn't know how old it was. He said it didn't matter.

With the cheese in front of me, I point to it and ask him, "Do you want some of this on your slice?"

He shrugs. Like he actually considered it.

I clear my throat, grab the fork next to me, and get ready to dig in when Paige interrupts. She stands up, makes the classic time-out hand gesture.

Paige says, "Okay. Okay. Let's talk this through one more time before you take that bite." And then she proceeds to recount, in her own verbiage, the story. Everything. How it got to here. How Adam is a duplicate, even though Paige says he looks nothing like me. The things Razor told me. And how eating this cheese will allow me to activate Tad's ability.

When she's done I nod and say, "Pretty much it."

It's amazing how well she knows me and how much she'll take at face value.

Paige sits back down, says, "You're still even more insane than ever before."

"At least this doesn't involve cracking my head open," I say.

Paige shrugs. "Really," she says, "this might be worse."

I take a forkful and she stops me again. Adam looks all irritated.

"Wait!" Paige leans forward. "What are you going to be focusing on?"

"Vauxhall," I say. "I just need to."

"What about the other yous? You know, there are still like three out there."

Adam perks up. "Three? I thought it was two. Who's the third?"

I look to Paige and then my mom. They both have this pained expression. Both of them are wondering what to do next. Both are stunned that Adam hasn't realized it yet. He doesn't get that he's number three. Of course, they don't know him.

"Seriously though," Adam says.

I say, "Oh, it's this one dude I met downtown the other night."

"We going to meet up with him? Another brawl?"

"Maybe," I say. "But I don't think he's going to be a problem like Tad."

Then I turn to Paige. "I just need to focus on Vauxhall, okay? It'll help me focus. Thing is, I think Grandpa Razor's just trying to distract me. Thinks I'm like his hired gun and I don't trust him. I need to see Vauxhall."

And with that I take a bite of the cheese.

It doesn't go down easy. Feeling the grubs or maggots or whatever in it moving inside my cheeks might be the most up-setting sensation I've ever experienced. I chew the cheese slowly though. Making sure to get the full flavor. Every greasy mole-cule.

And almost immediately the effects appear.

While it's the same vehicle as Grandpa Razor, what I see isn't the future. Eating the cheese, this gastromancy move, I can send my mind outside my body. I can remote view. And it's fucking incredible.

I've read about out-of-body experiences. Never had one de-spite all the head injuries, but even the descriptions you read can't prepare you for just how cool the real thing is.

Imagine downloading yourself into a computer and then being able to fly around, bend every law of physics, and just flit through every surface. Like you were made of cloud or something. Light as nothing. A fleck of dust in the vacuum.

I make my way through the front door and out into the night air.

Drifting over the lawns and trees, I swing over Leetsdale on my way into Cherry Creek. Hovering above the cars is surreal. So peaceful only a few feet up above the turmoil of everyday life. The air is still here. The sounds softer.

I'm headed to Cherry Creek 'cause that's where Vauxhall is.

I don't get how the homing deal of it works but pretty much all I have to do is think of Vaux, see her in my mind, and this kind of mental GPS springs up. It's not visual, just a sense. I home in on her. Track her like a fish swimming upstream.

She's at a sushi place with her mom.

I drift down through the roof. First it's pebbles and then it's insulation and then a fluorescent bulb and then a fan blade and then I'm in the room.

Vauxhall is sitting by the window.

Her mom's eating a California roll with tons of ginger. Vauxhall isn't eating anything. She's looking out at the cars passing by. Looks worried.

I want nothing more than to touch her. To kiss her.

I try.

Nothing doing. I'm not only invisible but I'm also intangible. Less than dust.

I hover a few inches above Vauxhall. Watch her eyes watch the street. Watch the slow rise and fall of her chest with each and every breath. It's nice to observe her like this. Without her being aware of me, she's different. Not being watched, she's more re-laxed.

Her mom takes a sip of water, asks, "You read that letter yet?"

Vauxhall turns to her. Shakes her head. "No. I don't want to."

"Who do you think it's from? I mean, wouldn't it be just easier to open it and find out? You're making such a fuss over it."

"Mom, I'm not comfortable with it, okay?"

Mom shrugs. She stands up. "Be back in a sec."

Then she walks to the bathroom.

That leaves us alone. I lower myself down to where Vaux's mom was sitting and stare at Vauxhall from there. She looks back out the window. Totally concentrating on something.

Then her phone buzzes. I can't see who's calling but she answers very plainly.

"Hey, Leif." She doesn't seem happy about the call. It's all perfunctory.

I move in across the table, place myself right next to the cell so I can hear.

The voice on the other end is a guy's. Leif. Uncommon name.

He says, "Guy is a complete unknown. Flying way below the radar. I don't know anyone who's ever met him. At least not in our circle. But what's weird is that someone saw him driving around with Adam today. And there's this suggestion that he knows Grandpa Razor and the Diviners."

"That would make sense," Vauxhall says. "But what if he's here to intervene? Try and stop us?"

"I don't think you need to worry. It's already too late for that. Probably he's just crushing on you and he's making stuff up. You know, sometimes guesses can turn out right."

"He knows me. He knows me from somewhere. I can feel it. I got this really weird feeling today, just before dinner. It was like I was thinking about him, trying to place his face, you know, when suddenly there was this shock of recognition. I was sure for a second, just a split second, that I knew him. Knew him really well. But it disappeared really quickly. Only a flash."

Leif is quiet. Then: "Why do you think he showed up now?"

"Who knows? He sent me a letter. I haven't opened it."

"Are you kidding me? Why not? What if this guy knows?"

"He doesn't. Trust me. I'm just spooked, I guess. I'm worried it will have all this personal stuff in it. And that will make me feel crazy. Either he's spying on me and getting all these details or maybe I really do know who he is and I just forgot. That would be even worse."

"Let me read it."

"No. I don't want to—"

And suddenly I'm yanked out of the restaurant.

Pulled back across the rooftops and the treetops like I'm attached to a bungee cord and its elastic has given out. I'm snapped back, quick as a blink, to the kitchen table, where my eyes open and I've still got a little of the cheese in my mouth.

I spit it out and grab a glass of water and down it while Adam, Paige, and my mom stare at me. Their faces full of questions.

I put the glass down. Say, "It worked."

"And?" Paige is first to ask.

"I saw her. At dinner. She was on her cell, talking to a guy named Leif about me."

"And?" my mom asks.

"That guy knows something more. He's in on this. So is she. I just can't piece together how. Why she'd go to Grandpa Razor. Why she'd want to hide something."

Adam, finished with his slice, feet up on the table, says, "Did the guy sound gay?"

"What?" I ask. Offended like that should matter.

I look to Paige. More out of habit than anything.

"All I'm saying," Adam says, "is that if he's gay, he's probably this one dude I met once at this used-book store. His name is Leif and he's very gay."

"What are you talking about?" Paige asks. This is her about to blow up.

Adam puts his hands up. "Whoa, don't bite my head off."

He looks to me to protect him. I got nothing.

Then he says, "Listen, I just brought it up 'cause this dude is into weird stuff. Same kind of stuff Grandpa Razor and his crew is into only it's kind of more metaphysical. You know, like New Age business. Dreams and like other worlds just behind the mirror sort of stoner stuff. Guy even says he's been in contact with like other beings. And he—"

I tune Adam out.

Can't help it.

It's late. I can't think straight. Not after everything that's happened. Not after the last twenty-four hours. And what really makes me feel like I'm slipping is that I only have like a day and a half left to get Vauxhall back and absorb the duplicates.

Like Adam.

Watching him getting into his story, I can't help but feel bad about what I'll have to do. This guy is going to vanish. He's going to wrinkle away into nothingness like Tad did and it'll be me who makes him go. I feel bad about it. I kind of want to keep the guy around; maybe there's a way I won't have to absorb him. Perhaps the universe will be just fine with two of us. Like twins. And he can go live on the opposite side of the country if that makes it better.

I'm dwelling on this, plotting out how I'm going to save him, when he says something that makes me snap out of it.

He says, "Yeah, Leif calls him the Enigma. Like he's a band."

That has me by the throat.

I interrupt Adam. Ask, "What'd he say about the Enigma?"

"Uh, you know, just goofy stoner stuff." Adam looks blank.

"I need to see this Leif. Tomorrow, early, we're going to the bookstore."

The perpetual sidekick, Adam is like, "Right on!"

Paige pipes up. "I'm coming too."

I tell them I need to rest up. Need to unwind, even if it's for a second. My mom is happy with this. I can tell the way she's been watching me, listening to me, that I probably look bad. If it isn't the bruises from the battle today then it's just the stress etching out lines on my face. I'll bet I have gray hairs.

My mom gives me a kiss on the forehead. Says she'll check on me.

By the time I leave the room Adam is already asleep.

Head on the table, drooling like a baby. My mom, bless her heart, grabs a blanket from off the couch and puts it over him. He snores something.

I head to the living room and collapse into an armchair, flip out the footrest, and flick the television on. Just for old times' sake, I go to the Spanish language channels and try to find a soap opera. Something really outrageous. Doesn't take me long.

By the time the first commercial for a Mexican soda comes on, Paige is sitting in the chair next to me, snacking on popcorn.

Old times. Same Paige, only back at the start.

P.B.V. Or Paige Before Vauxhall.

She says, "When you talk about this Vauxhall girl, you sound just like you did when you were all gaga over that one chick at Rocky Mountain Records and Tapes."

"No. Vaux's nothing like that girl."

Paige scoffs. "How's that? Thought you said that girl was the most beautiful girl you'd ever seen? I think the word was 'sub-lime.'"

"Well, she was nice to look at but . . ."

Paige chews a handful of popcorn, says, "Yeah, she was a pirate whore." Then, "Isn't this like the fifth time you've been in love, Ade? What about the waitress? Wasn't she the One?"

"Not the same. She was so needy."

Paige says, "Pier whore."

This is Paige being a bitch. This is Paige busting my balls.

And we've had this conversation twice now.

She's talking about Halifax. Mom and I went there shortly after Grandma died and spent a week traversing the quiet city. One night we had dinner in Lunenburg. This little picture-perfect fishing village of a couple thousand people. Right there on the ocean with all these North Atlantic barnlike houses and hundreds of tiny boats bobbing on the water. We had salmon and lobster at a restaurant on the outskirts of the town. Old Bridge Restaurant. Nothing classy. Everyone on staff was family. The mom welcomed and sat us. The dad and brother were in the kitchen. Cousin was bussing. Daughter was our waitress.

She's why Paige is bringing this up.

This girl, the Old Bridge daughter, was maybe sixteen and had blond hair in curls and lips like ruby pillows. I couldn't take my eyes off her the whole time we ate dinner and lay awake all night thinking about her. I had these fantasies of taking her away. Stealing her from her home in the middle of the night. Plucking her from the Old Bridge and throwing her apron into the ocean. Paige and I talked for hours about how I would do it. How I'd get hold of Mom's credit card. How I'd book the flight. Rent the car. Where I'd take her. I talked this way for weeks.

"Interesting." Paige smiles. "And Kate?"

Here we go again. Déjà vu. I tell Paige, "That was different but not like this. Vauxhall's a hundred times better. Kate was cute but she wasn't into me. It feels really weird talking like this. Like you don't know Vauxhall."

"Um, I don't. Besides, Kate's stunning and she's really into slasher films, right?"

I nod.

Paige says, "Damn, she might have been made for both of us."

I say, "She didn't like me, Paige. Let's move on."

"Kate was a definite wharf whore."

I put the TV on mute, turn to Paige.

"What's with all the nautical whore stuff?"

Paige snickers. "Me and Veronica came up with it. Total ranking system for hoochies. First level is sailor whore. That's just plain funny."

"And then pirate whore?"

"Right."

"Then I came up with dock whore. You know, so slutty she didn't even make the boat. But it didn't sound nearly as good as pier whore. Just conjures up the right images."

"And then?"

"Then wharf whore. I mean a pier can be classy. But a wharf."

"Nice. And if Vauxhall doesn't end up with me, she'll be what?"

"Barnacle whore."

"Wow."

"The thing with the barnacle whore is that she's on the wharf. And I see it as totally being decrepit, sinking into the waves and all in shadows, but not really. She's like so low she's clinging to the side of it just above the waterline."

Paige laughs and laughs.

I un-mute the TV and on the screen there's a lady with big red hair screaming.

I don't say anything, just reach over and take Paige's hand. Squeeze it.

She smiles. Says, "Me and Veronica, we're going to get her back for you. We're going to do whatever it takes. Tomorrow, the next day, no matter how much time, we'll be skipping school and running all over town but we'll get her to love you again. I don't understand what happened, but it doesn't matter. I believe you, Ade. Always have."

I close my eyes.

For the first time in what feels like weeks, I feel okay.

I feel like everything might just be fine.

I wake up hours later.

The TV is off and Paige is asleep on the couch behind me under a blanket.

Adam is still at the table. The puddle of drool under his face the size of a dinner plate. I grab a napkin and put it nearby.

Mom's in bed. Holding the Revelation Book to her chest.

She looks very calm. It's three in the morning.

I get to my room and crawl into bed and almost immediately I'm out cold. No dreams. No settling in. My head hits the pillow and it's black. Pitch, wonderful black.

I'm not sure how long I'm asleep when I hear the noise.

It's a snickering.

Covered mouth, trying-to-be-quiet laughing.

I open my eyes and it's too dark to make out anything but the glint of teeth in the half-light. And then a familiar voice says, "Damn, dog, you've taken it to the next level."

Gordon. Of course.

There's a sudden arc of light. Bright like a strobe.

And a shock.

My right arm feels like it's on fire.

And before I conk out I realize he's just tasered me.

SEVEN

I don't know how I get out of my house.

I'm guessing it's through the window.

And I'm assuming that my mom didn't hear anything. That Paige had gone home. That Adam was knocked out somewhere. Hell, even if he'd been on the floor of my bedroom he might not have noticed me being abducted.

Regardless of how I left, I wake up in Gordon's car.

Backseat.

He's behind the wheel and Jeremiah's riding shotgun.

They notice I'm awake right away. Before I can say a single word, Gordon drops a few bombs on me. Staring, wild-eyed, in the rearview, he says, "You've been making real waves. Stirring it up! I've been getting calls all day about you. Shit, homie, I guess you didn't know that Tad was a close friend of ours."

"I thought I was a friend of yours," I say.

Gordon laughs.

"Of course," he says. "But things have changed. Seriously, man, I can't believe that you'd do this after all we showed you. What happened in that bathroom was a miracle. We all saw amazing things that night. You, you saw the afterlife, for fuck's sake!"

"How do you know what I saw?"

Jeremiah snickers. It's a sinister sound.

"Bro," Gordon says. "That's my ability. I can see other people's visions as they happen. Kind of like wirelessly. I have the password to your head."

And that cracks him up.

"But what I can't believe is that you'd throw all that away for a girl. I mean, if you were really one of us, you'd have embraced losing control. If anything, a vision like that should have made you über-psyched to just let loose. Should have."

Jeremiah spins around and shoots me a grin. "We're the Pandora Crew, Ade. Devoted to breaking down the order of things, liberating the chaos energy inherent in the process of creation. What you did tonight, that just really made our job tougher. It's like you turned on us, man."

"Jeremiah's been pretty upset," Gordon adds.

We're cruising on I-25. Near the stadium. Across from the amusement park. I'm not sure where we're going but after the whole mall incident, I'm not sure it's a good thing to be with these guys alone.

I say, "I don't really have time for all this."

Gordon says, "All this? You don't even know what we're doing."

"Tell me."

Jeremiah says, "Normally we wouldn't want to spoil the fun, but considering the situation, you might as well know. We're taking you to the Glove. We're going to fix things."

"Fix things?"

"Yeah," Gordon says. "Make it chaotic again."

I straighten up. Stretch out. "I hate to break it to you guys," I start. "But I don't think I suddenly got everything all lined up. If anything, after my visit to the Glove, it got considerably more messed up. Haven't you all talked to Grandpa Razor?"

Gordon smacks his forehead, all over the top. Sarcastic as hell.

He says, "Take a look at Grandpa, Ade. Does he look messed up to you?"

"Not really."

Jeremiah laughs. Brays like a donkey.

Gordon says, "Don't make this hard on us. The Glove will explain it all."

Downtown flashes by outside.

The night being ripped apart by the lights and the noise.

"What do you two know about the Enigma?" I ask. See if I get a rise.

For a beat neither of the Pandora boys speaks.

Their silence is telling.

The car exits the highway and at a light, Gordon turns around and looks at me. I haven't seen him looking this severe. It's like I stabbed him in the back or ran over his mother. He says, "You're effing around with the impossible, Ade. You don't do that. Everyone knows you don't do that."

And he leaves it there. Pushes the car fast onto 15th.

I toy with the door, test to see if it's unlocked, consider, even, jumping out onto the street, rolling away from the car. But the child safety locks are engaged and, besides, Jeremiah is looking back at me. Taser in hand.

We get to the Glove's apartment and Gordon opens the back door for me.

Like we're on a date.

He even does one of those butler bows. The kind I imagine Grandpa Razor's Ralph does all the time.

Gordon says, "This won't take but a few minutes."

I follow them upstairs to the Glove's loft. Place looks exactly as I left it only the isolation tank is upright and the floor's been mopped. The Glove is sitting on a folding chair in the middle of the room. He's not wearing his gas mask.

He motions for me to come over to him. Points to a folding chair leaning against the wall opposite. I grab the chair, unfold it, put it down in front of him.

The Glove is still remarkably ugly.

Face just a sad distortion of scar tissue. A car wreck of a mouth.

"I'll admit," he says. "Some of this was my fault. I should have given you more direction. Should have been a little more thorough. But I figured after the time before, there was little chance anything would actually work."

"Why am I here?" I ask.

"Because I want to help you, Ade. Gordon and Jeremiah have filled me in on everything. It's amazing how quickly information gets around these days. There's no need for you to try and self-correct the present. No point in battling your parallel-universe selves. Just get back in the isolation tank and we'll do it over again. There may be some slight changes in the present but I guarantee what happened last time won't happen again. You'll get your girl back. Everything back."

"If that's true, if it can all be fixed so easily, why didn't Grandpa Razor send me back to you in the first place?"

"He likes his new station. His new appearance. You understand that, right?"

"Yeah but . . ."

The Glove stops fucking around, pulls a gun from out of nowhere. Handy trick.

He says, "Get in the tank. It's ready."

"You said you already did this five times with me. I remember."

The Glove grins. "Yeah. That's where they came from."

"But why don't I remember doing that?"

" 'Cause it wasn't this version of you."

"Well, then, which version was it?"

The Glove pushes the gun into my gut. "Just get in."

"Okay, okay." I put my hands up like I'm in a movie. I'm not sure why I do it but it just feels right. Probably just a programmed response after all the cop shows I've watched.

The Glove says, "Move."

I stand up. Start walking.

Gordon snickers. "Damn, dog. In your face!"

The Glove marches me across the room to the ladder.

"Climb," he says.

I climb.

And at the top of the tank, right at the edge with the water lapping around my shoes, he says, "Get undressed."

I turn around. Look him in the jaundiced eyes.

"This isn't going to work," I say.

"You don't have to believe to make it work, Ade. All you need to do is get undressed and I'll knock you out. When you wake up, everything will be back to normal. Either that or I can shoot you in the gut, then knock you out, and kick you into the tank. You'll bleed to death but not before you reverse the past."

I look to Gordon. Jeremiah. My so-called friends.

Gordon says, "Don't look at me, dude. I can't help you now."

Jeremiah says, "Just hurry up."

The Glove puts the gun against the side of my head. Barrel cold as ice.

So I undress. Pull off my shirt and pants but leave on the boxers. Gordon catcalls. Jeremiah says something about getting me on a stripper pole. They both find that hilarious.

The Glove, not laughing, says, "In."

I slide down into the tank. The water is warm and salty as before. I'm floating high up in it and the sensation is just as weird as before, like swimming in clouds. The Glove leans down and pulls a flask from his hip pocket. He hands it to me.

Gun pointed at my left eye, he says, "Drink."

Inside is the same stuff as before. The psychedelic cocktail.

Gordon says, "Chug!"

Jeremiah joins in. "Chug!"

Stuff smells terrible and I raise it to my lips but hesitate.

The Glove lowers the gun, pushes it against my forehead. "Drink."

I drink. It's sweeter than last time. He's changed the recipe.

I hand the flask back to the Glove and he smiles. I've been in enough fights to know that look. This is the moment. His smile, it means that he's won. It means that deep down he's convinced the whole thing is over and all he needs to do is slam me over the head with the butt of the gun. Already his muscles are starting to relax. He's breathing deeper. His brain is moving on to what happens next, what happens after I sink to the bottom of the tank. This is the moment.

And I use it.

I grab the gun and pull fast. Pull the Glove right down into the tank with me. He hits the trigger and there's a muffled boom as the gun fires, the bullet passing through the hull of the tank and slamming into the hardwood. A stream of water shooting out.

He's off balance, confused. Swallowing salt water.

I twist the gun away from him and I climb over him to get out of the tank.

I fall down the ladder, my feet slipping, and crash on the floor.

The gun skitters out of my grip and slides over near Gordon. He reaches down and grabs it but before he can even point it at me, I'm up and running. I round the tank, headed for a door on the far wall.

From the tank I hear the Glove cursing. Shouting, "He can't leave!"

Gordon and Jeremiah run after me, gritting their teeth.

Gordon holds the gun high, finger on the trigger. The look in his eye tells me he'll kill me.

I reach the door, open it, and dive inside. It's the bathroom. Shit.

Of course, that's when the drug that the Glove gave me starts to work.

My vision goes blurry. My legs turn to jelly. Head spinning, eyes rolling back in my head, I feel like I'm either more stoned than I've ever been in my life or that I'm going to pass out. Wind up choking on my own vomit in the Glove's bathroom.

That last thought is what helps me keep upright.

I peek out the door, see Gordon and Jeremiah fishing the Glove out of the tank. They know I'm stuck, that there's no way out from here, so they're taking their time.

I need to move.

And I try. I creep out of the bathroom but I'm so woozy I fall. So instead of creeping, I wind up crawling out. It's actually better because I make it to the futon mattress before they notice I've left the bathroom.

I find my way around the mattress and over to the mini fridge.

Every step is nauseating.

Every step it feels like my head is going to explode.

After the day I've had, this is the last thing I need.

God, do I want to just freaking sleep.

I stay behind the fridge as long as I can. Already I'm starting to shake, goose pimples popping up all over my body. I'm going to freeze to death if I don't move.

Too bad I'm seeing things.

It's the mushroom soup for sure but I'm seeing insects crawling up out of the floor. They glow in the dark and they have really long, ticklish antennae. Even though I know the bugs don't exist I can still feel their little feet all over me. Their shells knocking against my toes.

Gordon's at the bathroom door. Playing the badass killer, he kicks the door open and dives in with the gun in his hands. Of course, I'm not there and he looks stupid.

"Shit!" he yells. "Not in here."

The Glove, now super ugly and dripping wet, is beyond pissed. He swings his fists at Jeremiah and clocks the dude. Jeremiah drops to the floor holding his mouth.

"Find him now or I'm going to pull out your eyes!" the Glove screams.

Nice guy.

I know I need to move so I take a deep breath and kick all the insects off my legs and dash toward the tank. Amazingly, they don't see me right away. I'm able to get my clothes, unceremoniously dumped on the floor, and make it halfway to the front door when Gordon fires and puts a hole in the hardwood just inches from me.

I keep going.

Jeremiah beats me to the door, blocks it with his body.

The drugs kick into overtime and his face turns into a psychedelic swirl, like what you see on the bottom of a cup of rainbow sherbet. I actually want to laugh but stop myself. That would look crazy.

At the last second, maybe ten feet from Jeremiah, I turn to the right.

I imagine it looks like something a running back would do.

That's how it feels. Feels like I'm kicking ass.

And I head for a window over the sink in the corner of the room. I'm not sure how it's going to go down, and it isn't until I've actually jumped and I'm in midair, but I don't actually think about whether the glass will break. Even more, I don't bother worrying about what'll happen when I get outside. Might be a long, eventful fall.

I hit the glass and it shatters.

Also it cuts me up something terrible.

Like diving through a thorn bush, I can feel the claws of glass etching into my skin. Tearing deep, leaving long and bloody streaks.

But I'm out.

I'm. Out.

And the fall isn't bad. I wind up only dropping ten feet to the roof of the neighboring apartment building. I don't pause. Also I don't hit the roof and roll like I'm an asskicking action star. I pretty much belly flop on the pea gravel of the roof and it hurts like hell. Knocks the breath out of me.

But I don't have time to suffer and complain.

I'm up and limping behind a swamp cooler on the roof before Gordon or the Glove even sees me.

Getting down off the roof is easy. I find a staircase on the backside. First I throw my clothing on and then I slide down fast as I can. Run down the alleyway like a freak, trying my best to stay in the shadows.

The insects were trailing me for most of the run but now they're gone.

Before long I'm out and feel safe.

I make my way on the path by the Platte and don't even bother dodging the hoboes.

Only when I've got several miles between me and the Glove's place do I check my cell phone. I'm not sure why. Maybe it's 'cause I'm worried the light will be glimpsed, it's a dark enough night, or maybe it's because in the movies, when a hero stops to check his cell, that's when he gets killed. That's when the monster busts out of the bushes.

Good things the drugs have worn off.

I've missed three calls.

The first is my mom. Second and third are Paige.

I'm just about to dial home when I'm caught in the high beams of a car. I'm ready to spring when a girl yells my name. The voice is familiar but I'm still not trusting my ears. Then she yells again, "Ade! It's Belle!"

And that stops me.

She gets out of the car and looks basically the same. Dressed just as sexy as always, her hair down like before, but for some reason, she's cuter. The trashy thing she had going, the thing that seemed almost innate, is gone.

Belle's fresh.

And beautiful.

EIGHT

We're on Speer heading out of the city going very fast. I've got all the windows down, the wind's rushing in, and Belle's hair's swirling around like a messy halo.

The smell of her hair is intoxicating. Soothing.

We've been talking about what just happened.

Belle is dumbfounded but I don't want to get into the details of it all. I only give her bits and pieces. This is because I'm just too tired of explaining everything. I ask Belle why she was there.

"To help you, of course."

"Thank you. Who told you I—"

"Grandpa Razor. He figured you needed backup."

"He was right."

Belle lights a cigarette. It's her car, I don't make a fuss.

Then she starts up with a conversation I'm sure we had last year.

She tells me that discovering the Diviners has been a Godsend. She tells me that it's given her new perspective on her life and her relationships; that it made her look at me in an entirely different light. She says, "I wasn't sure of you, Ade. I wasn't convinced you could actually do something, at least not until recently. Whole time we were together, I knew you were kind of disgusted by me. I thought about explaining it but you wouldn't have listened. You were just too into your own thing to care. Me, I just liked you enough to hang around and I hoped you actually might be someone. Like really someone."

"Like Gilberto?"

She doesn't respond.

Somewhere near the Convention Center, Belle turns to me and says, "Grandpa told me some of what you're dealing with. About the other versions of you. At first it made my head hurt. Like when people talk about how space is infinite and if you think on that too hard it just makes you sick. Existentially sick. But I get why you'd want to fight it, to save the present. Also Grandpa Razor agrees that if you really want to try this, really want to dig down into the heart of it, you should let me take you some places you're not going to want to go."

"Like where?"

"You remember that time I took you over to my friend Colin's place? You know, Colin with the one lazy eye? Wait, no, of course you don't . . ."

And I don't. I can't recall anyone with a lazy eye.

"Well, let's just say he and his buddies freaked you out."

"I can deal with freaky. If it'll help, I can deal with it. But I have to find the others, the duplicates first. Before it's too late. You haven't happened to see any guys who look amazingly similar to me, have you?"

Belle laughs. "I'd think I'd remember if I had."

I find myself looking at Belle differently. Not in some sexual way, it's more comfortable, lived in. I think that really, for the first time, I'm seeing her the way she wanted me to the first time.

She's not the trashy vixen. She's not the control freak.

We're like partners in this. We're playing detective together and sitting here, Belle's hair sashaying and her dressed so sexily, it's honestly surprising I'm not thinking what most guys would be. But looking at Belle, I can only think of how much I want to be with Vauxhall.

I can only think about how badly I want to show her that I can do this.

I'm so looking forward to what comes next.

A few blocks from my house, Belle slows down and looks over at me, puts her hand on my thigh, squeezes, says, "This Vauxhall girl is totally not for you."

"No?"

"You're moving up, okay. Even though you all have some bad blood, the Diviners are enthralled by you. This is a whole new world. You need someone who can understand that. Who speaks your language."

"Like you?"

"Sure. Already, I've had like two lucid experiences that I'm convinced are the first stirrings, you know. The first suggestions of me developing powers."

"You're crazy, Belle."

"Why's it crazy to want to be special? To be amazing?"

"You're already amazing how you are. You don't need that Gilberto idiot giving you drugs to make you any more special. Besides, what I have has been the biggest curse. Not a gift. You're going to end up—"

She cuts me off with a finger to my lips.

Smiles.

Then Belle tells me that lately she's been trying to touch as many things as she can. She tells me she took E a few weeks back, not her first time, and she really just wanted to cling to that touching sensation thing. She says, "Do you ever think about how instant the sense of touch is? I mean the only time you really ever feel something that way is when you're in direct contact with it. Scary how fleeting that is, isn't it?"

"I guess."

She squeezes my thigh again.

"Sometimes touching is so beautiful. You want that feeling to last forever. You want to just wrap yourself in that feeling and always be in contact with it. Thing is, as soon as you move your hand away, it's gone. As if it was never there."

Belle takes her hand away.

"Do you even remember what my hand felt like there? The weight of it? The warmth?"

I shake my head.

Belle says, "Our brains just don't store that info. It's pretty much only the other senses. Visual mostly. Sometimes smells. Also sounds. But sounds can be so tweaked with memory."

I ask Belle where she's going with this.

I suggest I should probably get home sooner rather than later.

"I want to kiss you again."

"I knew that's where you were going. Listen, I really appreciate your picking me up and helping me out with this thing—"

"This Vauxhall girl," Belle interrupts. "She's not your type."

"How's that?"

"She's an actress. A fake."

"Oh yeah?"

"Totally." Belle snorts.

Looking straight ahead, my eyes narrowed down to nothing, I say, "Belle, I love Vauxhall. I've loved her since long before I ever met her. Nothing, not a single thing, will change that."

We get to my house.

And when I get out of the car she gets out too.

She takes my hand and says, "In Polynesia there's this ritual where a young kid, a teenager, as part of his becoming a man, has to keep his hand on the first woman he sees. Has to keep it there for as long as possible. And then, when either the woman is just too sick of the guy standing there or the guy just gives up, he needs to go back to the village shaman and describe exactly how the woman's skin felt. Describe it in detail. Later, after a few more rituals, he's blindfolded and taken to a hut where there's like five women. He's supposed to touch just the shoulder of each of the women and tell the shaman which one was the one he had his hand on for two days or whatever. If he can do it, he's passed the test. If not, he's still a boy. Most teenage guys don't pass. Takes them years."

I say, "Interesting."

Belle smiles and says, "It's not true but it should be."

She kisses me on the cheek.

I say, "You're going to make Gilberto totally jealous."

That makes her laugh. Crack up.

"I'm not with Gilberto," Belle says. "That was so long ago. Besides, Ronny hates the Diviners. He thinks they're a bunch of posers."

"Ronny?"

"He's an oneiromancer. Sees stuff in dreams. He can actually go into them too."

Belle pulls out her cell phone and slides through the photos she's got in a folder labeled RONNY XOXO. She finds the one she's been looking for and taps it to make it bigger, then hands the phone to me. "That's Ronny," she says. "Dreamboat, right?"

I look at the picture. Totally expecting to think the guy's a dog.

But I don't.

I don't because he looks exactly like me.

NINE

Belle isn't exactly sure why I'm making her bring me to meet Ronny but she's kind of intrigued by the thought of us two meeting.

"Really," she says. "It'll be kind of weird."

"Why?"

"I don't know. I've just told him a ton about you but you've never met him and honestly I think it could get awkward."

She doesn't realize just how awkward I'm going to make it.

That I'm going to absorb Ronny with a fist in his chest.

Belle tells me that her new man lives in a strange place. Basically, she tells me, he isn't paying for the lodging that he's enjoying now. She says, "Yeah. He's a squatter. But his place is freaking rad."

Freaking rad is the University of Denver.

We park in a neighborhood and wander onto campus, making our way along the concrete paths past immaculately trimmed bushes and burbling fountains and freshmen getting high. We sneak into the cafeteria and the whole way Belle says nothing.

The cafeteria is empty.

Just the buzz of the freezers and the reflection of the moon on the cold linoleum.

"Midnight snack?" I ask.

Belle says, "Come here."

We walk over to the far wall where a bunch of unused chairs are stacked. The wall is wood paneled. Little squares maybe four by four feet and each bordered by stylish edging. Little wooden windows to nowhere.

And Belle pushes in on one and it moves.

On a television show I saw this is how people escaped from prison.

In a comic book I read this is how the superhero gets out of the mad scientist's underground lair.

Belle motions for me to follow her and we climb through the hole where the wood panel was. Inside it's dark but there's enough light filtering in from somewhere up above that I can see. Behind the wall, it's just an empty space that's maybe wide enough for us to sit side by side. And the floors covered in at least three inches of dust bunnies and bits of plaster and insulation.

"What now?" I ask.

Belle pushes the paneling back in place, sealing us in. Says, "Now we go up."

About ten feet above us is a passageway.

At least I think it looks like it's a passageway but really it might just be a painted black square. We climb up to it using the scaffolding inside the walls. It is fast climbing. The beams are evenly spaced and when we reach the black square it is indeed a passageway. Just big enough to crawl into. It's dark and Belle heaves herself in and starts crawling down the length of it. I follow.

We've gone about twenty feet when I ask, "Where exactly does this go?"

"It's a surprise."

"And Ronny lives up here because . . ."

"Because he rules."

Of course. Just what I was thinking.

The creak of us moving through the substance of the building is all I hear. As we crawl I try to imagine where exactly we are. I don't have the faintest idea.

The passageway bends and turns. I imagine it's around walls. Maybe through rooms. I can't tell if we're under the floor or in the ceiling but I suppose that's the same thing when it comes down to it. Some parts of the passageway are dark. Really dark. Others not so much. Light seems to leak in from little cracks in the sides of the passageway like we're passing through windows.

After nearly five minutes of crawling Belle stops and reaches up and pushes away another secret panel. The she stands up and climbs out.

Her head reappears briefly and she says, "Up here."

I stand up and look and Belle's sitting in a small box. At least to me it looks like a wooden box just big enough for the two of us to fit in. I climb up and in and we're squished inside.

"Jesus, Belle, this is ridiculous."

Belle smiles and says, "Push the trapdoor closed."

I look around.

"The one we just came in," she says. "The door panel is under you. You're sitting right on it."

I pull the panel out from under me and push it back into place.

It snaps in almost soundlessly.

"Good," Belle says. "Welcome to Ronny's."

With that she pushes on one of the walls of the box and it

creaks open like it's on hinges. Actually, it is on hinges. It opens up into a beautiful large and very brightly lit room. The room is so bright that I'm squinting for the first few seconds as we crawl out into it. The thing I notice first is that it's carpeted. And then I notice the bookshelves, tons of them, filled with books. The lair of a nerd. And then I notice the massive backward clock.

We're behind it. On the other side of the clockface.

But there are no gears. No machinery. Whole thing is cosmetic.

Fake.

Last I notice the guy sitting in a leather armchair surrounded by all his books and smoking a pipe. Yeah. Ronny is my age, my clone with my face and my build, and he's smoking a pipe. Wearing a tweed jacket. He blows some smoke and then nods to me.

The only difference I can see between us is that he's got a wisp of a beard.

Even on the best of days, trying my hardest, I couldn't grow anything resembling facial hair. But this me, well, he's not bad. It looks good. Distinguished.

"You must be the infamous Ade," he says.

Then, the professorial version of me, he places the pipe down in an ashtray and stands up, reaching out to shake my hand. It's crazy how much he looks like me and even crazier that neither he nor Belle notice it. I'm shaking hands with a mirror image and I'm the only one aware of it.

It's like I'm crazy.

"Nice pad," I say. "What's the deal with this?"

He looks around the room. Smiles. "I kind of carved this place out myself. Discovered it and made it mine. I consider it like being inside my own head. Tucked away from the distractions of the world. Until you got here, Belle was the only other person that knew it existed."

"Must get loud during lunch."

That cracks Ronny up. My laugh only more hearty.

The scene is so surreal and I'm so tired I mentally do a pause and think about whether I'm dreaming. I move my eye around and there's no blur. That means it's not a dream.

Which reminds me. I say, "I heard you can see people's dreams."

He laughs. It's subtle but obnoxious still. Looking at Belle he says, "I can. But I don't just see them. I go into them. Inhabit them."

My memory is jogged. And then I get it. Dude's one of the psychic parasites that the Metal Sisters thought I had. The thing they assumed my dad was.

"You know the Metal Sisters?"

"Yeah." He does his laugh again. "They're idiots."

"They think people like you, guys with your ability, are just parasites. Hangers-on. That you're like gutter psychics."

Belle looks at me, shocked. I'm in Ronny's inner sanctum and I'm dissing him.

She says, "Ade. Seriously?"

Ronny waves her down. "It's okay, Belle. He's just speaking his mind." Then he turns to me and says, "Have a seat, Ade. I'm curious to know more about you."

I sit on a couch.

"How'd you smuggle this furniture up into here? Way we came in, wouldn't work."

He nods. "It was difficult."

Then he sits and takes his pipe up again and lights it and puffs and asks, "What brings you over here? Something you'd like me to see?"

"No," I say. So tired. So ready for this to be done. "I'm here to absorb you."

"What?" He raises one eyebrow. All quizzical.

I shrug to Belle. "I figure there's no point in beating around the bush any longer." Then to Ronny, I say, "You're a part of me. A part that broke off. And while I'm sure you're a super nice guy and you seem really well read and educated and I totally dig your little Batcave here, I've got to tell you that I'm here to stop you from existing."

Belle is shocked. Actually gasps.

"I'm not happy about it either," I say. "But it's you or me."

Ronny looks at me like I'm on drugs. He says, "I don't get it."

I stand up, stretch, ready myself for a fight. "There's nothing to get," I say. "I'm going to absorb you, cease your existence, and ensure my own. It doesn't have to be painful."

To Belle, Ronny says, "This dude's nuts, Belle. He's going to kill me?"

Belle shakes her head. Can't speak.

"I won't kill you," I say. "Just end you."

Ronny stands up. Puts the pipe down carefully and takes his jacket off. Folds it carefully and places it on the chair. And that's when I notice that Ronny is freaking ripped. Guy looks like something that walked out of an '80s action movie.

"You happen to be screwing with a bartitsu master."

He stretches.

Says, "It's similar to jujitsu though there is boxing and stick fighting mixed in."

He begins to walk around the periphery of the room.

Says, "It was developed in England in the eighteen hundreds for close-quarters combat. Something very steampunk about it. But the fact is, if you think you can walk in here and kill me, you're very mistaken."

And then he stops, bows to me, and puts his hands up.

Makes the universal come-here-asshole hand sign.

This isn't going to be easy. Not that Tad was the most difficult fight I'd ever been in, but this one is certainly shaping up to be the most damaging. I've never been in a fight with a martial arts guy though you'd assume I would have by now. I figure the way for me to survive this is to let him do all the work; if I can tire him, slow him down, let him think he's got me, then maybe I can get the upper hand.

Too bad I'm so sluggish. Tired.

Too bad this has been the worst week in my entire life.

I make the first move and it's an ugly one. I go for a jab and totally miss and Ronny brings his right hand down so hard on the back of my neck that it feels like he's snapped my spinal cord. I go down hard. Inhale carpet.

He already assumes he's won.

Says, "Are you done, Ade?"

I respond by standing back up. Getting back into position.

Dude's as quick as a viper though and he punches me in the left kidney.

The pain is like being knifed. I know that feeling.

I crumple but stand again.

Ronny looks to Belle and shakes his head. "He doesn't learn quick."

Belle says, "Ade, please. You're acting crazy."

Ronny jabs and gets me in the shoulder but I manage to swing at the same time and box him in the right ear. I can tell it stings by the face he makes.

He backs up and shifts his weight.

I use the pause to catch my breath and rub my shoulder.

Ronny, chatty, says, "Unlike you, I'm not the murderous sort. I have got great endurance and we can play this game all night if you like but you'll leave here in one piece. Hopefully, when you've come down off whatever drugs you're taking, we can have a conversation like two civilized guys."

"This is your last night, Ronny," I say. "Sorry, bro."

That pisses him off and he lunges again.

He gets me in the stomach this time. I vomit into my mouth and fall backward into one of the bookcases. All these paperbacks tumble down over me.

I stay there, spit onto the carpet.

Ronny shoots me a mean look. Like how could I dare.

Then, using the bookcase, I pull myself back up.

Then I spit again.

Ronny says, "You're not a nice person, Ade."

"Listen. I know what I am. This whole thing, it's a mistake. I made you and I'm going to unmake you. Belle, I'm sorry, he seems cool, but he's me. Just another version of me. And I can't have him ruining my life."

And with that I leap.

I've kind of perfected this move. I go from standing, seemingly slowed down and paused, to jumping in like a split second. In like a blink. Back in the day I used it to get out of something that wasn't working. Like when I was fighting with these hockey dudes and none of them would hit me in the head. It was just my liver and lungs taking the brunt of the attack and I had to get out. Never used the move much, never needed to.

Certainly not on the offensive like this.

It works. Ronny is surprised. I land on him, knock him flat, and try to just end it by getting my hand in position over his chest. Turned to the side like I'm going to chop him, my hand starts to flicker and glow. His chest wobbles with light.

He notices and kicks me off.

Shit.

Ronny screws up his face and looks down at his chest. Normal. He asks, "What did you just do?"

I don't bother answering.

Instead I attack him again, this time swinging with a big leather-bound book that I randomly pull off the floor. I hit him upside the head and he falls to the right but doesn't go down. He swings back like a metronome and catches me on the jaw.

That drops me.

And he looms over me, standing on my arms, and pulls back his hand and, mimicking the same move I made, puts it flat and then slowly moves it toward my chest.

I try to kick but my legs are ineffectual. Dude is made of steel.

The closer his hand gets to my chest, the more it starts to glow.

It shakes like a candle flame.

And my chest starts to glow too.

Ronny asks, "What happens if I put my hand right into your heart, Ade?"

I say nothing.

Ronny asks, "Will you cease to exist? Will I unmake you?"

His hand gets closer and closer.

It's practically bursting with light. Practically aflame.

His hand only two inches from my rib cage, Ronny says, "I wouldn't."

And then, unbelievably, he pulls his hand away.

The glow stops.

The flicker subsides.

"I'm not like you, Ade," he says. "I don't know what's going on here, but I won't kill you. I hope that after you've caught your breath, you'll talk to me. Tell me why you're really here and what you—"

Ronny's a nice guy. A good guy. But he stops talking because I get my right hand loose, and without hesitation, with only Vauxhall's face in my mind, I slam my fist into Ronny's chest and instantly he's gone.

Flash.

Bang.

Poof.

I stand up and hobble over to Belle. She looks confused. Like she's going to cry.

I sit down on the floor next to her and say, "He was a good choice, Belle."

Belle looks down at me, tears ringing her eyes.

She says, "Where are we? What is this place, Ade?"

I don't know what to say. "It's Ronny's," I try.

"Ronny who?" she asks.

Then it hits me: Ronny doesn't exist anymore. And now he never did.

CHAPTER FIVE

ONE

Dear Dad—

I'm trying to figure out the best way to get this to you. Since there is not inter-consciousness mail service, I'm writing it for myself and then I'm hoping the next time you pop over in my head and I'm not here—is that even possible?—you'll notice it and pick it up.

I don't even remember where we left off but there's a lot I need to tell you. I don't have much time. Pretty much today is the last day and I don't want to do it in a letter. If everything works out, I'll drop by. I've been going to Mom for help and she's been really cool. Cooler than she's been in years actually. Maybe I've been awake more now and maybe I'm just starting to see her for real.

I certainly hope so.

Anyway, why I'm writing isn't to tell you all that but because I was thinking about your accident and I was wondering that if I ever had the ability to change the past, to go back and make it so it never happened, would you want me to do it? Would you want me and Mom and your life back?

I'll catch up with you soon.

Love,

Ade

TWO

Belle drops me off just as the sun is burning a hole in the sky.

She's still confused about what we've been up to all night.

Remembers nothing up to the point that I absorbed Ronny.

Weirdly enough, she's fine with it.

Guess she's been in that situation enough times to not care so much. She's already made mental assumptions. Some of them she's shared with me.

I'm closing the door to her car when she says, "I hope we used a condom."

"Jesus, Belle," I say. "We didn't do anything."

"Well, what was that love pad we were in?"

"I already tried to tell . . . Never mind. Listen, thanks again for picking me up. I need you to do me one last favor. That cool?"

She winks.

"Okay," I say. "I need you to go downtown and check out this bookstore for me."

"A bookstore?"

"Yeah. It's on Broadway. I don't know the name of it but it's near the Mayan Theater and there's a guy who works there named Leif. I need to talk to that dude and I'd love for you to break the ice."

"Wait? Why? What are you going to be doing?"

"It's complicated. I promise I'll fill you in on it all later."

Belle shrugs. She asks, "Used or new?"

"What?"

"Used or new books?"

"Used, I think."

"Cool. I've been looking for a copy of this one book I had as a kid. It was about this detective who was a ghost and he had this dog that always was with him. Don't know why but that book's been in my head lately. Can't get it out."

"I know what you mean."

Belle grabs my hand and squeezes it. "Whatever happened last night," she says, "I want you to know that I've missed you. That no matter what you need to do with this Vauxhall girl, when you're done I'll be here. I know who you are, down deep, and no one else will ever get that close."

She blows me a kiss. I close the door. She zooms off.

And for a second I stand there on the lawn and think about how easy it would be to just stop at this point. Two me's down and three to go. I don't know if I'm up for it. Not in one day. Vauxhall seems so far away. Like she's drifting out of the solar system and I don't know if she'll ever come back. I think about how easy it would be to just call Belle and tell her to turn around. To tell her that I quit and that she's right, that I'm fighting for something that I don't know if I'll ever have again.

Something that I messed up. Something maybe that I shouldn't get back.

Like I said, I only think that way for a second.

Vauxhall swells back into my mind, pushes Belle out, and that has me running back to the house. I unlock the door and stumble into the house, ready to get a few minutes of sleep, but head to the kitchen first.

There's a note from my mom. She's at church. Back again at dinner.

She even draws a smiley face.

I sit down at the table and my eyes are already closing when I notice there's someone sitting on the back porch.

My first reaction is to scream inside.

I can't deal with something else.

Can't deal with another twist.

What I want to do is throw something. Not in a Jimi kind of rage but just in an I-don't-think-I-can-handle-this-anymore way. It's been too much. Minute after minute weighing down on me like boulders.

I pull myself together and open the back door.

The dude on the porch grins seeing me. He's got long black hair, dark rings around his eyes, and he's wearing a red and silver robe. There is only one person this can be: Heinz von Ravengate.

He hugs me and nods and I invite this dark magician into my house. We head into the living room and Heinz takes a seat in my mom's favorite armchair and I lie down on the couch. Getting my feet up, the stress is starting to melt away.

"I was worried after your letter," he says. "You never followed up."

"Man, Heinz, things have been crazy."

"Tell me."

I close my eyes and think about telling him everything but realize I don't have the time. Instead I probe the new memories, Ronny's memories, that have flooded my brain. In them I find his ability and how it works. What I need to do next is figure out what Vauxhall knows, what she's up to, and why she's talking to Grandpa Razor. I know that and maybe I'll know how to get her back. I open my eyes and turn to Heinz and ask, "Have you ever been inside someone's dreams?"

"Yeah," he says. Pretty confident of himself.

"Easy to navigate?"

"Uh, yeah. Should be. Look, tell you the truth I've never actually, like really really, gone into someone's dreams but I've kind of done it. It was with my ex-girlfriend and after this one ritual we had a moment, only a few seconds, but it was amazing and we were in each other's minds. It was . . . cosmic."

I say, "I'm pretty tired and kind of jacked up, been a terrible night, but I need to get inside someone's dreams and I know how to do it. Just this is the first time and I know that I need to only be in for ten minutes. That cool?"

Heinz smiles. "Of course, man. I've got no plans."

We've got to do this fast though.

If Mom came home and saw a Satanist in the house she'd flip.

"Awesome. Seriously though, it can only be ten minutes. Don't ask me how I know that, it's complicated, but it can't be a minute more otherwise I'm liable to get stuck. Or worse."

Heinz pulls an old-school watch on a chain from his pocket.

He says, "I'm on it." Then, after a beat, he says, "So how does it work?"

"The same as all the rest of it. No spells, just strange physics."

"Shouldn't it be nighttime?"

"Doesn't matter. Dreams are still there. Stay with us at the back of our minds."

"Dope. So, what's next?"

I tell Heinz I need to make a mental picture of the person I want to bond with first. I tell him that the next step is getting myself unconscious rapidly and I can't just fall asleep, that doesn't work. I say, "Hang on, let me show you."

And then I throw myself forward and knock my head against the beechwood coffee table between us. I did this at least ten times last summer. And I always hit the same corner. If I do it with just the right oomph I'm able to knock myself out but not get anything more serious than a bruise.

My head hits.

My skull rocks.

It's been a freaking long time since I've done this.

But it works. I'm out cold and in the darkness, I see only Vaux.

THREE

When the black clears I'm in a field.

It's cold and I can see my breath in the air. The field is empty. Long ago harvested, now it's just frozen dirt and skeletons of leaves but in the middle of the field, a few hundred feet from me, there's this pipe.

Sticking up out of the ground, it's a cylinder at least ten feet long and wide enough to climb into. It's got a lid, like a submarine door. And this rusty door is hanging open on its hinges.

The clouds swirl overhead as I walk across the field.

I wonder why Vauxhall's dreaming of this place. If it's somewhere she's been before. If it has a special significance. And while it's cold, there's something beautiful in the chilly emptiness of this place.

I walk up to the pipe and I kick it. The clang resounds across the field.

A bit panicked, I look around to make sure there's no one there to hear it.

The field is empty.

I climb up onto the tube and look down into its interior. It's dark. Very dark.

I look back around at the field again.

What am I supposed to do here?

Will Vauxhall show up? Do I wait?

Instead I decide to check out the pipe. I lower myself in and back against the cold metal. And above me, written on the inside of the pipe in white chalk, it says, "Imagine you're underwater. Make it warm."

Weird.

But it's her dream, so I close my eyes. I imagine the tube is filling with water.

Nothing happens.

I think about closing the top so I stand up and inspect the rusted hinges of the cylinder's submarine door. I know that if I close it, if I really close it, there's a good chance I'll be trapped in here. There's a really good chance that if I close the lid on this tin can I'll suffocate inside.

I sit back down into the cylinder and close my eyes again.

I take a few deep breaths and laugh to myself. Think about water. And still nothing is happening. I consider that maybe all the action is somewhere else. Maybe I need to leave the field. Maybe this dream is bunk.

But the urge to close the lid is really strong.

And it's compelling enough that I reach up to the lid to pull it down.

I don't actually touch metal though. I touch skin.

Warm skin.

And I hear a familiar voice.

"It won't work if you just lock yourself in there. Chances are you'll just suffocate."

It's Vauxhall.

I open my eyes and get up. Vauxhall is standing next to the tube. She's wearing a black swimsuit and has sunglasses on. I almost faint dead away looking at her body. I can only imagine she's freezing in the middle of this chilly field.

"Hi," I say.

"What are you doing here?"

"Thought I'd come by and visit you. You get my letter?"

Vauxhall, the her inside her own head, the dream identity, smiles, laughs. She's so comfortable here because this is her world. Here she is queen and anything that happens, everything with the exception of me, is under her control. Or so she thinks.

"I got your letter," she says. "You're quite the pest, aren't you?"

"I love you. Have loved you for years."

"Yeah. You mentioned that. Karl isn't too psyched about you showing up. He seems to think it's more than just you being a stalker. He thinks you might actually be trying to stop us. Stop what we're doing."

"What are you doing?"

Vauxhall goes, "Yeah. Right."

Then she grabs hold of the submarine door. She says, "You need to settle down into the tube and then close your eyes. You need to think of the one you love and hold that memory and then, this is the crucial part, you need to recite the formula."

"What formula?"

"See, you've never been here before. You're an interloper."

"Interloper?"

"Big word, right?" she says, grinning. "Tricky thing about this pipe is that if you don't do it exactly right, if you take a wrong turn or something, you're likely to lose your only means of getting back out. Either that or you'll really mess up and lose everything."

"Like what?"

"Like what it is you want."

She hands me a scrap of paper. On it is a mathematical formula. Something with a lot of letters mixed in with the numbers. It looks painfully like calculus. Never passed that class. Never even went more than three times.

"I don't have to solve this, do I?" I ask.

"No. But you do have to repeat it. Read it."

"You ever been in here?"

"Oh, yeah, tons."

"What happens?"

She says, "Don't worry. You'll be fine."

I nod and swallow hard and then slide down into the tube. Vauxhall says, "Memorize this fast. Hurry. I'm closing the lid."

I read over the numbers and letters, trying to memorize them. I read them backward and forward, the slip of paper trembling in my shaking hands.

"Got it?" Vaux asks.

I mumble something. It's more a groan than actual words.

"See you later."

And with that she closes the lid of the cylinder. It's pitch-black inside. I feel the paper and the rough and cold edges of the tube.

Vauxhall shouts, her mouth must be right against the edge of the lid. "Repeat the formula. Hold the book. Keep repeating the formula."

I do.

I recite the numbers and letters as I remember them. Over and over until it becomes a mantra and then the number and letters lose their meaning. I'm just making sounds now. It's like a birdsong, just notes. Just my mouth moving.

Inside here it's dark enough that I see little stars. Little flashes of imaginary light drifting around me. It's my eyes trying, desperate to find something to see.

And that's when I start to wonder about the air.

I wonder how much there is and where are holes for breathing. If any.

Soon I'm sweating.

I'm about to panic when I feel something warm around my feet.

At first I think it's just my sweat. Or maybe I'm just imagining it.

This warm feeling, it wraps my feet and then my calves and then thighs. It's water. And soon it's at my back and under my head. First thing I think is that I've peed myself. But I haven't. And the water is getting warmer. Not hot. Just like bathwater that's sat for a while. Room temperature.

And this cylinder I'm in, it's filling up.

Before long the water's at least an inch deep and it's lapping at my ears. For some reason I decide to sit up. I sit up and as soon as I do I realize I've made a huge mistake and that I'm gonna bang my head on the inside of the cylinder. I brace myself for the impact and more for the loud clang I'm sure I'm about to hear. But it doesn't happen. I sit up fully and I hit nothing.

Makes no sense.

I reach up to feel where the top of the cylinder should be and it's gone. I can't see my arms but I fully extend them and touch nothing.

The water is filling up the cylinder even faster.

Soon it's inches more and rushing in. Fast like a little raging river.

Rapids all around my thighs and pushing up against my back.

That's when I start to slip. I start moving downward with the water. I know the cylinder isn't long. Maybe it's ten feet. Enough that I know that if I slide down more than four feet I'll hit the bottom. I slide, anticipating my feet touching the smooth metal of the cylinder's bottom but I don't touch.

I keep sliding.

I slide faster and faster and soon I've gone at least ten feet and still no bottom. Still touching nothing and it's still as dark as the inside of my stomach.

The water is fast.

Down and then the cylinder turns. Or maybe I turn.

I round a corner and I'm on my back sliding up the inside of the cylinder. The water rushing around me is so freaking loud.

I'm moving faster and there's a dip. Almost a drop.

I stay on my back and the water pushes me.

I'm in a water slide, I tell myself. That's exactly what this is. It's a water slide.

Two more turns.

One left, the next right, and then I'm slipping and sliding all over the place.

The water splashing in my face. My clothing drenched.

This has got to be a water slide but the lights are out. There is another drop, this one is long and I come down out of it faster. So fast that I'm having to wipe the spray of water out of my eyes. Clench my teeth. I'm loving every second of this.

And that's when I see light. It's a star at first.

Distant.

But it quickly grows. Bigger and bigger. A window then a door.

A door-size white circle.

Plain as day about fifty feet from me.

Thirty feet.

Bright enough that the slick insides of the cylinder are reflecting it. I can see my feet. My soaked shoes. I can see my hands.

Twenty feet.

The circle of light gets brighter and brighter.

I get closer and closer to it.

Ten feet.

And then there's a drop and I'm submerged in water. A rushing sound and I'm tumbling. I gasp and I stand and I break the surface and I walk blind. I can barely see with the water in my eyes and the light so bright and I'm coughing.

Choking.

I'm in a pool.

FOUR

With each successive blink I see more.

The blue of the water.

Light.

People. A lot of them little kids.

But some of them my age. Men and women, boys and girls. All in swimsuits. All splashing around and a few of them looking at me funny.

Pointing to my clothes.

I turn around and look back at where I just came from.

The water slide is a giant snaking blue tube slithering in and out of a number of similar blue tubes. They all empty into the same pool, the pool I'm standing in fully dressed. Every few seconds some kid comes tumbling out of the mouths of the slides. Most of them shouting as they crash into the water. They resurface smiling and sputtering.

The ceilings are glass. I can see perfect blue skies above.

The walls are white. White clay. Around the edges of the pool are decks. People sit in folding chairs and at picnic tables. Towels spread everywhere. There have to be at least two hundred people here.

The place is packed.

Unbelievably, it's Celebrity's Sport Center again. Just Vauxhall's version of it.

This Vauxhall, I guess she loves the place as much as I do.

I pull myself out of the pool and sit on the edge.

My feet still dangling in the water, I sit there and catch my breath and I start laughing. I can't believe what just happened. I laugh out loud at the fact that I just crawled into a rusting metal cylinder and was spit out into a giant swimming pool. Whatever leftover tension I had has melted away.

That's when I feel a hand on my shoulder.

I turn around and look up and there's Jimi Ministry in swim trunks and a white T-shirt. He's got sunglasses on and he's smiling. He says, "Welcome. Glad you made it. How did you figure it all out?"

I say, "Vaux helped me out. Where exactly are we?"

"This is the pool. A popular hangout at the Mall."

"Where's that? This?"

"It'll be better if you talk to Render."

And that's when my heart stops beating.

It can't be the same Render.

Can't be.

I haven't heard that name since Dr. Borgo's but the movie he showed me, the scientific video of the two-headed twins, one head shrinking to a screaming point, has haunted me. Infected my nightmares. And that name, Render. There is no way Vauxhall could possibly know about him. So long ago. But, if my dad knew . . .

"Can I change first?" I ask, standing up.

Little rivers of water are draining from my socks and shoes.

The tips of my fingers are raining down water.

"No, we're going back on the slides." Jimi grins. He takes off his T-shirt and sunglasses and sets them on a lounge chair. He says, "Let's go."

"Don't all the slides go to the same place?" I ask.

"No. Only most of them," Jimi says.

I follow him around the side of the pool.

We pass a few groups of teens and they look at me funny. Some of them laugh. We pass families eating lunch. We pass people who are sleeping in the sunlight streaming down through the glass ceiling. I see a girl my age with short brown hair. She smiles at me as we pass.

"Everyone here is cool," Jimi says.

We walk over to a series of ramps that lead to where you can get on the slides. As we make our way up, my shoes are making that sloshing sound on the ramp. Little kids go running past us. We go up and up, at least twenty switchbacks on these ramps.

Finally we get to the top and I look down to see the pool below.

Everyone looks tiny.

At the top there are six entrances to six tubes.

Big maws with rushing water in them and short lines of kids

ready to take the plunge down. We get into the third line to get to the third tube.

We don't talk as we wait.

It's just the sound of rushing water and a thin lifeguard with glasses who sits on a stool by the entrance to the slide. He has a walkie-talkie and about two minutes after someone has disappeared inside the slide the walkie-talkie buzzes to life. Then the guy with glasses looks up and says, "Next."

The kid in front of me steps up and soon he's gone.

I'm next but now I'm stressing about Heinz. Surely it's been ten minutes already. It has to have been. But I'm still here. And deep in Ronny's memory I can see that if you're in too long you get stuck. Stuck in someone else's dream and wind up a vegetable back in the real world.

He'll wake me soon. He has to.

I step up to the tube and sit down in the water.

The lifeguard asks, "Where's your swimsuit at?"

I shrug.

"Don't come in here again without your suit."

Jimi kneels down beside me and whispers, "When you get to the big turn, where the plastic plants hang down into the tube, you'll see a railing on the right hand wall. Grab it and pull it."

"Grab it and then what?" I ask.

The roar of the water rushing down the tube is so loud.

"Pull it. A door will open and you'll need to climb in."

"Climb in to what?"

The lifeguard says, "Next."

Jimi says, "You'll see. Go now."

The lifeguard's getting annoyed. "Are you going to go?"

I lie down and push myself into the tube and I'm off and running again.

On my back, the water spitting and frothing around me, I spin down the tube and up along the walls.

The slide twists and turns and I'm worried I'll miss the hanging plants. But then it levels out and I'm going down much slower and the slide begins a leisurely arc to the right.

That's when I see the plants.

Fake plants hanging down from a joint in the top of the slide. If you were moving too fast or not flat on your back you'd never see it. Just a cheap plastic green plant. And sure enough, to the right on the wall of the slide is a silver rail.

It's short, maybe ten inches long. Like a rail along the stairs on a bus.

I sit up and prep myself for grabbing it.

Unsure of what exactly is going to happen.

The rail gets closer and closer and I'm anxious that I'm going to miss it. In fact, I'm sweating about it. It gets close and I put my hand out ready to grab at it and that's when I slip. I slip backward, off balance, and I'm sliding past the railing.

I roll over onto my stomach and scramble; try to grab at something to stop myself. I'm crazy thinking that maybe I can crawl back up. Crawl against the water.

But it's so slippery.

It's like this, I push with my feet, the rubber soles of my shoes gripping the plastic of the tube, and I'm finally getting somewhere. Pushing against the water. Against the slickness of the slide, it's hard work. Exhausting but I'm pulling myself back up to the rail.

In less than a minute I'm there.

I thank God for the shoes.

I don't know how it's supposed to work but I pull down hard on the rail and it moves in the plastic of the tube.

Pop.

A circular hatch about as round as me opens in the slide of the tube and there's water running into it. It's dark but I push myself in headfirst.

Another slide.

It's narrow and I'm sliding down headfirst and it's faster than the slide I just came from. It's super fast and I'm spinning around the inside of the tube, up on the ceiling and the walls and soon I don't know which is the top or the bottom.

It's so dark it's like I'm floating in space.

Then just like before I see a star of light that becomes a ball of light that quickly becomes a window then a door.

And then I'm out, splashing down into another pool.

It's not a big pool. This one is small. Maybe as big around as a big bed.

I'm the only person in this pool and it's lit from below. The whole bottom of the pool is lit up like there are fluorescent bulbs under there. I feel like I'm on stage.

Getting out of the pool and looking around only compounds the feeling.

Best thing I can compare it to is being in an aquarium.

It's a big space, one long corridor with the pool at one end. There are fish tanks lining the walls. Big tanks and small tanks.

Tanks with really colorful fish and tanks with lazy ugly eels. There are massive tanks as tall as I am and packed full of fish that dart around in bright flashes of color. There are tiny tanks, tanks no bigger than my hand, with a single tiny fish in them. No people. No furniture. The floor of the corridor undulates in the light reflected from the tanks. It's blue-green and the air is moist.

At the end of the corridor I see a green light.

It takes up the whole of the passageway. Like a green wall.

I walk slowly. Looking back over my shoulder every few seconds to make sure there's no one following me. The burbling of the fish tanks is somewhat soothing. I stop and look at an orange fish the size of my hand. Its mouth gulps like it's trying to say something.

Closer I get to the green light at the end of the corridor, the more anxious about it I get. Even from halfway back I can tell it's another tank. But this one is clearly massive.

It's even bigger than that.

I step out of the corridor of tanks and enter a circular room that stretches around into darkness on both sides. There is no ceiling. The walls just go up and up and up. The tank in the middle of this room, it practically takes up the whole space. Maybe ten feet of space around the edges. And it goes all the way up too.

The green light, it's coming from the tank.

The water in it shimmers with green phosphorescence. It's spooky. I walk up to the tank, the glass or plastic of it at least six or seven feet thick. Looking in, everything is distorted. I see some shapes but they could be just my eyes playing tricks.

I walk to my right, following the curve of the tank.

The whole while I'm looking inside. Trying to make out something.

There are these little colored dots. No bigger than freckles. They glow. Fade in and out and whirl with whatever current there is in the tank. They're hypnotizing. Standing there, staring into the half-light at the dances of these flecks of starlight, I'm super relaxed.

Chill as everything.

It hits me then that this tank, it's pretty much the same stuff I saw when Gordon and Jeremiah shocked the life out of me with the AED. After seeing me in the future knocking myself out over and over and over, I wound up in a dark place with glowing orbs that looked just like here.

How is that even possible?

This isn't the afterlife, unless Vauxhall has seen it too and is dreaming about it. No, it's something else. If this is what it looks like, then I didn't see out after my own death after all. No, what I saw was a big tank under a mall swimming pool.

And then I really see something in the tank move.

It's like the whole tank has shifted over to the left. What at first I took to be shadow or maybe murky water is really something in the tank. Something almost as big and thick as the tank itself.

This shadow moves toward me. I see skin. Rubbery flesh and then an eye. An eye as big as the clockface in Ronny's secret hideout.

I jump back, my skin crawling.

I want to run but my feet don't move. The eye, it gets closer.

Right up against the glass. Unblinking. Just a deep black pool inside a deep black pool. The glowing flecks spinning around it.

Then comes a voice. It says, "Ade?"

My heart stops.

The voice is in my head, it's echoing around in my skull, as deep and dark as the tank and the pupil of the eye.

"Ade?"

"Yes?" I say out loud.

"Welcome to Heaven."

My heart starts again.

The eye moves back, slowly dissolves into the murk. Then part of a tentacle glides past. The suckers, the suckers that I see, they're as big as dinner plates.

The voice says, "I'm Render."

The video Dr. Borgo showed me comes back. The little screaming head.

"What are you?" I ask out loud.

The voice says, "A person like you. But here, in this place, it's better for her to imagine me as a giant squid. Largest of my kind."

"Aren't you French?"

"Lost my accent long ago."

I look up, straining to see the top of the tank.

"It's fourteen stories," Render says in my head. "I make up about five stories of it. They gave me some room to grow."

"Vauxhall imagined you like this?"

"Yes."

"Pretty freaking weird. Why?"

"It's a dream, Ade. Why not?"

I think on that a moment but I don't like the idea that Render's in my head, I don't want to pause too long and give him time to poke around. I say, "I saw what you did to your brother. Not the nicest thing."

The squid makes a hmmm noise. Only it's underwater.

"That was a very long time ago," he says. "I've mellowed with age. Besides, what you're doing isn't much different. Taking out your twins one at a time. I doubt they enjoy your visits much."

"Why are you here? Vauxhall hasn't ever heard of you, has she?"

"No," he says. "I'm here on my own."

"Why?"

"Because Vauxhall needs me. She's got something very big brewing and I want to be a part of it. I want her to be successful."

"And Grandpa Razor, why's she seeing him?"

Render pauses. Then, "She was confused once but she knows what she needs to do now. Ade, your Vauxhall is a very, very powerful being. More powerful than you have ever imagined. And now, now that you've changed things, ripped into the fabric of reality, you've made her even more powerful."

"What is she going to do?"

"She's going to end the world, Ade. Apocalypse time."

I shake my head. "No. That's insane. And impossible."

"Not for her it isn't," Render says.

"But how?"

"With her mind, of course."

"Why? Why would she want to do that?"

"Ask her yourself," Render says.

On cue, Vauxhall, stunning in a fitted blue dress, walks around the side of the tank. She's smiling, her teeth glittering in the half-light like her diamond earrings. A fantasy.

She walks up to me and says, "You found it."

I point to the squid, to Render. "He tells me you're plotting something terrible. That you want to destroy the world. Why?"

Vauxhall isn't fazed. She says, "For this place."

"What?"

"This is Heaven, Ade. Have you ever seen it before?"

I think of drifting in the sea of black, of the colorful orbs.

I nod. "But this is a dream. It's a mall under an empty field."

"It's Heaven," Vauxhall says. "This is where I want to be. Where I want everyone to be. What I'm doing is for all of us."

Render adds, "It will be revolutionary. I'm so excited to be a part of it."

I pull Vauxhall aside. As aside as I can considering Render takes up almost all of the room. "Please. Tell me what you're doing. Let me help you."

"I don't need help," Vauxhall says. "We're all going to be fine."

"Who are the we?"

Vauxhall smiles. "My father and I, silly."

"But your father killed himself . . ."

Vauxhall screws up her face. Looks at me like I'm nuts.

Then she turns to the tank, the squid.

I get what she means but it's so freaky I have to say it. "He's your dad?"

Render says, "Yes."

Vauxhall asks, "How come you don't know that yet?"

"I just got here. Where I'm from, originally, your father is dead."

Render says, "Well, that's unfortunate to hear. I hope you're not trying to frighten my daughter with talk like that. As you can see, I'm quite well. I'm healthy, happy, and very busy."

To Render I say, "I've seen your handiwork."

"Hmmm," he responds. "An unscrupulous physician made that film. Took advantage of me. It's been copied thousands of times since then, and I wouldn't be surprised if every psychiatrist had a personal copy. Highly inappropriate. I was at a weird time in my life. I made some mistakes when I was younger but that's not the person I am today."

This is funny coming from a giant squid.

I say, "Grandpa Razor seems to think you're an evil bastard."

Vauxhall shakes her head. "Razor is the bastard."

"She's right, of course," Render says. "Let me ask you this, Ade. Was I the one who attempted to transfer your childhood to your half-brother's? Was I the one who set you up? Hit you? Tried to inject you with blood?"

I don't say anything. Don't have to.

Render says, "Of course not. I'm a ghost to you. This is the first time you've met me. I think it would be wise of you to question the information you're getting."

All of the threads suddenly start coming together in my head. Who is Render, really? He's not a squid, he's a guy. He's an old guy. He must be the one.

The Enigma.

Reading my mind, Render says, "Yes."

I turn to Vauxhall. "This guy is dangerous, Vaux. You can't trust him. Surely you know that? You can sense it, right?"

Vauxhall shakes her head.

"Listen," I say. "I need for you—"

And then suddenly I'm being pulled backward by something, back around the tank, then down the corridor lined with aquariums, and back into the pool.

I go under the water, like I'm living in reverse, and as soon as I'm under, everything goes black.

FIVE

When I come to, Heinz is kneeling down next to me and his face, the one that's supposed to be menacing and all Satanic, is a mask of pure fright.

This guy looks like he might puke.

I get back up on the couch and close and open my eyes a few times.

"You okay?" Heinz's voice is shaking.

"Yeah. How long was that? Felt like hours."

"Just ten minutes. Actually nine minutes and forty-two seconds. I woke you early 'cause I was a little bit worried. You were mumbling and everything."

"Thanks. It worked."

"What did you see?"

I motion for him to sit back down.

I say, "It was crazy. Another world but it felt completely real. Unimaginably real. A lot of the stuff I just saw you'd really dig. In particular the giant squid in a dark tank."

Heinz leans forward. "Suh-weet." Then he motions to his own forehead. "You've got a little—?"

I reach up and touch my temple, come away with a bloody finger.

"Nice," I say. "It's been a while."

He hands me a napkin. I don't want to know where it came from.

He says, "Teach me."

Heinz is pale white. Probably exactly how he wishes he looked all the time. His hands dance in the sleeves of his robe. This black magician, purportedly in touch with all sorts of demons and hellspawn and elementals (all of these have names and are listed in his illustrated brochure with sketches obviously copied from the Dungeon Master's Manual), has turned into a kid.

"To do what?"

"To do that. Your power," Heinz says.

"No."

Heinz gets off the chair and kneels down in front of me. "Please," he begs.

"I don't even know how it works. I was born this way. Remember, I was the one who wrote to you, asking you how it worked."

This Lord of Darkness shakes his head. "I have no idea but it rules."

I stand up. "Sorry, Heinz, I have to . . ."

Before I can finish he knocks himself out cold on the coffee table. Only he hits the corner much harder than I ever have.

The sound is downright scary.

When he comes to, after I've wiped up most of the blood, he's woozy and drooling. He says, "I didn't see anything."

"Most people don't," I say.

I get him packed up with a bag of ice and a towel we can afford to never see again. Then I walk him to the bus stop. He thanks me and then all embarrassed he waits for the bus and I wave to him from the living room window as he gets on board.

As the bus vanishes, I dial up Dr. Borgo.

He answers on the third ring.

"Been a while, Ade," he says. "I was worried about you."

"Everyone seems to be," I say. "I don't have much time to chat, but I need to talk to you about that video you showed me, the freaky thing. Render."

"Okay."

"Is he still alive?"

"He was a kid in the seventies, Ade. I'm sure he's my age. Early forties at the oldest."

"I've seen him. Talked to him."

"What?"

"Yeah, in a vision. Well, it's a little more complicated than that. I don't actually have time to deal with it, but who else have you told about Render? Who else did you show that video to?"

Dr. Borgo clears his throat and I can picture him rubbing his chin. "Uh," he starts, then pauses. "Actually, Ade. That's patient-doctor information. I can't tell you."

"You have to. It's a matter of life or death."

"Your life?"

"Everyone's."

"What do you know, Ade? Talk to me."

"I don't know the details yet. Trying to figure them out. But there is something going on, something bad, and Render is in-

volved in it. Tell me who you showed the video to, Doc. I think
I know who it is and I think I can help them."

Long pause. Dr. Borgo is stressing.

"Okay," he finally says. "I have a patient your age, just started
seeing him a few months ago. Deeply disturbed individual though
he appears to have an ability. Nothing like yours, something a bit
more, well, vaudevillian."

"Tell me his name."

"Karl. Karl Solitaire."

"We've met. One last thing, Doc. Why'd you show him the
Render video?"

Dr. Borgo chuckles though it's more from discomfort than
anything funny. He says, "For much the same reason I showed
it to you. He was having problems at the time, convinced that he
was changing radically. In his words, he'd had a premonition
that someone was trying to take over his life. Someone was at-
tempting to become him. He told his father and his father
mentioned Render. The big difference between your story and
his was that his father mentioned Render because he wanted his
son to overtake the person challenging him. It was a positive
thing."

I choke. Say, "Please don't tell me I've got another half-brother."

"I doubt it," Dr. Borgo says. "His father probably ran in the
same circles though."

"Any chance you've heard of the Enigma?"

Dr. Borgo is silent for a long time.

Then he says, his voice lowered like he's worried someone
might hear him, "He was an urban legend for a long time. You
don't often hear the words witch or warlock bandied around that

often these days. Conjures up all sorts of superstition and clap-trap. But from what I've heard, if the Enigma exists, he's the closest anyone alive has ever come to being a creature of myth. Personally, I think he exists. But I wouldn't know where to begin looking for him."

"Oh, he exists. I've seen him. You have too."

Dr. Borgo is quiet.

"I'll tell you later," I say. "When this is over, remind me to buy you a beer."

Dr. Borgo laughs. "You're seventeen, Ade. But I'll take you up on it."

I hang up and head to my room to clean up my wound and find Adam asleep in my bed. Dude's totally conked out on my pillow; there's a pool of drool on the sheet. Seeing him sleeping there is like an out-of-body experience.

I grab some bandages from the bottom drawer of my desk and use the mirror on the back of my bedroom door to clean up. The healing process, however, has already begun, and even though my forehead is all sorts of swollen and red, the bleeding is gone.

"You hit yourself?" Adam sits up.

The mirror image of me in the mirror behind the reflection of me.

Weird.

"Yeah," I say. "Something I had to do."

"This is all still about tracking down those other versions of you, isn't it?"

"Yes."

"Awesome. I was worried that was just a gnarly dream I was having."

I laugh. "Like the butterfly."

"Huh?"

"It's a Chinese proverb or something. This guy dreams he's a butterfly and then wakes up and thinks maybe he's really a butterfly dreaming he's a man."

Adam rubs his eyes. "What's that got to do with anything?"

"Never mind."

"So, what's next? This is like the last day to track them down, right?"

"Yup. Next I find Vauxhall."

"Cool."

I turn around, look straight at my duplicate as he gets up out of bed, fully dressed, and stretches, scratches at his chest. "Any ideas of where to find her?" I ask him.

"Yeah. She's in school."

I grin, nod. This is why I keep the guy around.

SIX

Vauxhall's taking a summer film class at Aurora Community College.

I leave Adam in the car and wander inside the building.

I find her in a classroom with a bunch of older students. Most everyone in there is like thirty or forty or almost dead. They're listening to a woman with big red hair lecture and point at a monitor behind her. On the screen is a flower in black and white.

I can't hear what she's talking about but I imagine it's interesting.

Vaux looks very interested.

Right now, I want to just bust into the classroom and jump on top of one of the desks and sing to her. I'm not sure what I'd sing but maybe the act would be the thing to break the dam in her memory. If anything, she'd never forget it.

But my voice is lousy and I decide to wait.

I give myself five minutes.

And even though that's a really long time to sit in a hallway staring through a tiny window into a brightly lit classroom, because I'm looking at Vauxhall the time passes in a blink.

I watch the way she takes notes.

Her hands moving through her hair.

Her profile when she raises her hand and asks a question.

The beat of her eyelashes.

The lusty swell of her lips.

The curvatures of her body.

And before I know it everyone jumps up, even the elderly students, and starts to push their books back into their bags. They file out into the hallway, most of them ignoring me, but Vauxhall waits inside the classroom to talk to the teacher.

I take a seat at the back and listen in.

To the teacher, Vauxhall says, "I really liked that last part about using the filters but I'm not sure which one would be the best. You think the orange for the panchromatic?"

The teacher thinks about it as she packs up. Then she pauses, says, "Definitely the orange. I'm excited to see what you've been adding to the film. Great stuff."

Vauxhall smiles, turns around, and sees me.

Her first reaction is shock. Almost panic.

And that makes me feel terrible. Horrible. But then her face softens and it's like she's mentally figured out how exactly she's going to handle this. Fact is: I'm expecting her to walk up and slap me.

I picture her all pissed off, the way she was last Date Night.

God, I've been such an idiot.

Vauxhall walks over and I brace myself but instead she sits down across from me and says, "What is it about you?"

"About me?" I ask, trying to be calm. Trying to hold myself together.

I want desperately to kiss her right now.

I physically need her. My mind having to battle my body back.

She doesn't play cute. Says, "You've been following me. I should be calling security right now."

"Why aren't you?"

"Because . . ."

"Because you know me?"

"Maybe."

And I can see it in her eyes. There's a glimmer of recognition there.

The dream, it's a memory now in her head. She can pull it back out and look it over and know that it's good. That it's true. She can see me in her head and realize, even if it's only slightly, that she knows me. I'm instantly familiar.

I say, "Architeuthis. At least, that's how I think you pronounce it."

"What?" Vauxhall leans in closer, like she didn't hear me right.

"That's the scientific name for it. The giant squid."

All the blood suddenly drains from Vauxhall's face.

She's caught in a tractor beam.

Her eyes go wider than I've ever seen them before.

Her mouth hangs open.

She's breathing all shallow.

"How . . . How did you?"

"Because I was there," I say. "I love you, Vauxhall, and I'm not going to deny it. I'm not going to hide my feelings. I have known you for years. We have been through amazing things together, crazy things. I mistreated you but I'm making up for it. I'm bringing down mountains for you."

Vaux doesn't know what to say. The love of my life, the girl who only knows me from a dream, sits back in her chair and says, "It couldn't have been real."

"It wasn't. Just a dream. But I was there."

"In the mall?"

"Yes."

"And Render?"

"Yup."

Vauxhall asks, "Want to see a film I made?"

"Of course."

We go to the back of the classroom where there's a bank of televisions.

She sits down at one of those TV/VCR combos with the tiny screen.

Vaux offers me the chair and I slide in close. Maybe only ten inches from the screen. The tape Vauxhall slides into the VCR part is labeled MODESTY BLASÉ. She tells me it's a joke. A riff on a British comic strip about a fashionable spy.

"Hope you like it," Vauxhall says. "It's three minutes long."

"Rocking the old-school VHS, huh?"

"I like the texture of it," she says.

The video is grainy. As it starts Vaux tells me it was shot on video with a semi-fancy camera. "A Fuji DH-S1 they had at my old school," she says. The way she says it, it's obvious to her that I don't know my cameras. That she's just telling me because she's nervous. Because she cares what I think.

The first minute is of the sky. Black and white and shaking slightly. Little dribbles of color appear and then fade away. If anything, they remind me of the color flashes I've seen with good concussions. Strong concussions. Over this pretty much static scene plays music. A woman's voice humming. Vaux's voice.

"That's you, right?"

Vaux says, "Uh-huh. Watch this."

What the camera is looking at changes. Now we're staring into the ground. It's a hard cut. Just grass and farther in, awash in static, dirt. Another thirty seconds of this, just watching the grass grow, and something moves. A shadow. I hear Vauxhall scoot forward. The song she's singing in the film, it turns from just humming into something like be-bop. Something like scatting.

"Jazzy," I say.

She shushes me.

The camera cuts dramatically from the lawn and the dirt to the inside of a kaleidoscope. Looks like back when I could hit my head and see the future, back when I was going down the tube of light into the future. The spinning colors pull back around the edges of a tunnel. We're looking down this psychedelic circle and Vauxhall's there in the center of it. Dancing. On the soundtrack, her cooing and syncopating get louder and louder until she's shouting. Her getting closer and closer as she fills out the tube. I'm hypnotized.

Closer and closer, Vaux is most of the screen now.

She's wearing black. Her face with so much makeup I can hardly tell it's her. The mascara blown out around her eyes making them look twice as big. Her lashes as long as my fingers. Her singing, it becomes yelping. Screaming. Screeching. And then something incredible happens. Something impossible.

Her face is superimposed over the city.

There smack against the mountains, the skyline I've grown up with.

And all of it suddenly crumbles. Towers teeter and fall.

The whole city comes down in a massive plume of dust.

Her face over it all, looking on sagely like some ancient goddess.

The camera moves in.

Zooms to her lips.

Lips as bright red as nail polish. Lips as big as my hands.

Teeth as bright as suns beneath.

Vauxhall screams one final scream and then she swallows the camera. Honestly. The last five seconds are her lips and teeth and then inside her mouth and then inside her throat and then nothing. Darkness.

Behind me, Vaux says, "I didn't eat the school's camera."

Film over. Credits.

I turn to Vauxhall, my jaw dropped. "That was amazing."

"Thanks."

"How did you—"

"Convinced this gastroenterologist my mom knows to scope me."

"Are you serious?"

"Cool, right?"

"Yeah, but the thing with the city? The destruction?"

"It's like CGI."

"Like?"

Vauxhall crosses her arms. "You were in the dream. I told you what I'm going to do. Why are you here, Ade? Why did you come to talk to me?"

I lean in. She knows what I want to do. Why I'm here.

Vauxhall leans in, pulled by some gravitational force toward me.

This is it.

This is how I get her back. This is how I fix everything.

And at the last possible moment, Vauxhall pulls away.

She shakes her head.

"You're here to try and stop me. Grandpa Razor sent you, didn't he?"

"You can't end the world, Vauxhall. I've only just found you again."

Her eyes tear up. She says, "Don't think of it as ending. Think

226 | K. RYER BREESE

of it as being re-created. Being remade in a better image. It's so damaged now. So unhealthy. We'll redo it better. I have the power to do it. It's for the better. Please don't make it such a bad thing. Don't make me sound like a monster."

I grab Vauxhall's hand. Hold it tight.

She doesn't pull away.

"Your father, the Enigma, he's putting you up to this. He's controlling you."

"No," she says. "I make my own decisions. Besides, I'm not the only one who wants this. I'm not the only one who wants to shift the world to a better place."

"Who else?"

"Karl and his father."

"His father?"

"Yeah. He's brilliant. Used to be a physicist. He's the one who figured out the mathematics of it, gave me the formula."

"There's a formula to end the world?"

"There's a formula for everything."

I shake my head. "Please, Vauxhall, let me prove the world to you again. The mall was beautiful. I loved visiting there but it's not the world. I want to stay in the world. And I want you to be here with me. We can fix it other ways."

Vauxhall thinks about it. Then, she asks, "How did you get in the dream?"

"I have powers too. Powers like you."

Vauxhall looks disappointed.

"What?" I ask.

"That's what Karl's father warned me about. He said that

someone might come, someone with abilities like mine. Someone who would challenge me. Do you ever read comics, Ade?"

"Yeah. But not much."

Vauxhall says, "There's this one, it was from way before I was reading comics, but it's pretty good. It basically starts with an all-powerful being called the Monitor. He was like a god, had the ability to oversee all these different parallel universes and all the other superheroes who live in them. At the start everyone assumes he's a bad guy, but actually he's a good guy, trying to save all these hundreds of superheroes from destruction by the Anti-Monitor. The villain is everything the Monitor is but in reverse."

"You saying that's me?"

"Karl's dad said that someone like the Anti-Monitor might come to stop me."

"But you're not saving the world, Vaux. You're the one destroying it."

Vauxhall pulls her hand away. "You don't get it at all."

She stands, gets ready to leave. I reach out, grab her.

"Please, tell me about Karl's dad. Is he like Render?"

"Not really. He knows them but he's more of a . . . science geek. In a cool way. He has this place downtown, his studio, where he has his experiments. Does stuff with isolation tanks and—"

She stops, seeing me shake my head. Start laughing.

Karl's dad, of course, is the Glove. Unbelievable how small and twisted the world is. If I wasn't so in love, I'd be tempted to just let Vauxhall go and destroy everything.

Vauxhall looks at me funny. "What?"

"I know Karl's dad."

I stand up and hold her. We pause there, eye to eye, our faces only inches apart.

"Give me time to prove the world to you, Vauxhall. One chance. Just one."

"How?"

"Karl's wrong. His dad is wrong. Your dad's wrong. They're all using you. Please, give me one night and I can prove the world is a wonderful place. I'll show you that the beauty of your dreams is still here in this reality. I promise."

Vauxhall whispers, "Okay."

And then she pecks me on the lips. The kiss is so fast that it feels like a hummingbird just flicked by my face. But it instantly recharges me. It sends electrical currents spiraling through my body and makes me shiver like a sugar rush.

"Tell me where to find Karl," I say.

Vauxhall says, "Don't hurt him."

I say, "I won't."

"He's with the Diviners and his dad. They have this show they do downtown. They do it every month. Called the Destiny Show."

SEVEN

It's bright outside, the sun burning down everything in its path, and I squint walking back to the car.

Adam's there, playing on his cell, but he's not alone.

I can see the shapes of two other people packed into my car.

There really are only two people they can be.

Gordon and Jeremiah.

Adam sees me, waves. He shouts, "Hey! These guys need to see you. Something really urgent, I guess. I invited them in."

I lean in and look at the new guests.

Gordon nods. He's got a gun.

Jeremiah nods too. He's holding a knife.

Jesus . . .

I say, "Let's just finish this here."

Gordon says, "Oh, that's exactly what we plan to do. Get in the car."

I shake my head. "No. You two get out."

Gordon looks back to Jeremiah. Jeremiah shrugs.

They both get out. The lot is empty. Just cracked pavement and a few wisps of clouds rolling overhead. It's a scene straight out of a spaghetti western.

Gordon points his gun at me, says, "We wanted to help you, Ade. We wanted this to all come together simply and you just didn't get it. Like, I'm confused about just how stupid you are. Every step of the way, we have held your hand and helped you become something new, but then you betrayed us. We can't forgive that."

"I won't let you use Vauxhall to end the world, Gordon."

Jeremiah says, "But it's going to be so much fun!"

From the car Adam yells, "Dude! I've got your back."

Gordon points the gun at him. He shuts back up.

I say, "I figured you guys were just in this for kicks. I never thought there was a real, honest-to-goodness plan at work."

Gordon laughs. "It's a hell of a plan, man. But the credit goes to the Glove."

Jeremiah nods in agreement. "Dude's a genius."

"He knew about the whole thing with you and your half-brother and he asked us to give you a nudge. Push you a little bit and get you to see the next step. Weird thing is he knew exactly what you could do if you were given the chance. See beyond this life. Shit, that's huge. Also Glove's the one who got in touch with the Diviners. He knew you'd come to them for help and he made sure he was the one you'd turn to."

"Why? Why'd he want to fix things with me? Why not just end the world without going through all this ridiculousness?"

Gordon looks at the time on his cell. He says, "I'll save the exposition until after you're dead. You don't need to understand everything, smarty pants."

I put my hands up. "Give me one second."

"What? Seriously?" Jeremiah asks, rocking on his heels. "I wanna do this!"

I turn to Adam. Say, "I just need to tell him something."

Gordon says, "Tell him from here."

"It's private," I say.

Jeremiah laughs uproariously. "Ha! They're homos or some-thing!"

I say, "Just let me tell him something."

"Fine," Gordon says. With the gun he motions for Adam to get out of the car.

Unlocking the door and stepping out, Adam says, "I'm not so sure—"

"Move it!" Gordon shouts. "And hands on your head."

Adam puts his hands on his head and walks over to me. The crunch of pebbles on the hot asphalt is nearly deafening. He stands in front of me and mouths: *What?*

I say, "Adam, you're an awesome guy. I appreciate everything you've done for me and I'm not ever going to forget you."

Adam screws up his face. "What the hell, bro?"

"Sorry," I say.

And then I raise my hand and fast as possible I dash it, glowing and shuddering like heat above a highway, into Adam's chest. He vanishes with a flash and a pop.

Gordon and Jeremiah stand there stunned. Confused.

I don't wait for their reaction but throw myself to the ground, head first, a move I haven't used for about two years but totally perfected in the abandoned lot behind my dad's hospital. It's ugly, leaves some nasty marks, but it works.

My head hits the asphalt and the cracking of my skull is like a gunshot.

Black.

Beautiful, instant black.

And then, the world reforms.

Bit by bit, piece by tiny piece, all the molecules of the parking lot and the sky and my car and Gordon and Jeremiah, settle back into place and I drop down into it.

Right behind Gordon.

"I got teleportation, asshole," I say as I wrap my arm around his neck and choke him until he loses consciousness and goes limp. Doesn't take long. The gun drops out of his hand and I let him fall to the ground.

Jeremiah looks at me, terrified.

I'm a monster.

The destroyer.

He drops the knife and it clatters. He says, "Yo, man. Look, I really didn't—"

And then he runs. Just books.

I watch him go. His outline getting blurrier and blurrier in the heat.

And then my cell rings.

Belle.

"Hey," I answer.

"I'm at the store," she says. "That Leif dude works here. He's kind of a nice guy. Anyway, he knows you. Got skittish when I mentioned your name. When you coming down here?"

I get into my car. Start it up.

Weird thinking that Adam was just sitting here only a few minutes ago.

"I've got to go downtown to some show or—"

Belle says, "There's a show going on right here. In the back of the store. It's called like the Destiny Something or Other. I don't know, looked sketchy."

"I'll be there in an hour. Hang tight."

"Cool."

Belle hangs up and I toss my cell on the passenger seat. It hits something metal. I look over and find that one of the Pandora Crew left a little present. A silver box with some masking tape and my name, written all sloppily, on the top.

I pick up the box and open it.

Inside: An index card pulled from my mom's wall. It's dated for tonight and the vision was from ninth grade. It's obviously one that I'd forgotten about, but I'm not sure how. I must have been even more messed up than I remember.

The card says, "On a beach with a gun. Vauxhall is there. We're fighting and something is hovering in the sky above us. Very strange and uncomfortable. Thankfully it's short. I'm hoping it's just a game. Just a trick. Halloween? Scary."

It wasn't a dream.

It was a memory of a vision.

EIGHT

I pick up Paige at her house.

She's stoked to see me and gives me a big hug.

I can't tell her how elated I am. "This is almost over," I say.

"What's the show we're going to?" she asks. "I love shows."

We walk into the theater at the Litmus Test Café's Destiny Show and my skin is already crawling. The place is packed with a football team's worth of fakers.

All the folding chairs, all in hasty rows, are occupied by the people who are keeping me down. All these prognosticators and gut readers. All these tea freaks and sandalwood buffoons. All these crystal hummers and attention seekers. All of them the kind of people the Diviners would love to see me become.

All of them looking for fame and fortune.

None of them looking for meaning.

It's also pretty obvious that most of them don't recognize me.

I ask Paige to have a seat in the back. She lets me know she'd rather sit up front.

"Someone's got to watch your back," she says.

"I don't know what'll happen here," I say. "But I need you to be safe."

"Wait? Why'd you bring me again?" she jokes.

"Paige," I say sternly. It's the only time I've ever talked to her like a dad.

She sits in the last row next to a woman with a red-feathered hat.

I walk up front and take a seat while the conversation rattles around me.

There is a stage. It's one of those high-school deals painted black with cheap floor lights and there's a deep red curtain hanging as a backdrop. Curtain is old and dusty. If anything, it lends the place a kind of nasty cabaret atmosphere.

And the place is boiling. There are only these little cheap fans onstage so everyone's fanning themselves with scraps of folded-up paper. The audience is just this sea of multicolored waves.

So who do we have for this afternoon's entertainment?

The Diviners, Karl, and the Glove.

Gilberto's sitting in a leather armchair smoking and acting sophisticated. He is wearing a suit but no shirt underneath. He is wearing a fedora as if an afterthought.

Next to him, sitting on a stool that looks very rickety, is Lynne. She's got a flat blue dress on. If she could, clearly, she'd just evaporate right there.

And next to them, a bit farther to the left, is the Glove. He's squatting like a toad with sunglasses on and a mask to hide most of the worst of his scars.

They don't notice me until I sit.

And when Gilberto sees me he points me out to the Glove and the Glove stands up all menacing but Lynne pushes him back into his chair. From as close as I am, I can see her mouth: *Just wait.*

That's when Belle sits down next to me.

She says, "Looking good."

The show starts, the lights fade on and off a few times, and then a guy with a red polo shirt and a soul patch steps up onto the stage with a skinny microphone, the kind you see in old music videos.

He doesn't introduce himself but everyone here seems to know him.

This guy just starts in. "Thanks again for coming. First off, I want to thank the Glove for being here today despite his busy schedule. Really, I think we should all give him a decent and heartfelt round of applause."

And the crowd erupts.

Cheering. Catcalls.

The Glove just nods slowly. The way he does it, it's like he's been expecting this treatment forever and now, only right now, he's finally getting it. He looks super proud of himself sitting there. He waves to the crowd and the guy with the mic brings it over to him, hands it over carefully. The Glove says, "Thanks."

More clapping. More waving.

I notice the Metal Sisters are sitting three seats away from me. Anka's there with a big purple hat with black fake flowers in it. Slow Bob too.

The Glove says to the emcee, "Spence, I'd like to formally welcome everyone to the event tonight. I want everyone to know that I really appreciate all this group has done for me and I want to let you know that I'll be available afterward for questions."

Cue audience clapping.

The Glove continues: "But let's just get into it, shall we? We have a special guest here in the audience tonight. He's someone a few of you may have heard about. Special is, I think, an appropriate label. Spence, I'd like to introduce Ade Patience."

And the Glove points over at me.

Then he hands the mic to the emcee and Spence looks at the crowd before focusing in on me. He says, smile so wide, "Ade Patience, welcome."

Cue scattered applause.

Gilberto stands up, takes the mic from Spence, and squints to see me as though I'm miles and miles away. He says, "Ade?"

And to the audience he says, "You guys might've heard about Ade here. Pulled off a pretty amazing feat a little while back. We were hoping he'll be on this stage soon. But, well, things have kind of gotten funky."

People in front of me turn around to look.

Gilberto continues, "Ade here thinks he's better than the rest of us."

Cue audience groaning.

Cue audience shock.

Gilberto, strutting, says, "Ade breaks the rules. He's a cowboy and doesn't believe in getting in touch with the deeper aspects of the universe. The real machines that move the life. No, Ade still thinks that he has that power in his hands. And it's those hands that seem to be a real problem, as our friend the Glove can attest."

I stand up.

I say, "I'm here to change everything."

Cue audience gasping.

Cue Paige clapping. Hooting.

Gilberto shrugs. Looks to Spence. He says, "What does your supposedly being able to do the one thing that no one in the history of divination has ever been able to do have to do with you destroying the Glove's studio, with you beating him senseless and trying to—"

I interrupt right there. "He's a liar."

I say, facing the crowd, "How about you tell everyone about your hired thugs?"

The Glove makes that harrumph sound.

I say, "How 'bout you tell this wonderful audience of all your followers how you held a gun to my head and tried to force me into your tank? How you tried to stop me from escaping by sending the Pandora Crew over to kill me?"

Cue audience mumbling.

The Glove chuckles, says to my back, "I don't have to stop you."

I say, "Fact is: You don't want me around because I don't fit into your neat understanding of how all this works. You don't want me around because I'm becoming more powerful than you could ever imagine. And I'm taking Vauxhall back. I won't let her be your weapon."

Cue audience shock and stuttering.

The Glove laughs so hard he chokes. He says, "You have no idea what you're talking about, Ade. You're so far off it's not even—"

238 | K. RYER BREESE

"Why don't you tell me then what's going on?" I interrupt. "Tell us all."

I step up on the stage and stand right in front of him.

"Tell us all," I say.

And that's when his son, Karl, comes storming up onstage from out of nowhere.

He grabs me by my arms and it looks like he's going to throw me over the edge of the stage but instead he holds me there. Tight. His face, my face, is so close that my head starts to spin. Of all the duplicates, he looks the most like me.

Through gritted teeth, Karl says, "She'll never be with you."

And suddenly my arms start tingling.

My feet feel like they've fallen asleep.

The back of my throat dries up.

Karl says, "You have no idea what I am capable of."

And he narrows his eyes and the process speeds up. I watch in horror as the skin on my fingers starts to shrivel, to get old. And moles pop up and grow big like mushrooms. And liver spots yellow my once-smooth skin.

Right in front of all these people, in the glare of the lights, Karl is sucking the life from me. He's aging me to the grave.

In his eyes, he seems so joyful.

I try to break loose but can't.

I've gotten so weak.

In his eyes, I see myself. Myself graying and dying.

I start to shake like I've got palsy.

My eyesight darkens, begins to fade.

"This is the end, Ade," Karl says.

And it is. I start to fall to the floor, drooping in his hands like an empty suit.

Every color bleeding out.

Every sound getting tinny and distant.

I don't see the baseball bat swing but I hear the sound it makes as it thuds against Karl's chest and sends him sprawling backward, wrenching his arms from mine.

I collapse but with his fingers off my skin, I start feeling better almost immediately. The colors return. The sounds grow closer and closer.

Someone steps up onstage between me and Karl.

Someone with a baseball bat.

I look up and I can't describe how beautiful it is to see Paige standing there. She looks down at me and smiles, puts her hand out. I take it. She pulls me up.

The audience is stunned into silence.

I step over to Karl and then, my legs rubbery, I kneel down beside him.

He looks at me, eyes wide, trying to catch the wind that Paige just blasted out of him. His face purple, he tries to speak. Nothing comes out.

I raise my hand over his chest.

My hand flickers like the sun through leaves on a windy day.

Karl grimaces.

The Glove, behind me, shouts, "No!"

But I do it. I drop my hand into Karl's chest and he fades out. Absorbed.

Again the Glove yells, "No!"

But the instant Karl vanishes, it is as though he never existed in the first place. Gilberto looks around confused. Spence even more so. They don't know who he's yelling about. All they see is me, returned to my normal youth, leaning down with my hand on the stage.

That means something.

If the Glove knows Karl is gone, then . . .

I stand up, all the bones in my spine cracking into line, and walk over to the Glove. "Who are you?" I ask him point-blank. The place so quiet you could hear clouds passing by outside.

The Glove says, "I'm surprised you can't guess."

I look at him closely. Carefully in the light.

"You can't be," I say.

"Why not?"

My eyes roam over his twisted face looking for similarity. Finding none.

"You're old," I say. "You look nothing like me."

He says, "That's because I am nothing like you."

And yet my hand begins to glimmer and flash.

His hand does the same.

Both of us move at the exact same time.

Both of us shove our hands into each other's chests.

That's when everything explodes in a fireball of brilliance.

NINE

I'm in a blank space.

The kind you see in movies or on television shows when the

protagonist disappears into the void. Usually it's just a white room. Sometimes it's black.

This is blank.

Like water. Just nothing.

A true void.

The Glove is standing next to me in the space. He looks peaceful.

"What is this place?" I ask.

The Glove says, "Think of it as being on pause."

"We're stuck. This forever?"

"No." Then he says, "But I figured it had to happen sooner or later."

"What?"

"You." He continued, "This was the fifth time I tried and, honestly, I thought I succeeded. The Pandora boys were certain you'd go along with it all once you got a hint of what was happening. It was never about you destroying your copies; that was Razor's deal. For me, it was about restarting the present. Getting back my life."

"What happened to you?"

The Glove wipes his face and in this place, this absence of anything, all the scars come away with his hand as though they were fright house makeup. And under, it's my face. Exactly the same without any of the slight differences that Tad or Adam or Ronny had. He is my exact replica. He is me. Just twenty-odd years older.

"I'm your future, Ade."

I step back. The wheels in my head spinning so fast I can't make sense of anything. Maybe it's this place but I feel like I'm falling.

"I don't understand."

"It's complicated but . . ." He looks around. "We have the time." Then he says, "I am what you would become if you hadn't erased the past. If you'd have let Jimi's anger, his childhood, infect you, let it metastasize in your mind, this is what you'd look like. Who you'd be. And my life was miserable. This anger ruined it, corrupted me. You wouldn't believe the things I did. Terrible things. It wasn't until I was forty that I discovered the ability. I met an old man, twisted physically from his abilities, and he taught me how to use what I had to actually change time. At first it was seconds. I could maneuver ten seconds into the past. Then it was twenty. Soon I could manipulate time, actually erase it. I'd do something I was ashamed of and then change it. Make it so it never happened. I went back in time to exactly this moment, when the change started. That was the first attempt. Right now. Seventeen years old. And from there, I started erasing the past. I've been stuck here for ten years. Who knows why, funkiness of the universe and such. And just like the old man who taught me, the power has slowly twisted me into . . . Well, into what I was before."

"How come I've never had visions of myself like you?"

"Because I've been here. Stuck. Removed."

"And Karl? Clearly not your son."

"No. But I helped him along. He considered me kind of a father. It was a last-ditch attempt to figure out an alternate solution. Clearly it failed."

The two of us standing in this emptiness, I ask, "Okay. So what happens now? Did we just blank each other out? Are we dead?"

"No, but only one of us is going back."

That throws a wrench into the conversation.

The two of us hovering in nothing and the Glove, this anger-scarred forty-year-old version of me, narrows his eyes and says, "Hang tight. This is going to get interesting."

The Glove brings his hands together like he's harnessing some chi. Like he's one of those old dudes you see in the park doing tai chi, moving in underwater motion. And the air around his hands, if there's even air here, begins to gleam.

I start prepping myself for the inevitable attempt to absorb me. The inevitable push into my chest.

But he's fast. Lightning fast. Before I can even back away or get my hands up in defense, he whips out and pokes me with his index finger on my forehead. The speed of it, the pain that follows, is like a snakebite.

And bam!

Suddenly we're not in the void anymore. No, now we're on a playground. More specifically we're on the playground at Montclair Elementary and we're duking it out, real honest fisticuffs, in the pea gravel. And the Glove isn't an old scarred man anymore. He's young. Both of us are. Both of us eight years old, mirror images of each other down to the underoos, and we're fighting for our lives.

I pull him down and get on top of him and start smashing him in the face with a little metal toy truck that I drag out of the sand. He grimaces, this little kid face grimace, and kicks me in the nuts.

But before I even roll off to the side, my arms instinctively wrapping around my stomach, he touches me again and we're gone.

Crash!

We smack down on a green somewhere in New England. From the few seconds I spend looking around, I can tell it's a college campus. There are students with backpacks gawking at us, the two identical twins wrestling on the lawn. We're both older, maybe sophomores at this school.

The Glove—it's almost difficult for me to tell the two of us apart—has me in a choke hold. He's squeezing hard. Like his life depended on it and I'm about to black out, go limp, when I manage to reach up and touch his forehead with my middle finger.

"Fuck you," I say.

And wham!

We fall into a swimming pool. It's hot and humid out and immediately I can tell this is North Carolina. I've only ever been here once, my uncle's place on the beach in Kill Devil Hills but I know the look of the pool. We're ten years old and churning up foam in the shallow end, both of us holding our breath.

I come up out of the water first and step back from the Glove.

Gasping for air, feeling like Jimi must have, I say, "I . . . can do whatever . . . you can. And more likely . . ."

The Glove says, "Let's see."

I realize then that I don't need the concussions anymore. My powers, the ones before I went and erased Jimi's corrupted childhood, are back. No need for a head bashing, no need for any blood, now, like any good superhero, I just need to think it and it happens.

Before the Glove can even blink I'm behind him.

Teleportation.

I bring my hands down, my hands together, clasped in some sort of wrestler move, and slam the Glove on the back of his head. He splashes down under the water and attempts to swim away, but I grab him by the ankle and haul him back to the surface.

He flips over and grins, some blood between his two front teeth, and says, "You're too weak. Your blindness for Vauxhall is what will kill you."

And then he hits me in the forehead.

Thud!

We wind up in a movie theater only a few months back. It's this horror flick that Vauxhall really wanted to see, something that if I'd actually been watching it I would have been plugging my ears the whole time. Reason I didn't see it was us making out in the back row. The Glove and I tumble into seats up front. Knock over this one chubby guy's massive bucket of popcorn.

As the movie spools, the light strobing around us, we roll out into the aisle where the stickiness of the floor catches us and the popcorn comes to pieces in our clothes.

Someone yells for us to get down. For us to shut up.

Me and Vauxhall in the back too wrapped up in tonguing to even notice the brawl going on up front.

The Glove gets the upper hand and slams his palm into my forehead.

And we're back, struggling on the stage in front of all the prognosticators who came to hear the Glove and Gilberto tell them how to use their magic.

As soon as we're back, everyone stands. Chairs topple over.

Gilberto shouts something I can't hear.

As we fall off the stage and smack hard down on the floor, I see Paige and Belle running over. I'm not paying attention, my hands just in a flurry of motion, and miss seeing how the Glove gets me on my back. His hand, shivering in the air like an insect's wings, about to pierce my chest.

I'm weak, worn down by the fighting.

Not sure I can push him away.

So I cheat.

I teleport behind him and pull him to standing. The Glove is back in his scarred and run-down body. No one else but me knows who he really is. No one else sees the truth of the almost mythical struggle that's going on here.

The Glove says, "Regardless, she'll destroy you."

And that's when I punch my hand through him.

The light opening up around my fist, his body a black hole, and before I can even register the image, he's gone. Not even a puff of smoke like in a magic show.

I catch my breath for a second as Paige runs over and puts an arm around me.

"The hell just happened?" she asks.

Of course, the Glove never existed now. This show wasn't about him. The past has been erased; all of my duplicates are gone. It's over.

Paige helps me to a seat but I don't want to sit down.

I have something left to do here.

Something I've been meaning to do for a while now.

I pull myself up on the stage in front of a totally bemused

Gilberto and take the mic from Spence. As I'm standing there, wobbling and covered in sweat, people start to clap. Probably they think this is part of the show. Just a little sleight-of-hand entertainment. Maybe some performance art.

Into the mic, I ask, "How many of you can change what you see? Regardless of how you see it?"

Nothing.

"How many have tried?"

A dozen hands.

Gilberto, behind me, stands up and cups his hands over his mouth and says, "Can anyone out there remind Ade of the rules?"

Then to me, he's like, "I know I can. We're here to talk about seeing the future. Not messing with it. You've been there already, Ade. Been there, done that."

"No," I say. "Actually, I am here to mess with it."

Someone in the audience, a guy with a ball cap, yells, "Sit down!"

And another, a woman, stands and says, "There's a reason it's a rule."

Cue murmured agreement.

Heads nodding.

Into the mic I say, "I know that. I know what the rule is. And I know that a lot of you don't know who I am. Maybe you do and you've heard a lot of bad things about me. Most of those things are probably true even. But tonight everything changes, it changes because the world is different now."

The guy in the cap shouts again. "Go home!"

A kid I didn't see in the back yells, "Moron!"

There's shouting breaking out all over.

Insults. Slurs.

Behind me Spence calls out, "Now, people. Come on. Let's bring this to—"

I interrupt him by heaving one of the fans off the stage and it shatters loud. People stand up ready to leave.

I raise my hands to quiet them and then step forward to the edge of the stage and say, "The deal is simple: If you get caught up looking for the future in everything, dreaming about how good the future must be, then you lose the present. You doom yourself to inexperience. You fail. And if you get too caught up looking into the past, then you lose the present. That's why the past always repeats itself. 'Cause we're too focused on trying to think it away. Trying to explain it."

There are a few grumbles.

I say, "Seeing the future locks it in. It's what makes it happen. Before you see it, the future can be anything. Just as the past can be accepted. It can be defanged."

People sit back down.

Some are even nodding.

I say, "Close your eyes to the ending. Make it up yourself."

The tide has changed.

Now there's more nodding. Even a few claps.

At this moment, I'm a rock star.

I say, "Seize the now."

Cue audience applause.

Behind me, Gilberto's like, "That's why Ade won't be wealthy."

Mic to my mouth, I step off the stage and wander into the audience.

I say, "All of us hoping for that next great thing as though this isn't enough. We're always trying to open that lid. Ask yourself this: What'll happen if you don't see it?"

Belle, hand raised, says, "You can change it."

Cheers.

Hooting.

Here, right now, I can't be defeated.

I can't be stopped.

I smile, turn to Gilberto, say, "That's right. When you haven't seen the future, when the outcome hasn't already been decided, you can change it. You want to help people? You want to help yourselves? Show people how to live for today."

More applause.

Paige stands and soon half the place is standing and clapping and even Spence is nodding in agreement, his feet tapping. In the spotlight, I'm a superhero.

From her chair, Belle asks, loud, "What if you've already seen it? How do you change that?"

Cue sudden quiet.

Belle, louder, asks, "How do you change the future?"

To Belle I say, "That's the easiest part. You don't."

Gilberto snickers.

Paige smiles.

To the people, all watching me, I say, "You're the people that other people pay to see the future. Or the past. You'll find what they want in the random pages of books, in the guts of animals, in names, in computers, or observing birds, or watching melting wax. You will boil a donkey's head and look at its eyes. You will use rainwater. Stare at blemishes. Run your fingers along the navels of your clients. But does any of it mean anything if it can't be changed?"

But before any of them can talk, before a single mouth opens, I say, "You don't change the future, you change yourself. What you all need to understand is this: Right now, all that matters is right now."

Then: "I have to save the world now, people."

Cue standing ovation.

Cue me throwing the mic.

Cue Belle nodding knowingly. Smiling.

Cue Paige giving me high fives.

Cue me vanishing like a spark.

TEN

There is nowhere else to go but to find Vauxhall.

I think of her and go.

I have what I need.

The abilities that will see me through the rest of this.

And I have never been as confident as I am now. Even though teleportation takes a fraction of an instant, there is still time in the space between spaces to think. And my mind, suddenly finding itself relaxed, unburdened by the duplicates and the sickness that was Jimi's history, sends itself back to the mall.

To the water slides.

Back into Vauxhall's dream world beneath the barren field.

It is exactly as I left it last time. Kids splashing around in the shallows, teens lying out on towels under an extremely bright sun cascading its light through the windows, and everyone loving every minute of their life. This is Heaven.

At the slide I wait in line maybe two minutes before the bored lifeguard motions for me to go. I don't sit down. Don't lay the mat flat. I just run and jump into the slide's open mouth.

Screw the mat. I'm going commando.

I yell at the top of my lungs and I spin wildly down the slide.

It's an exceptionally long ride down.

Me turning over and over, my arms and legs extended like I could take up the whole slide. I feel sorry for any kid at the bottom when I come tumbling out.

In this bright blue wonderland I only think about how goddamned giddy I am.

I think about Paige and another part of me, some deeper, maybe more mature part, smiles. I need to tell her that I appreciate her.

That I understand her.

That I am always going to be there when she needs me.

Things I don't think to tell her.

And Mom. My poor mother. Her eyes turned to the sky. Her faith in me and the blinders she wears. The bitter part of me that's been so confused by her, about how she's lost herself in this all-consuming quest for salvation, for a few seconds it retreats and underneath is the boy who laughed at his mom's silly jokes and her weird habits. Underneath, still bright and shiny as though it was protected all this time, is me and Mom the way we used to be. Us ridiculous and dangerous.

And Vaux.

I replay the peck she gave me.

Our brand-new first kiss.

In my mind I replay it again and again.

Reverse it. Zoom in.

Turn the volume up.

I replay every conversation we've ever had in the fifty-two seconds left on the slide. How in love I am right now can only be measured astronomically. I imagine things exploding in the depths of space. Nebulas bright with color blossoming in the cold and whole new planets whirling into formation from out of nothing.

This love is the love of creation.

It's the new me finding my feet and running to Vauxhall and sweeping her up in my arms and never ever letting her go.

This is the new Buzz.

I come out of the slide, my head spinning.

My legs in the air, head back and soon underwater, I splash out the way kids do. The way I did when I was ten. In the blue it's all gurgles and burbling.

I burst out of the water smiling, my arms raised like I've won some race.

Some award.

My smile the goofy smile of an awkward kid.

A touched kid.

And I find myself standing on a bus platform downtown.

I've jumped off here before.

Standing next to me is Grandpa Razor. No Vauxhall in sight.

He's wearing a suit. It's hard to get used to this new, spiffy Grandpa.

He says, "She's not here."

"You're a mind reader now?"

"No, but I have some of this plotted out."

"That's impossible."

Grandpa Razor, still looking freshly minted, says, "I've seen what you've seen, Ade. Been in that head of yours. Did you forget that there's always a link? A permanent connection between you and me? I've seen what happens here, that's why I'm waiting for the number ten bus with you."

"I can teleport now. No buses."

Grandpa Razor gives his classic laugh. "Ha. Yes, of course you can. But not right now. Now you're going to ride the bus and then you're going to take some pills and then you're going to kill the Enigma."

"You're nuts."

The platform is practically empty. There's a dark-skinned woman at the opposite end with three small children. She's eyeing us. Pulling her kids back.

Grandpa Razor asks me how long I can hold my breath.

"Look, I'm going to bail."

And just before I close my eyes and teleport again, Grandpa Razor says, "You've seen this before, Ade. You know how it goes."

With that, he pokes me in the neck with a needle.

It's not a syringe. I can feel the difference.

And I can see it.

It's an extremely long needle. Not like a knitting needle but like a regular needle, just seven inches long and the width of a hair. Like he plucked it off his silver dome.

Thing is, with the needle in my neck, I can't move.

I'm paralyzed.

That shouldn't matter with teleporting 'cause it's mental but it does.

"None of your powers will work with this in," Grandpa Razor says, stepping in front of me. "It doesn't have a name and I only stumbled on it by accident. In reality, this needle is used for acupuncture. But it can do some amazing things if placed properly in a subject with abilities like ours."

I hear the bus before I see it.

It hums and rattles and is preceded by a draft of cool air.

Almost like it's pushing a breeze in front of it. Grandpa Razor puts a cell phone in my pocket. This cell phone, I've seen it before. The vision.

Grandpa Razor, again anticipating, says, "It's me on the other end."

I want to ask him why he sounds so different.

Why in the vision, when he calls, his voice isn't its usual jacked-up self.

He answers, as though he knows exactly what I'm thinking. Says, "You underestimate me, Ade. I find it insulting that you think I'm so limited."

Then he moves the needle slightly, just a millimeter, and suddenly I can feel that my legs will move. Grandpa pats me on the shoulder. The way family would. He says, "All aboard."

The bus is empty.

We get on and the dark-skinned woman with the kids doesn't. She just watches us as the bus pulls away and makes the sign of the cross. I walk to the back and Grandpa Razor follows. He sits next to me and pushes the needle back.

The bus starts up.

The cleaned-up Grandpa Razor says, "You're doing the right thing."

Then he opens a small envelope. There are three red pills inside.

"You're wondering what these are for, right?" he asks. "They're an insurance policy. I can't very well keep this needle in you for the next hour or so. No, I need you to do what I say, when I say it. These pills you're about to take are synthesized equivalents of the ground puffer fish that practioners of voodoo used to create zombies. It doesn't actually work that directly but it can shut down your, well, central processing system and then I can override it using a new ability I just happened to glean from a rather handsome duplicate I absorbed. It takes a few hours to settle in and you need to be in a dark, safe place. I've arranged something for you."

Grandpa Razor does his classic chuckle. And coughs.

He takes two of the pills and puts them in my mouth and since I'm unable to move, he grabs my face and makes me chew them. There's just this hideous-tasting paste in my mouth until he remembers to move the needle a tad to allow me to swallow.

I do. It's awful.

Grandpa Razor nods. Slowly.

The bus heaves through the city and then we're out in the open.

"We're almost there," Grandpa Razor says.

I'm desperate for something to drink. My stomach feels like it's eating itself.

And I'm feeling tired.

It's an unnatural tired.

It's a drug tired. The lights inside the bus start swirling and my vision starts to fade. Grandpa Razor says, "Get ready to be reborn, Ade. Reprogrammed. You're the only one who can do this. The only one she really trusts. The one that, deep down, she already loves. I don't want you to panic but, from here on out, it's going to be a horror show."

My eyes roll back into black.

The darkness feels uneasy.

I hear laughter.

CHAPTER SIX

ONE

Dear Ade—
  Wake the fuck up.

                                                                    Ade

TWO

I snap to in darkness.

It's hard to say if my eyes are closed or if it's just that dark.

I move my fingers to my face and they're open. I touch wet eyeball. The feeling isn't pain but shock.

Then I want to panic.

My eyes aren't covered.

I'm not tied up.

I move my legs and find that I'm closed in by something. Something hard.

At my thighs and the bottom of my feet. I kick and my feet kick something hard. I reach out with my hands and only a few inches from my face is hard.

Above me is hard.

Below me is hard.

Wood hard.

It doesn't take me more than a minute to know I'm in a box.

It doesn't take me more than a few seconds later to know I'm in a coffin.

I panic.

My throat closes up. By reflex.

Stomach starts to move up into my chest. Emptying all the acid it's got into my lungs. The feeling is drowning. But not in water. It's in fear.

The kind of fear that doesn't let up.

It's not the shock scare of a movie. The madman behind the door or under the bed to lick your hand. It's the fear you get when you first fall asleep and dream you're falling. The fear you're going to crash. The fear that is relentless and makes your whole body buzz with a dark energy.

Now I scream and the scream reverberates in the box under how many tons of dirt I can't guess.

The scream seems to go on forever after it's left my mouth.

Like all my body is screaming too.

The scream fades slow. It hums in my ear.

The darkness crushes me.

I push up as hard as I can with my hands and the wood above me gives. It moves. Something shifts above it. Like soil moving. Or sand.

I take a deep breath.

Scream as loud as I can and push again and this time the top moves.

Not up but over. Over to the side and a cascade of sand avalanches around me. Into my eyes and my mouth. I try to close my mouth as fast as I can but it's still filled with sand. Sand that I choke and sputter and cough on.

I lurch up and out of the coffin.

Up and out of the sand like a magic trick.

Fresh air overwhelms me. I breathe it in with my nose. My mouth still full of sand that I'm trying to spit out. Big globs of wet sand that come out slowly in my spit.

I retch. Dry heave.

I try and clear my eyes out with my hands but it just gets more sand in. Sandy tears are running down my cheeks. Sandy spit dribbling down my chin. I can only imagine what I look like.

A few more coughs.

Hacks and most of my mouth is clear.

I was buried in the clothes I was wearing and I wipe my eyes with my shirt. Feel like I'm scratching my corneas but when I open my eyes I can see just fine.

I stand up and of course I'm on a beach.

The beach.

How many times will I be here?

How many times will something terrible go down on this stretch of sand?

The moist air licks at my lungs. Fills them with its deep primal scent.

On the horizon, maybe only a few thousand feet away is the tennis court. The lights are on. I hear insects buzzing.

I feel around in my pockets. The mobile phone. Grandpa Razor's phone. It's still there. I feel around in the other coat pocket and find a gun. I take it out and under the pale light it's black. Black and featureless.

Just the heavy shadow of a gun.

He says, "And on the third day he rose."

The feeling that comes over me is like hypnosis.

Them swaying.

The moon falling.

Lake splashing.

The stalks of the reeds whistling.

No wind.

Just rustle.

Grandpa Razor saying, "Ade, you're going to save the world. You're going to do what none of us have been able to. Your destiny awaits you, my friend. Go kill them and then come back here. You will succeed."

The moon falling.

This is hypnosis.

And the pills.

My mom once told me that we're hypnotized every day.

Every day we walk and think and don't pay attention to where we're going and yet we still get there. It's like when you drive one route all the time. The same route. It just becomes second nature. The right at the light. The right at the stop sign. Left at the church. And when you're busy or deep in thought or on the phone you don't even pay attention to where you're driving. The left at the church.

It's hypnosis. The body acting on the some baser quiet level regardless of directions from the mind. And that's just what starts to happen.

The drugs for sure. I start walking toward the tennis courts.

Grandpa Razor behind me saying, "Be strong. You're a hero. Destroy them."

I walk forward and reach into my coat pocket. Both hands.

One grasps the cell because I'm sure it should be ringing by now.

The other is on the gun.

This is the now and this is how things are supposed to play out. I'm locked in on this. I let my body move with time and let the future take its course.

There can be no deviation now.

Not with Grandpa's ability washing over me.

I get a few hundred feet from the tennis court and I can see Vauxhall and the others. Clear under the bright vibrant lights. It is exactly how it should look. I stop when the phone begins to vibrate.

I don't answer with hello.

I don't answer with anything.

Just put the phone to my ear.

Automatic.

"Destroy everything," Grandpa Razor says. "Leave nothing behind."

I realize now what it means.

His voice. His message. This is how his ability works.

I don't say anything because I'm on autopilot now. I just breathe into the phone and walk to the tennis courts. Grandpa keeps his chant going in my ear.

I want to fight it. Want to stop my feet but I can't.

I want to throw the gun into the lake but I can't.

". . . destroy it all."

I get within fifty feet of the courts and move faster.

". . . nothing behind . . ."

I walk onto the court. Vauxhall turns and looks at me and smiles. Render is there, of course. Just as I saw before. He walks up, says, "I don't think so, Ade."

Face to face at last.

The cell phone buzzes.

The voice says, "Nothing left . . ."

And Render steps up to me and raises his hand but doesn't touch me. He doesn't need to 'cause I go flying back onto the court as though he punched me.

He smiles. Super proud.

Vauxhall looks down at me sadly.

"Destroy it all . . ." Razor on the cell says.

I pull myself back up and step closer to Vauxhall. She shakes her head. And then she raises her hands to the sky, to the moon. A shadow falls over the court, something massive moving over us. I don't bother looking up. Not yet.

I can hear Vauxhall's breathing. I want to kiss her but I can't get close.

Grandpa is controlling me.

He's in my head, jerking me around like a puppet.

Focused in on the love of my life I say, "You can't do this."

"She can and will," the woman standing near her says. This woman is wearing sunglasses and a hat. It's hard to tell how old she is but she's so pale.

On the phone, Grandpa Razor says, ". . . everything. Destroy it all . . ."

Render says, "You can't stop this, Ade."

Again Render steps over to me and sends me sprawling across the court without even touching me. This time I have trouble breathing but I pull myself up.

Moved against my will.

Whatever is floating in the sky above us, it makes a humming noise.

And the louder the humming noise gets the more I can feel my own body coming back to life. I can actually feel my nerves awakening, shaking off Grandpa Razor's control. It's not all the way. I have to struggle against it. Have to really focus hard and it's painful. Like having hot sauce pumped between my ears. But I'm moving on my own.

The cell phone in my hand buzzes. Grandpa says, "Kill her first."

I'm able to drop it down into the sand.

I walk back onto the court and stand in front of Vauxhall and say, "I love you and I won't let you do this. No matter what happens next, I'll get you back again. Even if it takes a thousand years."

And that's when I pull the gun from my pocket.

This part isn't under my control. This isn't me pulling the gun. The humming of whatever is drifting over us has subsided and I'm losing my grip on my own neurons.

Vauxhall says, "Don't."

Grandpa Razor makes me pull back the hammer.

Render raises his hands and Vauxhall's face falls, her lips tremble. And that's when a sudden burst of light explodes from the air around her, encasing her in a glowing bubble of energy that lasts half a second before jettisoning up into the atmosphere and leaving the court dark.

For the first time I look up and I see what looks like the moon.

Infinitely black and hovering just above the treetops.

It moves slowly and I can see the jagged surface of it.

"Excellent," Render says, and a giant smile breaks out across his face. A beaming smile. The kind that dads give kids who bring home good grades or kick the winning goal. It's a smile that says accomplishment. Then, looking at me, he says, "You're too late."

The hum of whatever's above us increases. It's practically shattering my eardrums and it's just in time because the spell breaks. I'm able to force Grandpa Razor back out.

Right here, right now, it's over. Whatever the drugs he gave me were.

The swaying.

The track.

The programming.

It ends.

But the gun is ready and to my horror I see that I've pulled the trigger. The very moment that Grandpa Razor left is the very moment my finger moved. And in super-slow motion, as though all time has slowed in a vacuum, I can see the bullet leave the barrel of the gun. The bullet's trajectory has it going directly into Vauxhall's chest.

I don't even have to think about what I do next.

It happens.

I teleport and reappear in a flash. Right in front of Vauxhall. The gun I was holding drops down onto the court. Clanks. And the bullet hits me square in the shoulder.

Time speeds back up and I fall to the court, blood gushing out of me.

Vauxhall screams and drops to her knees and holds me. Render walks over slowly, his hands down at his sides, and they're glowing red. Like they're on fire.

"Ade, it's time to die," he says.

And he holds those burning hands up and they crackle in the air, as though they're chewing up the oxygen around them, lit cigarette tips on every finger.

"Move it, baby," he says to Vauxhall. "We both knew this was going to happen."

Vauxhall stands up between me and Render. She says, "No."

Render narrows his eyes and Vauxhall is flung out of the way like she was tissue paper. She slides across the tennis court and comes to an unconscious stop.

Render grins and I teleport.

I appear behind him but he's already turned around and grabs me by the neck with his burning hands. The feeling is like wearing a necklace of melting metal. The skin on my neck starts to blacken and char. The smell is a BBQ in hell.

Render raises his other hand and extends his index finger.

Angles it toward my right eye.

He's going to blind me.

Reading my mind, he says, "Oh, it'll be worse than that. I'm not stopping at the eye."

I cringe and try to teleport again but while the space around me starts to shake I can't actually move. The background wobbles in place but nothing changes.

He's holding me here.

Render says, "Even with all of your fancy abilities, you're no match for me. I am the non plus ultra. I am the culmination of everything. Grandpa Razor told you as much. Why he sent a child to stop me is beyond all reason."

And that's when a voice speaks up from the darkness.

Grandpa Razor, somewhere behind us, says, "There was a very good reason."

Render lets go and I drop to the court.

He spins around to see Grandpa Razor standing there.

Razor says, "The word of the day is distraction."

And then he clamps his hands down hard on Render's head. The way a basketball player grabs a ball when he's about to throw. A shimmering white light radiates from Grandpa Razor's fingers and Render's mouth drops open. He's gagging.

And he doesn't have a tongue.

It's a tentacle.

I move over to Vauxhall. The sun is rising. The light is changing. Pink on Vauxhall's beautiful pale face. I hold her in my arms and watch the sun rise.

A few feet away, Grandpa Razor's hands are smoking atop Render's head.

And Render's head is starting to shrink.

Getting smaller and smaller in Razor's hands. The tentacle in Render's mouth whips around wildly, like it's got a life of its own. Looking for an exit from the ever-shrinking mouth in which it's trapped.

Render's eyes bug out. Look like they might explode from his head.

I can't watch, and I turn back to Vauxhall. I run my fingers over her face. Brush the hair from her forehead and watch as her eyelids flicker. She wakes up and sighs.

I ask her, "Are you okay?"

Crying, she says, "Yes. Why did you do that?"

"Which part? Try to shoot you or catch the bullet?"

She smiles.

"You're too late," she says. "It's already done."

"What's done?"

"The world, he's ending it," she says. "He got inside my head."

Vauxhall cradles me.

I notice I'm getting blood all over her and want to apologize but she speaks first. Says, "I'm like a prism. Others, my dad, they can use me, send their abilities through me, and I magnify them. Making them more powerful. I get this high from it. For the past few years I was with the Diviners and then Grandpa Razor but all of them just used me, they only saw the end result of my power. Only saw what they could gain from it. And then my dad came back into my life, convinced me that the only way to stop it was to stop everything. To move everyone to Heaven . . ."

Then she looks up into the sky.

The black sun hovers over us. Floating toward the city.

"What is that?" I ask Vaux.

She says, "It's the doorway."

"How do we close it?"

Vauxhall says, "We can't."

And that's when Grandpa Razor starts laughing. His sickening, throat-clearing gargle. Render's head is the size of a tennis ball and it's shriveled down like an apple left in a desert. Wrinkled and hideous, the tentacle twitches between his puckered lips.

This Grandpa Razor, he's got crazy powers.

I'm guessing all the messing around I did only made them worse.

Grandpa lets Render go.

The abomination falls to the ground and shatters into a million pieces as though he had been made of ceramic. One of the Render pieces rolls across the court and hits my shoe. It's one of his tiny eyes.

Vauxhall gasps, covers her mouth to stifle the scream.

Grandpa Razor turns to us and says, "You did this, Ade. You made me what I am today. I really appreciate all of your work though I realize you did it for entirely selfish reasons. You couldn't overcome Jimi's past by yourself, you sort of let it take hold in you, and then, when it got too heavy, you decided to opt for the easiest, most destructive solution. In the process you made this place and it is in this place that I will prosper."

He walks over to us.

Steps on Render's eye. It crunches under his leather shoes.

Then he leans down, looks at my wound. Scoffs. Says, "You'll be fine. Then, what Vauxhall here has unleashed, through her daddy's will, can only be stopped from the other side."

"Other side of what?" I ask.

Grandpa Razor says, "Of reality. She's pulling it all down and bringing it into her dreams. While that sounds wonderful on paper, in the end it leaves quite a vacuum here. No one likes a vacuum. That being said, if it's truly too late and we're all doomed to live in someone's dream world, it may as well be mine, don't you think?"

He chuckles and spits on the court.

Then he says, "But let's not get ahead of ourselves. First things first."

His hands glow with the white light. Smoke curls from his fingers.

And that's when we vanish. Both Vauxhall and I.

Though we're not there to see it, I can only imagine the fury painted on Grandpa Razor's face. He's probably screaming into the sky right about now.

THREE

We appear on a sandbar in the middle of a shallow sea.

It's day and bright out.

So bright that the air is flat and colorless.

The water around us is light blue and crystal clear. Only four feet deep at its deepest and surrounded by strange rock formations like from a Southwestern landscape.

Red sandstone bubbles with nothing growing on them rise like the humps of marooned whales hundreds of feet above water.

"Where is this?" Vauxhall asks.

I smile.

There are river stones, large as houses, piled one upon the other and melded together in fascinating shapes like arches, tunnels, slides, bridges, and grottoes.

While the rocky outcroppings are barren the sea around us bubbles with life.

This goes on for miles, every direction we look.

It is a wonderland.

"This is my place," I say. "Welcome to my dream. I made it just for you."

Vauxhall looks around again.

And she kisses me and it's not just a peck.

This is our first full-blown kiss. And we collapse into each other. All the stress of the real world, all the stress of death and destruction washes away as we embrace, our fingers warm against each other's bodies. Our tongues dancing.

That's when Vauxhall notices my shoulder.

The wound is gone.

"How?" she asks.

"I make the reality here."

I point out across the vastness of the sea to a cluster of islands.

Archipelagoes.

"That's where we're going," I say. "Walk or swim?"

Vauxhall takes my hand. "Walk."

We step off the white sand of the beach and wade into the shallow water.

It's warm.

Bathwater.

Little waves crash along our shins and calves but out at the archipelagoes we can see huge fifty-foot waves breaking in enormous plumes of mist.

"How did we get here? I mean, how did I get here?" Vauxhall asks.

Little neon-red fish nip at our toes.

"I'm not sure how it works," I say. "I just thought of us being here and . . . here we are."

"Are we really, really here? I mean, are our bodies here too or lying back there?"

"No, we're really here."

"Crazy."

"Yeah."

"And what are we going to do? Will we go back?"

"Yes. We have to. I just want to spend some time with you first."

Vauxhall stops walking. "But what about back there? Will it be destroyed while we're here? Will everyone be sucked into Razor's dream?"

"No. That world is basically being paused. Kind of . . ."

"Kind of?"

I say, "Don't worry about it. Everything will be fine."

She says, "No. Tell me."

So I tell her how it works is that we're only gone a fraction of a fraction of a second. I tell her that while it feels like we're gone for hours, days, it's really only a blink in reality. I say, "It's like we're moving at the speed of light here."

"How do you know all this?"

"I don't know. Just, I kind of inherited it."

We walk in silence, trudging through the sand and sea, trying not to step on spiky coral protrusions, just enjoying the warmth and the peace.

When we reach the rock outcroppings of the islands, we see they're bigger than I thought they were before. The waves are even bigger.

We make our way up to the first of the large formations using cracks in the rocks. It's tough going and as soon as I start sweating I take hold of Vauxhall's hand and teleport the two of us to the top.

She hugs me.

Standing upon the rounded hump of rock, staring out over the vast blue, we can see past the enormous breakers and into the deep blue-green distance.

The sun dries the last drops of salt water from our skin.

We sit down, Vauxhall in my lap.

She says, "This place is amazing. Better than mine."

"No," I say. "Not at all. This is nice for now. But it's not real. It's always like this. Nothing ever changes."

"But that's great. That's what I want."

I run my hand through her hair, so happy to have her back. I say, "It gets boring after a while. If we stayed here, we'd drive each other crazy. We'd wind up wishing to be back. In the real world, even with all its problems, there is change. And change is what keeps us alive."

"I hate change."

"I used to hate it too," I say. "But that's only because I was afraid of it. When you let other people make your decisions for you, when you let the world run on its own course, then it gets scary fast. But if you take control, if you set your own course and push through all the horror, see the beauty in the simplest things, like this place, then you learn to live for change."

"I don't buy it," Vauxhall says.

"Come on," I say. "Let's go."

"Where?"

"There."

And as I turn around, Vauxhall turns with me.

There is a door behind us. Just standing there on top of the rock. No walls around it. Nothing nearby.

Vauxhall looks at me, says, "What's in there?"

I tell her that the way it's going to work is that I'll open the door. I tell her there will be blinding light and the noise of a thousand mountains crashing to dust, noise that might make her want to scream until our eyes burst.

I say, "Trust me."

Vauxhall says, "I don't know . . . I . . ."

"We're skipping into another dream. It's the only way."

I stand up and take her hand and she stands up next to me.

Her eyes are jewels in this light. Her skin glistens with salt crystals.

"You will follow me through," I say. "I will step across and you need to just watch the back of my head. Ignore everything else. And remember to just walk naturally. When I step, you step."

"Okay."

That's when I wave Vaux over to the door. I open it quickly.

The light inside is shockingly bright. And the noise. It's unlike anything. It's the sound of the universe being shredded. The sound of creation breaking.

I turn to Vauxhall and say, "It's going to be fine."

Then I step forward. Swallowed by the light.

We're stepping into oblivion, the place between places. This is the void that the Glove and I were in before bouncing around in time. We're stepping over a thin crack between nothingness and everything.

Right foot first into the light and the noise is gone.

Sunlight again.

It takes my eyes a long time to adjust. I'm squinting through tears. I just close my eyes and wait for the tears to stop. Then I feel a breeze on my skin. My hair moving.

Vauxhall is right behind me. Eyes still closed tight.

"Go ahead and look," I say. "It's incredible."

We're standing on a high cliff overlooking a wild and colorful landscape that stretches off into infinity beneath a neon-blue sky. The terrain undulates with hills and between them there are meadows and forests, ponds and stretches of what look like beaches.

There is vegetation everywhere. And I see places where the hillside has been worn away and the rock below is deep red. Or in other places it's a faint purple. In a few yellow clay. And there are turbulent streams and birds calling from the treetops.

Vauxhall says, "This still your dream?"

"No," I say. "It's yours."

Vauxhall laughs. "What? I've never seen this."

"Turn around."

She does. The door is gone and behind her, only about a mile away, is what looks like the mall. Heaven. We can see the glass windows of it and inside, tiny as ants from this distance, are the people playing in the pools, sliding out of the slides.

It's not the same as Vauxhall's heaven but close.

Very close.

"This is my dream," she says. "This is Heaven. Why'd you bring me back . . ."

She stops short, noticing the details of the building are different. Noticing that the slides aren't quite the same. That the water's color is a little darker.

"Where are we?"

I say, "We're not dreaming anymore. This is Bermuda. A hotel."

"The real world?"

"Yes. I teleported us here."

"But the door . . ."

"That was an illusion."

Vauxhall turns to me. "Why are you doing this?"

"Come on," I say, and I take her hand and teleport the two of us inside the hotel.

We're standing by the pool and the kids are splashing everywhere and their raucous shouts echo but the sound of the water gurgling is soothing. The air feels heavy, soft. The smell of chlorine isn't overwhelming but intoxicating.

Vauxhall leans down, touches the water.

A red drop splashes down beside her.

Blood.

She looks up at my shoulder. I look over and see it's gotten worse. My shirt is soaked with gore now and it's still running fast.

Vauxhall jumps up. "Oh my God," she says. "We need to get you to a doctor."

"I'm okay," I say. "Listen, I want you to stay here, just for a little while."

"Why? Where are you going?"

"I have to stop Grandpa Razor. I have to go back."

Vauxhall takes my hand. "I don't want to be here without you."

"Please, Vaux," I say. "It's safer."

"But I started all this."

"Not what's happening now," I say. "I started it and I'm finishing it."

She frowns, looks at my wound again, and grimaces.

"I'm worried. Please be safe," she says.

And I kiss her again before I vanish.

FOUR

I show up downtown by the art museum.

And the black sun, really it's more of a black hole, is hovering right there, churning up the streets like a tornado.

People are being pulled out of cars and whisked up and into it.

This looks like a scene from a blockbuster movie.

The air vibrates with the sound of the black hole.

Everything electric.

And while it looks like something I've seen before on television, the sounds tell me it's all too real. Screaming. Thousands and thousands of people screaming as they're being pulled skyward. Pulled into the dark iris floating over us.

The sounds of sirens too. Every siren on every car is wailing.

Trees have been uprooted.

Masonry is crumbling.

Streets are buckling.

This is Armageddon.

I find Grandpa Razor, his hands raised in triumph, standing in the center of the street directly below the swirling frenzy in the sky.

I walk up to him just as a minivan filled with people is wrenched into the atmosphere. I can hear their screams recede as they vanish into Grandpa's dream world.

He notices me right away and smiles this massive grin.

It's like he's conducting the madness.

"Do you know what's on the other side?" he shouts.

It's clearly a rhetorical question.

"My dream," Grandpa Razor says, "is to live in a world where I am like a pharaoh or a sultan. Where people build temples in my honor and bow before me wherever I walk. Does that sound terribly unreasonable?"

"Yes," I shout back.

Grandpa Razor says, "You have so little imagination, Ade. This could have been yours as well. You made the template I'm using here. It was your twisting and fracturing of time that has allowed all of this. I'm surprised you're not joining me now. First, we take this city. Then the next. And the next. If you join me, it'll go even faster. We'll have the whole world in a matter of days."

"I'm here to stop you."

Grandpa Razor bellows. It's not a laugh but a roar of triumph. "Join me and I'll let you keep her. This is all because of Vauxhall anyway. You love her so blindly that you'd doom the world. That's fine. It's reasonable given the state of things. If you join me now, I'll not only let her live but I'll let you have her. The two of you can escape to your little island paradise and swim all day long. You can have her, Ade. It's the only offer I'm making you."

I teleport right in front of him.

Only feet away.

He's eyes are gleaming and up close he looks even younger than he did before. His skin is more supple. His hair not as gray. His teeth sharper.

"You can't stop this. It's in motion now. Vauxhall's power infused it and you can't take it back out. There is no solution to this, Ade."

I teleport directly into the space he's standing in now and he flies backward, dislodged. He knocks his head. Gets a nasty scrape on his cheek but he's up quickly.

"Fighting me will only delay it. And not even that long," he says.

The wind tries to strangle us it blows so hard.

More people fly up into the dark circle.

Around us, cars are being wrenched up from the street and slam into buildings before breaking apart. The pieces spin like leaves caught in eddies.

Grandpa Razor launches himself at me, grabs my left hand.

He holds it for only a second but it's enough to suck the life from it completely. My hand withers like sped-up documentary footage of a rotting plant. It's black and then it's white and flaking apart before the wind blows it away.

My hand is gone.

Just a stump in my sleeve now.

Grandpa Razor says, "I can do anything Render could. But even better. Even stronger. Your girlfriend's power will be the death of you."

I teleport away, behind him.

I wrap my right hand around the back of his neck and use the ability I took from Karl. It doesn't work. Nothing changes and Grandpa Razor slams his elbow into me, sending me sliding back against a curb.

I struggle to stand up but he's too fast.

He grabs hold of my right leg, on the calf, and he does his wicked magic. My leg withers and drops to dust. My pant leg empty and flapping like a flag in the gale. Oddly, it doesn't hurt.

Grandpa Razor leans down in my face, says, "Is this really how you wanted to go out? Me tearing you apart, piece by piece? How pathetic."

He grabs hold of my remaining leg and pauses.

"I don't blame you," he says. "I know that deep down, you're just a slave to your emotions like all the cretins in this world. You'll enjoy serving me."

His hand on my leg, no power shifting through it, this is my moment.

I realize that regardless of what happens next, regardless of how crushing it will be, I have to make the only move I have left.

I look up into Grandpa Razor's eyes, the black pit pulling in clouds behind him like an evil halo, and I say, "This never happened."

I go back.

Send myself back to the end of the school year.

In the few milliseconds that I exist, I erase.

I erase everything that happened from the moment right before Jeremiah interrupted Date Night. The moment all of this changed. Went downhill.

All of it.

Down to the last second.

The Delirium never happened.

Borgo never showed me the tape.

I never plugged into an AED.

My powers are stripped away.

And erase.

Each one vanishing.

And erase.

Along with my memory.

And then—

CHAPTER SEVEN

ONE

Dear Jimi—

Sorry I was such a dick and missed your birthday. I feel really sucky about it. I know that lately I've seemed like I was trying to avoid you but really I wasn't. There's been some kind of nutty things going on in my life and I just need to deal with them but haven't been.

You surely know what that's like.

Anyway, I've been getting some therapy to resolve those issues I told you about. It was working really well when you were coming to the sessions with me. Helping me to deal with the stuff that you were there firsthand for.

I'm hoping maybe you'll do that again now that school's out.

Oh, also, let me know when your next play is. Vaux said the last one was just amazing and I don't want to miss the Shakespeare one you're doing. So call me.

About Gordon and Jeremiah. Yeah, I was hanging out with them for a little bit but decided it wasn't really the best thing for me to be doing. I met a guy once who had been in a mental hospital after getting totally depressed and when he and a buddy got out, first thing they did was grab a beer and head to a party. Not the best idea. Dude was picked up by the cops three days later trying to slash his wrists. I guess what I'm saying is that I need to walk a different path now. If I'm going to deal with what I've been given—and I'm not blaming you again—then I need to change my life.

I heard a few rumors about the Glove character (where do they get those names?) from Gilberto. He said the guy had these amazing abilities that I should really consider using but I don't think so. It's sketchy. Messing with time can just really fuck stuff up. Have you ever read that "All You Zombies" story? Jesus . . .

Anyway, I'm hoping you'll come to the swim meet.

Talk to you soon, bro.

Ade

TWO

Mom is back from church early and I find her already barbecuing in the backyard.

Telltale plumes of rich smoke and her wearing her apron.

I give her a kiss on the forehead and ask her if she checked the mail. She says no but tells me that I shouldn't be so stressed out about it.

She tells me that the things most worth waiting for usually take the longest. Even college applications. She says. "Psalm Thirty-seven. Don't be impatient for the Lord to act."

"Okay. I'll check the mail anyway. People going to be here soon?"

Mom says, "You haven't been in your room?"

"No."

"Check it out."

I smile and head back inside. There's nothing for me in the mail so I go to my room and I'm not the least bit surprised to see Vauxhall sitting on my bed. She's got a laptop and a crucifix lying next to her.

I come in, kiss her, and point to the crucifix.

"Your mom gave it to me," she says. "Sweet, right?"

"What are you going to do with it?"

"Haven't decided."

"Thought you were going to the art museum with the crew?"

Vaux says, "Nah. Eve's busy with work. Elise and Sam are doing God knows what at the farm. Everyone accounted for."

"Glad you're happy," I say.

"I am?" Vaux winks.

"Nice to have so many friends?"

Vaux sticks her tongue out at me.

I sit down and she puts the computer on my lap, says, "Press return."

I do.

On the screen a video is playing. Something Vaux's been working on for a few weeks. It's an end of the year project for her filmmaking class and she's been talking it up something crazy but not given me any details. The titles pop up, white on black, and the movie's called *Heavy Metal Affair*.

"Catchy title," I say.

"Just watch. It's only fifteen minutes long."

The first three minutes are of Vauxhall prepping for a date.

Putting on makeup and then driving.

Running red lights.

Then it cuts to me talking on Oscar's roof from the party six months ago.

I look haggard. Horrible. All the things I told Vauxhall about my mom, about my dad, about my childhood, they're all there in wispy digital color.

I tell Vauxhall that this is totally embarrassing. I tell her that I don't know if I want anyone seeing this. I say, "I mean, it's well filmed and all, but really?"

Vauxhall says, "You're the main character. The hero."

"There's a plot?"

"Don't be mean. It's avant-garde. Just follow along. Piece it together afterward. Preferably in your sleep."

"—"

Vaux pushes me. "Just watch it. You're going to love the next part."

The feeling I get is déjà vu.

It's a shiver and shake that makes my arms jump. What I see is what Janice described the time she hid out in the back of my car, the time she tried to make me as miserable as possible. It's Vauxhall talking to the camera.

The camera following her down a hallway.

Her saying spiteful, nasty things.

And then it ends with her kissing Jimi and slamming shut a door.

I pause the video, look at Vauxhall, and laugh.

She grabs my hand, holds it to her mouth, kisses it all over, says, "It was just acting. Just a scene. Jimi's so gross. I would never, never in a million—"

"I'm not worried, Vaux."

Score one for changing the future. A big middle finger to Janice.

Vauxhall asks, "You're not upset, right?"

"I'm not. Not at all."

"Good."

There are more scenes with me.

More of my long stories with my face all blotto and my voice wavering. Scenes that, if anything, hammer home the reason I've stopped knocking myself out. Scenes that remind me that I don't want to ever look that wretched again.

And then there's an action sequence.

Vauxhall in her Negative Woman getup, her all mummified and doing these crazy high kicks with the camera swooping in, and her punching plaster-faced dummies where the film's all sped up.

It ends with stock footage of a nuclear blast.

"I love it," I say.

Vauxhall cuddles up to me. "I knew you would."

I put the computer down and push Vauxhall back on the bed.

Lying on top of her, I kiss her neck and her ears.

I kiss her eyes.

I ask her, "Do you ever get sick of seeing just my past? You're bound to run out of things to see soon. Then the high will be gone, and maybe, maybe you'll start wanting someone else."

Her face pressed against mine, body filling the gaps between us, Vaux pushes her hips up and narrows her eyes. "I won't ever get sick of you, Ade."

I ask, "Any of my old memories make you upset?"

"Not yet."

"Wouldn't that be nice just to be able to be with me and not have to see anything afterward? Just to be able to relax and not have the high, not have the weight of that on you?"

Vauxhall says, "I haven't seen anything for weeks."

"Seriously."

"Yeah. You're all out."

"And?"

"And what?"

"The high?"

"No high."

"Why haven't you told me?"

"You never wanted to know. You told me not to tell you about what I saw."

Our lips touch. "You miss it?"

"No," she says. "I don't at all."

My hand finds its way under her shirt right when my mom calls for us to come to dinner. She shouts, "Food's getting cold!" She then stamps her feet and says, "There will be no fornication in this house!"

Vaux sighs. "You need to save your energy anyway."

We run into Paige and Veronica in the kitchen.

After hugs and air kisses, Paige pulls me aside and asks me if my mom made her famous ribs. She says, "I just want to know because last time I had them I was a farting freak."

I nod slowly. "Poor Veronica."

Paige hits me. Hard. "You pumped?" she asks.

"I'm calm. Not expecting much."

"Well, it's your first meet. Maybe tonight all that living healthy will pay off."

Outside, Mom's got the table set up with one of those plastic outdoor tablecloths that looks good but rips easy. There are places set with plastic forks and knives and paper plates. A pitcher of lemonade twinkles on the table.

Someone in the driveway behind our house is revving his truck.

The smell of exhaust mingles with the tang of barbecue sauce. This is summer.

We all sit and as Mom's loading up plates with beans and coleslaw, Belle and Gilberto and Lynne walk in. They've brought wine and a fruit and cheese plate. Belle stinks of pot smoke but my mom hugs her tight regardless.

All of us sitting around the table.

All of us, addicts and charlatans and dykes, sharing a meal.

All of us not so dangerous now.

Paige and Veronica tell us about their trip to Ecuador last week with Veronica's family. They tell us little stories about nude beaches and surfing, about making out when the folks weren't looking. Paige says, "It's amazing what two girls in love can get away with when they're playing friends."

The conversation just flows.

All of us relaxed, all of us laughing.

My mom, sitting at the head of the table, surveying the scene, looks very content. She listens intently, laughs along, and writes everything down in a journal she keeps wiping baked beans off of.

When it's time for dessert, I head inside with my mom to bring out the brownies and cookies and pie, and I ask her what the journal is.

"Not another Revelation Book, right?"

Mom smiles, shakes her head. Picking up a plate of brownies, she says, "A book of patterns. It's amazing how the good Lord's worked the tapestry. But if you look close, you can see the binding. The materials."

"What are you talking about?"

"Patterns. Numbers. The past reaching forward. You ever notice the numbers? Outside, today, they're speaking the same the number of words. Each sentence is fifteen words long."

"Didn't notice, Mom."

I peek outside and see Gilberto smoking.

I ask Mom about the code. About the numbers.

The past six months, Mom's been pretty much lost in a fog.

She didn't talk to me for two weeks after the slideshow presentation and my revelation. She spent the whole time at church. Me, I was eating fast food the whole time and hanging out at Paige's and heading home to change clothes every now and then. When she started talking to me again it was as though nothing had happened. She didn't bring up my visions but looked at my eyes and scanned my face. Probably just force of habit.

Wasn't until two months later that she mentioned the Rapture, mentioned how eager she was to leave. And even though the Revelation Book never reappeared, Mom was back to her old self as though it was a coat she took off for a little bit, got chilled, and then put on again. In her way, she's very comfortable.

Today, even though I don't really want to know and really don't want to feed her obsession, I ask Mom what her new discovery is.

"It's fifteen," she says.

"Why fifteen?"

"Fourteen is Christ. Fifteen, that's now. It's the name of God. Take a look at the Bible. Galatians. Hosea. Exodus. The flood. The prophets. Feast of Tabernacles. Matthew. The height of Bethany where—"

"Mom, what are you trying to tell me?"

Tears suddenly running down her face. Tears smacking down on the powdered-sugar tops of brownies. Mom's choking them back and failing.

I put a hand on her shoulder and she says, "For a long time, things weren't the same at church. With the congregants. They were so disappointed. It was like being put back out into the desert to wander. And then, thank God, this. It's a message, reminder of the power of faith. How our choices change the world."

"Fifteen?"

Smiling up at me, face soaked, Mom says, "Peace. Serenity."

"—"

"Salvation."

I hug Mom tight, the brownie plate biting into my chest. She trembles then pulls away quickly and wipes her eyes and sniffles.

Then she turns to bring the plate of brownies outside, says, "Started when you made your choice, Ade. When you didn't kill Jimi."

And then she's outside, back out in the sunlight and the flickering of bright green leaves and the smell of honeysuckle, and making small talk as though she'd never said a word.

I saw my dad last night.

Went to the hospital and visited him inside his head. He was sitting on a patio of a hotel overlooking Paris, the Eiffel Tower all lit up, and sipping a cocktail. Looked really good, really healthy.

We were sitting there and he said, "There was this video I saw once, it was when I was going to this shrink who actually understood people with abilities. He was this guy who had a hand in the scene, was the go-to dude for anything that prognosticators or psychics could need. Anyway, it was this nasty video about these French twins. They shared like one body and—"

"That's enough, Dad." I stop him there. "I don't want to have nightmares."

He shrugs and then snaps his fingers and turns out the sun.

The moon flies up into the sky like it's on a string.

He smiles at me, says, "There are some benefits to living in your dreams."

THREE

My first swim meet and it's a big one.

Dark outside, the windows of Celebrity are all fogged up and the fans are turning in the rafters something furious.

The place is so quiet, everyone so focused on the meet, that the sound of the fake waterfalls spilling their guts onto fake rocks is deafening.

It's us against George Washington and Coach has me swimming in the first lane, the outside one, where the slowpokes loiter.

There are no carrots here, no fine Beverly Morrison asses to follow.

I'm on the block and tensed to jump, my muscles all pulled to their limits.

On the chairs across the pool, Vauxhall and Paige and my mom are sitting with their hands in their laps, necks stretched out, none of them talking, none of them breathing. I'm watching Vauxhall and her eyes, the way she's holding herself. Sitting there she looks comfortable. She looks tamed in some way.

And then the gun goes off and every cell in my body jumps.

I don't feel the water going into it.

Suddenly it's just there all around me. There's the whoosh as I push and pull, the bubbles of legs kicking out in front of me. The beckoning of the black cross painted twenty-five meters away. Then I'm at the wall and I'm turning and I don't see anyone else. The pool, it's empty beside me.

I feel no strain. My breathing is so tightly controlled.

Everything in me sings in time, perfectly tuned. How good this feels, I can tell already why in the future I'll be jumping off of buildings and surfing. It's the adrenaline rush. It's just the replacement of the Buzz.

A minute.

Two minutes.

The race is over and I come up for air and hear the roar of the crowd, only it sounds like thousands of people. Taking off my fogged-up goggles, I look around to see that I'm second to last. Lane two, that guy's out of the pool toweling off already. He's shaking hands. Fact is: This has been the best swim of my life and I'm in fifth place.

Vaux waves. Paige waves. Mom smiles.

I pull myself out of the pool, the water beading and melting off, and walk over to where everyone's sitting. Some of my teammates, they pat me on the back. One of them says, "Good try, dude."

Vauxhall kisses me and hands me a towel.

One of our swimmers got in first and so the cheerleaders start getting funky. Them being Mantlo cheerleaders means they're extra loud, tattooed, and picking fights with the George Washington cheerleaders. One of them winds up in the pool.

I sit down feeling better than I ever have.

My lungs working exactly as they should.

My body moving blood and air and thoughts so smoothly.

The love of my life beside me.

My mom here and proud.

Paige happy.

I'm in the best place imaginable, the one place I was always supposed to be, the place everyone aspires to. I'm content. I'm satisfied. Anything could happen next. And I look at the pool, the surface of it calming back into a steady shimmer, and I think back to the Buzz and knocking myself out.

But then I look over at Vauxhall and I can see only love in her eyes.

I can feel it in my veins.

I don't need anything else.

BEFORE *PAST CONTINUOUS,* THERE WAS *FUTURE IMPERFECT*

Ade Patience can see the future. Pretty cool, right? There's one problem. In his latest vision, he saw himself murdering a kid from school.

— "Dark, funny, twisted…Brace yourself for a wild ride." =
—Josh Berk, author of *The Dark Days of Hamburger Halpin*

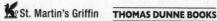